RETUR
MANOR

By the same author:

LURE OF THE MANOR

RETURN TO
THE MANOR

Barbra Baron

This book is a work of fiction.
In real life, make sure you practise safe sex.

First published in 1995 by
Nexus
332 Ladbroke Grove
London W10 5AH

Copyright © James Hallums 1995

Typeset by TW Typesetting, Plymouth, Devon
Printed and bound in Great Britain by
BPC Paperbacks Ltd

ISBN 0 352 32989 0

Chapter 1

Eighteen-year-old Ellie Branks was pruriently engaged in the act of soothing her seventeen-year-old dorm-mate's enticingly plump bottom with petroleum jelly. Georgina was lying face down on her bed with her navy-blue uniform skirt piled untidily on her broad hips. Her baggy, white cotton knickers were stretched tightly into the crack of her behind to expose her tortured buttocks; glowing bright pink, they were criss-crossed with thin, red welts, evidence of a recently administered caning by the perverted head-mistress of Chalmers Finishing School for Young Ladies, Miss Claire Petty.

The somewhat tubby headmistress was wont to administer bare-bottom thrashings to her charges for the slenderest of reasons. Poor Georgina's peccadillo had been nothing more serious than turning up five and a half minutes late for her music class. For this trivial offence she had been reported to Miss Petty, and shortly thereafter she found herself summoned to the awesome presence. Having been obliged to double her plumpish belly over the high back of the infamous, early-Victorian chair which was invariably used as a punishment aid, she had suffered the indignity of having her skirts raised above her bottom, drawers lowered down the backs of her chubby thighs, and then she was assaulted with the stinging pain of ten hearty swipes from the bane of Chalmers – the whippy cane which was housed in pride of place over Miss Petty's fireplace.

It was rumoured in the school that Miss Petty took the greatest of pleasure in caning the girls. This was, indeed, very true. But what was not known – for she locked her

1

door and proceeded to perform the smutty act in secret as soon as a thrashed girl was dismissed – was that the excitement she derived from the administration of punishment was entirely sexual. With each feverish slash of her cane the headmistress's eager pussy would get ever wetter and when the girl in question had received her punishment and been sent packing she would eagerly thrust two fingers up herself and furiously masturbate to orgasm.

Although Miss Petty's onanistic habit was unknown to her charges, a certain Lord Brexford and his young wife Sophronia were most familiar with it.

Chalmers sat close to the edge of imposing cliffs near the town of Deal, in Kent. Lord and Lady Brexford's slightly crumbling, grey stone Gothic mansion, Deal Manor, was perched imposingly atop a gentle hill in full view of the finishing school on the other side of a dense wood belonging to the Brexfords. The previous winter the thirty-eight-year-old, handsome and most salacious lord had taken possession of a high-powered telescope, his sole intention to use it to spy on the Chalmers girls. With it, the first arousing sight he had zoomed in on – for whippings and so forth turned him on massively – was that of Miss Petty in the process of administering a vigorous caning to Ellie Branks, and he had greedily ogled her subsequent onanism.

Shortly thereafter, Lord Brexford had made it his business to make the acquaintance of the headmistress of Chalmers. After quickly discovering that Claire Petty's sexual fantasies were most extensive, embracing far more than mere sadism, he had persuaded her – with the promise of regular invitations to the sex orgies which were a frequent feature of life at the manor – to send him girls for the purpose of seduction. The first – a virgin at the time as were practically all the protected daughters of the rich and famous when first housed at Chalmers – had been the pretty and most willing Ellie Branks, scion of a powerful north-of-England industrialist. Young Ellie had sacrificed her virginity with remarkable enthusiasm and relish.

Since then, there had been two other pretty young victims. One had succumbed to Lord and Lady Brexford's joint wickedness just before the Christmas holidays and the other a third of the way through the current, spring term. However, neither had proved quite so willing, or anywhere near as libidinously adventurous, as sweet Ellie. They had submitted to Jeremy Brexford's deflowering – under the greedy gaze of his wife – without struggle or protest. But they had exhibited a notable lack of eagerness and with the dark deed done his lordship had lost interest; neither of them had received a subsequent invitation up to the manor. However, Ellie had, on numerous occasions; the Brexfords delighted to sport sexually with her, and she took equal pleasure in indulging with them.

Ellie and Georgina had become lesbian lovers shortly after Ellie's introduction to the joys of sex at Deal Manor. Whenever the two were in one another's cuddly embrace, Georgina took raunchy enjoyment in hearing of her girl-friend's salacious exploits. A virgin herself, even though her disgraceful behaviour with Ellie was hardly indicative of one, she had long craved in vain to be asked to the mansion.

The late spring evening was warm and pleasant. Ellie was administering her loving and self-arousing attentions to Georgina's sore bottom close to a wide open window. In the dorm, only the flickering gaslight over Georgina's bed was on, and the rest of the room was in deep shadow. Pru and Toots, the other two occupants of the four-girl dorm, were in the games room playing ping-pong.

'Poor you,' sympathised Ellie. With four fingers she scooped a generous dollop of jelly from its tin and smeared it over Georgina's left buttock. As she began to smooth it in with the flat of her palm she commented, 'Such a pity that you don't enjoy a caning. For me it's a wonderful turn-on.'

'We can't all be as kinky as naughty you,' grunted Georgina. She wriggled her crotch sensuously against the white cotton sheeted mattress. The heat in her bottom was beginning to cool down pleasantly under Ellie's gentle ministrations. 'But I am enjoying this. Ooo – don't stop, there's a dear.'

3

'I just love to get the stick now and again. It brings me off a real treat, it truly does.'

Ellie was remembering the first time she had been caned, when she had discovered, to her delighted surprise as Miss Petty vigorously swiped her bare backside, that she was becoming more sexually aroused with every stinging, cutting slash. The pain had been incidental, the orgasmic contractions of her tight little virgin pussy all. She recalled shuddering through an explosive climax with her thigh tops tightly squeezed, rubbing together, and her hard little clitoris jerking on the back of the punishment chair before Miss Petty – who had realised nothing of her charge's pleasure – delivered the final cut.

'Now what? God, you're so dirty, don't you know it?' muttered Georgina; for having first pulled her girlfriend's knickers even tighter up into her buttock cleft, Ellie had then taken firm hold of their waistband, her intention most clear.

'It'll be much better with them off, dearest,' she softly murmured. In one smooth movement she dragged the baggy blue panties over Georgina's quivering bottom, down her snow-white, chubby legs and off one foot to leave them hanging around the other ankle.

Ellie herself was fully dressed in her uniform of smart white, buttoned-to-the-neck starched blouse and heavy, ankle-length, navy skirt. Her passion had been steadily on the rise at the sight and feel of Georgina's backside. Now that those lovely, silken, fat buttocks were perfectly naked, a naughty, provocative idea entered Ellie's sexually adventurous mind. Standing, she clumsily but swiftly unbuttoned the side of her skirt, fingers atremble. She stepped out of it, then hurriedly stripped off her knickers, leaving them on the linoleum-covered floor in the middle of her pile of skirt.

'Your bot's feeling lots better now, is it not, Georgy?' Ellie, naked from the waist down apart from her blue plimsolls, asked.

'Mmmm. But I do wish you hadn't stopped,' Georgina mumbled into her pillow. She turned her head, observing Ellie's lewd semi-nakedness for the first time. Her rosy red lips turned upwards in a lazily horny smile. 'Just what are you planning to do now, you dirty thing you?'

'Something, my darling, I think's going to be very, very nice.' Scooping a big dollop of jelly from the tin she began to smear it thoroughly over her downy, brown-haired pussy.

Georgina blinked several times in happy, randy surprise. She tittered. 'It's my poor bum, that's sore,' she said, 'not your twat.'

Meanwhile, up to his dirty tricks in Deal Manor, Lord Brexford had embarked on one of his telescopic prowls. Miss Petty's windows – a frequent browsing place   had revealed nothing for he was half an hour too late to have gloated on Georgina's thrashing – and the headmistress had long since frigged herself to orgasm and was dozing at her desk, her head cradled in her arms.

The lens of Brexford's telescope – an instrument meant for star-gazing and so powerful that he could zoom in to read the title of a book in the school library – paused briefly to hover at one of the games-room windows. His eye dwelt speculatively on the unbra-ed, bouncing tits of Ellie and Georgina's ping-pong-playing dorm-mates. Jiggling, hidden breasts surely being an attraction, but one of no more than passing interest, he moved on, window by window. After lingering here and there, but discovering nothing to excite him, he arrived at the window in Ellie's dorm which was wide open in front of Georgina's single, iron-framed bed. His thin, aesthetic lips tightened. His widely spaced, deep chestnut eyes narrowed, the one almost touching the eyepiece of the gleaming copper telescope moving in to clamp itself to it.

The lovely, libidinous Ellie and her puppy-fatted roommate were at it yet again, by the Lord Harry, the shameless little sexpots! But what on earth did Ellie think she was up to by smothering her sweet fanny with grease? Within his tight, drainpipe, brown velvet trousers Brexford's prolific cock stirred. Reluctantly deserting his telescope for a moment, he hurried to the door of the third-storey attic room

– which was devoid of furniture but for two ancient, leather-covered chairs with split seats from which horse-hair stuffing leaked – and shouted for Lady Brexford, whom he knew to be in her study almost directly below him. Then he strode back to his telescope and adjusted its focus to afford him a perfect close-up view of Ellie and Georgina.

'Your bum's still a bit sore, of course, isn't it?' Ellie was saying. 'And guess what – my twat's going to kiss it better.'

Planting her hands on either side of Georgina's shoulders, she carefully lowered herself over the girl's back. Ellie's soft, crinkly pubic bush was thick with the yellowish petroleum jelly. Georgina's rosy buttocks were smarmed and slippery with the stuff. Greasy pussy hair met smeared left buttock, first touching it gently and wiggling, then sliding up and down against it. Pouty lips closed in on pink, delicate ear to kiss wetly and nibble the lobe. As Ellie caressed Georgina's behind with her pubis, hips rocking as if in the throes of a gentle fuck, she whispered, 'Nice, no, is it not, dearest?'

Nice it most certainly was. Georgina could not see much, but she was overwhelmingly aware that it was her Ellie poised over her back, that it was Ellie's darling little fanny anointed with jelly and rubbing her tender backside – and that it could not have been anyone else. Her pudgy hand stole beneath and between her soft thighs to find her own pussy. Her neat-nailed, stubby middle finger began gently jiggling on her clitoris. Soreness magically soothing away to be replaced by sensations of utmost horniness; she groaned and whimpered into her pillow. The intriguing little diamond-shaped birthmark on Ellie's behind – so well known to Lord and Lady Brexford – jerked up and down.

'You've found something interesting down at Chalmers, have you not, you dirty man?' chirruped Sophronia gaily as she flounced into the room.

'Indeed I have, my love.'

Her husband's right eye remained eagerly glued to the

telescope. His right hand was clutching the bulging crotch of his trousers.

'Get it out, Sophie,' he said. His voice had harshened. 'Get my prick out, do.'

'My, my. It must be *most* exciting.' Lady Brexford's thick and wavy, shiny dark hair, a reddish glint in it, bounced on her emerald-satin-covered shoulders as, knowing exactly what was required of her; twenty-two-year-old Sophronia, lady by title but not always by nature, took hold of one of the heavy old chairs by its back and dragged it to Jeremy's side. It left a trail on the dusty floor of the seldom-attended room. 'But I absolutely demand a peek first,' she said.

'Be quick about it then, woman,' grumbled Lord Brexford, relinquishing the eyepiece to her. 'I find myself in the greatest of need.' Indeed, his hefty cock was positively straining at his flies.

When Sophronia's prurient eye attached itself to the telescope, the carnal encounter between Ellie and Georgina was getting steamier by the second. The jelly was fast disappearing into the soft, badly marked skin of Georgina's bottom, her middle finger was plunged deep in her pussy as her thumb gentled her hard little clit – and Ellie was excited beyond measure; she had contrived to open her thighs and wrap them around one of her girlfriend's buttocks so that her aroused clitoris was in direct contact with the slippery flesh.

Georgina became impatient for direct pussy to pussy contact. Rolling out from beneath Ellie she contrived her onto her back to fumble open the buttons of her blouse. Impatiently, tearing at the pearl buttons, she undid her own blouse and, with breasts wobbling, their large, pale pink nipples erect, climbed on top of her.

Tits crushed into tits, lips into lips, pubis into pubis. What was left of the petroleum jelly on Ellie's hairy mound mingled with Georgina's blonde hairs. Moaning softly, Ellie wrapped her legs around Georgina's plump thighs. Erect clitorises found one another to slip and rub together in a sensuous lesbian fuck.

'Enough of your gloating, wench,' grated Lord Brexford, impatient to get his eye back to the telescope and his pleading cock in Sophronia's mouth. Taking her by the elbow he pulled her away from the instrument. 'You must execute your wifely duties without further delay,' he told her.

He had meanwhile unbuttoned his trousers and he was urgently fishing inside them for his cock. Lady Brexford immediately, expectantly, running the tip of her tongue over her full, pretty lips, parked her lovely behind on the chair at his side. As the large, aristocratic, rapacious prick she knew and loved so well was dragged into the flickering gaslight, she angled the chair in front of her lord. Her shoulder was tucked into one of the wide-spaced, wooden legs of the tripod. As Brexford's eye glued itself once more to the telescope viewpiece, the glistening tip of his wife's tongue touched the little eye in the helmet of his cock to squeeze a tiny button of flesh inside. She freed his bulging balls from the waistband of his still buttoned underpants. She licked all over his bulbous glans, adding to its purply sheen, then she slid her lips slowly over it and drew as much of her lord and master's prick into her mouth as it could hold, almost to her throat.

Brexford muttered an obscenity. His eyes pigging on Georgina's fat and jerking buttocks with their tell-tale welts and rosiness, he grunted. 'The gal's just had a thorough trouncing, of that there's no mistaking. Dear Claire hardly lets a day go by without thrashing one or the other of the girls.' He stifled a groan. 'Suck me, my darling,' he gasped. 'Suck my dick. *Gobble* it!'

'Tell me again about that very first time at the manor,' muttered Georgina into Ellie's mouth. 'When you went and lost your cherry. Tell it to me nice and dirty.'

'They, they got me squiffy,' panted Ellie, squirming beneath her. 'They took me up to Lady Brexford's bedroom and laid me on the bed. She, she touched my titties all over. She . . .' Her words tailed off into a lengthy, happy sigh.

'Yes, yes, don't stop. Don't stop, Ellie.' Georgina's hips were rocking faster, all of her considerable flesh was wobbling.

'. . . she put her hand up under my skirt, all of the way up and right into my drawers. She played around with my cunnie. She squeezed it and called it a furry little rabbit. She got a finger in it. She . . .'

Georgina stopped her words with a passionate kiss on the mouth. Her tongue rooted its way around in the space between Ellie's lips and gums. She panted, 'And all the time *he* was watching, wasn't he? That dirty, dirty man Lord Brexford was watching, and leering at you both, wasn't he? Wasn't he? Tell me.'

'Yes. He was sitting on the edge of the bed, close to us. He had a hand over his thighs on his . . . his thing. He . . .'

'Cock. Ellie. Call it a cock, why don't you.'

'Yes. He was rubbing his, his cock. Then while she was undressing me, he got the thing out. She began licking my cunnie and pushing the tip of her tongue inside and he closed his fist around his cock and began to, to *wank* it. It was enormous. Georgy, it was as big as a peeler's truncheon, I swear it.' Ellie's eyes were wide and shining at the memory as the two greasy young pussies, slipping and sliding against one another, neared orgasm, their sweet juices oozing and mingling.

Up at the manor, the aptly described dirty, dirty man, his lady wife's soft and pouty lips slithering up and down his hard-on, her tongue flickering on the hot flesh as she gobbled him, was also approaching climax as he leched on the sight of the genitally locked girls. He of course had no way of knowing that Ellie was at that moment in a fever of lust brought on by something more than the excitement of her lesbian tussle, that she was gabbling away in words as dirty as she dared utter about Lord Brexford himself, about her admiration and lust for his cock and about how he had taken her virginity with his wife looking on and playing with herself. Had he known that amusing little fact, Lord Brexford would surely have been most gratified by it.

Sensing that her man was about to come, Sophronia energetically wanked Jeremy as she sucked him, whilst down in

Chalmers Finishing School for Young Ladies the brides of Sappho were shifting position. Georgina clambered over Ellie to move around and duck her mouth to her pussy. Ellie clasped the fat, tortured buttocks, raised her head and thrust her tongue deep into Georgina's cunt. They busily, greedily ate one another to rapid, explosive, consuming orgasm as the peeping Tom in the sexual observatory at Deal Manor erupted copiously into his wife's mouth with three massive grunts, and she gluttonously swallowed the semen down to the last delicious drop.

Ellie and Georgina lay very quiet and still, mouth to pussy, for long moments. At last Georgina rolled her chubby self slowly off her girlfriend; she produced a lengthy, most contented sigh.

'That was so marvellous,' she murmured, sitting up. 'Cripes, it was good, good, good.' She began to button her blouse – then her euphoria was suddenly ruined as her thrashed bottom protested at being sat upon. She leapt to her feet, hands jumping to her backside, rubbing as she went, 'Ow. Ooof!'

'You're going to find it a bit difficult to sleep tonight,' observed Ellie, eyeing the striped, blotchy buttocks with renewed and considerable interest.

'Pity I'm not like you. Pity I don't enjoy it. Lucky you.'

Ellie nodded agreement. She shrugged. 'Maybe you should do something bad again when you're better. Get another whacking. Perhaps you'll learn to like it.'

'No way. You must be potty.'

Ellie giggled.

'I'm still a virgin, too, damn it,' complained Georgina.

'Not with me, you're not.'

'You know what I mean.' Contriving her foot into the unoccupied leg of her knickers, Georgina hauled them up and into place. They were so voluminous that they went up and over her navel, covering her belly. 'Why can't *I* get an invite up to the manor? Why always you?'

'Maybe you will, one day.'

'No.' She sighed. 'I'm too fat for them, that's the real truth of it.'

'You're not that fat, Georgy. You're a bit plump, that's all. Nice. I love you the way you are; I wouldn't want you to be any thinner.'

'I'll never be invited. Still, anyhow I'm going to get very close to the house tomorrow.' She produced a twisted, little inward smile. 'I might even get to lose my cherry at last.'

'How's that? You never told me anything about it. Who's the lucky boy, then?'

'Thomas, one of Lord Brexford's stable lads. He sent me a note – that's what made me late for Music. I'm going to sneak out tomorrow and meet him. I know he wants to do me.'

Ellie chuckled. 'I hope he does. It's what you need, Georgie. A proper seeing-to. But you'd better not lie on your back underneath him. Your bum's going to be awfully sore come tomorrow, for sure.'

Rubbing her buttocks with a wry little smile, Georgina commented, 'My twat as well, I hope.'

Chapter 2

The century-old stables of Deal Manor were on the edge of the oak and beech wood, not far from the house itself. Sneaking through the trees to arrive at the stables unseen was not too difficult – getting out of Chalmers presented the far greater problem; Georgina had ripped her navy skirt at the knee whilst scrambling over a wooden fence which was fashioned into spikes at its top.

It was lunchtime. She had used the excuse of a bad tummy-ache in order to stay away from the dining-room, though the only genuine ache Georgina was suffering was that in her needful, plump little virgin pussy. Mealtime, with all the staff and pupils crowded into one hall, was the safest period to get out of the school and also for a clandestine meeting with Thomas since the hour was not a usual one for horses to be ridden at Deal Manor.

The stable lad was not in evidence when Georgina arrived. The huge main doors were hanging open, and all six steeds were shut into their stalls. The horses – as fine a small collection of thoroughbreds as could be found in any gentleman's stables – peered at her over the gates as she wandered cautiously into the slightly gloomy interior and called out Thomas's name. Like most girls of her class Georgina adored horses. She had a stroke on the nose, a pat behind the ear and a cube of sugar for each of them.

Her petting of the animals was brief; it was not exactly what she was there for – she had come for a rollicking roll in the hay. Keyed up with sexual tension, nervous as a fox-cub, she became more and more dismayed as time dragged by and the boy failed to put in an appearance. Twenty

12

minutes passed by and there was still neither hair nor hide of him. She began to fear that he had been assigned some extra duties and that he was not going to show up at all.

But just when she had made up her mind that he was not coming, there he was with his off-tune whistle, his untameable shock of brown hair and an infectious grin behind which he was contriving to hide his nervousness.

Like Georgina, Thomas was a virgin. Apart from a couple of daringly snatched gropes with a less than willing village girl, his only truly libidinous experience had been with Georgina. She had actually – through his breeches it was true – had her hand on his straining cock. And Thomas, though that had been as much as she would allow him at the time, had explored beneath her skirt and had groped her heavy cotton drawers-clad pussy whilst she rubbed and squeezed him. He had very quickly come in his pants.

Today – and his nerves would no doubt have been worse had he known it – Georgina was determined to let Lord Brexford's stable lad go much further; all the way, if he so wished.

She fell upon him with such alarming rapacity that she all but scared him off. In truth, as far as the fair sex was concerned, Thomas was a most timid lad. To touch her tits that last time had taken him considerable courage. And when his hand had ventured stealthily beneath her skirt he had done so full of fear, holding his breath as it crept inch by inch upwards towards the treasured prize – and then he was attacked with paralysis when he reached her knickers. Now, having been in a mental stew on his short way from the manor – wondering if she had shown up, undecided what he would say to her if she had and building up his nerve for that first kiss – here she was with her arms flung around him in enthusiastic greeting, her lips mashing feverishly against his and her crotch eagerly bumping his groin.

His confusion grew worse when she broke away from him. With a panting sort of smile on her flushed face, clasping both his hands hard in trembly fingers and with her eyes jerking all over him but somehow not actually catching his own, she gasped, 'You really shouldn't kiss me like that, Tom. You really, really shouldn't. It's quite too daring, you know.'

Since it was unquestionably she who had been making all the action, his confusion increased. 'I'm a bit late,' he stammered. 'Sorry.'

She squeezed his hands as hard as she could. 'I have to be back immediately after lunch. We don't have much time.'

'It's all right. It doesn't matter.'

'Oh yes, it *does*,' she insisted.

He watched as her eyes ran down the front of his badly crumpled, collarless beige shirt and over his heavy belt to the crotch area of his dark brown corduroy breeches – where they dwelt fractionally, almost imperceptibly narrowing before sliding slowly back up to his face. 'Do you know what the time is?' she asked him.

His grandfather had recently died and he had left Thomas an almost new, gold hunter, of which he was most proud. He produced it with a flourish from a small pocket in the front of his trousers; it had no chain; that had been left to his mother. Pressing its ornate top button, he sprung open the case.

'It's twenty minutes to two.'

She tutted. 'Drat. It's very late already. Almost too late.' Her gaze fell on the open door of an empty stall. There was a big heap of fresh straw in a corner of it. She tugged his hands. 'Come on. In there.'

Thomas could hardly believe that this was happening to him. The last time he had had to overcome his fear before coaxing and cajoling a shy Georgina into accepting and returning – sexual favours. Now he found himself being hurried – more or less dragged – into the stall, where Georgina sank backwards and pulled him down with her into the straw.

At that moment she was recalling her randy grapple and her orgasm with Ellie of the previous evening and the memory was serving to increase her horniness. Kissing Thomas passionately, but clumsily, she closed her eyes. His

14

full lips were soft, and as yet his chin sported only a fuzzy, almost unnoticeable growth of beard; she might have been kissing a girl.

But this being was no female. There was a glorious, soft hump of genitalia which was anything but feminine squashing itself into her belly. She was determined that this was the day in which she was going to free this arousing, mysterious package, those provocatively named cock and bollocks – how she loved the dirty words – which she had so far only giggled and joked about with her friends and had never actually seen except on small babies.

They were side by side in the straw. Napoleon, Lord Brexford's favourite, six-year-old, chestnut-coloured stallion, was peering in at them around the half door of the next stall, his handsome head slightly nodding. He whinnied as, oblivious to her sore behind, Georgina rolled onto her back and struggled to pull Thomas on top of her, opening her legs as she did so. His crotch settled doubtfully into hers.

'How would you like to see my titties?' she asked him, very quietly.

How would he like to . . .? By golly, the lass was being astonishingly bold on this fine day. 'God, yes. Not half,' he gabbled.

She undid her crisp, white cotton blouse. Beneath it she had on a cream chemise. Taking hold of its loose, lacy bottom, she pulled the chemise all the way up to her neck to expose fully her large, globular, perfectly white breasts to the stable lad's hungry gaze. Watching his reaction she took her tits in both hands and lifted them, squeezing them together, offering them provocatively to him.

'Kiss them, why don't you, Tom?' she challenged him. 'Go on, do. They're lovely and soft and warm.'

This surely could not be happening. The closest Thomas had got to a tit since being breast-fed was to fondle it through a buttoned blouse. He kissed, gingerly, on the upper swell of one. She humped them up even further to shove them into his face. They smelt amazingly sweet to him, sweeter even than the fresh, clean smell of the straw.

'Kiss my nipples? Please?'

He dared.

'Suck them, do.' It was almost a command.

He felt as if he were standing back, observing himself, as he obeyed. He, Thomas Farley, elder son of a ploughman, was avidly sucking the fat teats of a rich man's daughter from a finishing school whilst his cock rapidly grew hard between her legs. As his mouth went from tit to tit and he licked and he sucked and he kissed, he replaced her hands with his to grope and fondle.

'What's that down there then?' exclaimed Georgina. 'Oooo! It feels so lovely and big.'

She had been working the front of her ankle-length skirt up to her belly and now she wrapped her bare legs around the backs of his rough trousers. His cock was digging solidly into her pussy.

Thomas's nervousness was by now swamped by his libido. He remembered how last time with her he had creamed in his pants. This time, he would do it in her hand. Maybe even in . . . but that did not bear thinking about.

'You know very well what it is,' he mumbled into her tit. He took a deep breath. 'Why don't you touch it, then?'

He need not have taken the trouble to ask her, for her hand had been in any case sliding determinedly in the direction of his groin. Her eager fingers had already reached the iron buckle of his thick leather belt. It crept lower to force itself between their mingling crotches. Its palm cupped his hardness. It pressed. It rubbed. It squeezed.

'Get off me, Tom,' she mumbled.

'Why? What . . .?'

'I want to do something. Lay down next to me.'

He sank into the thick straw by her side, his fascinated gaze rooted on the big, swelling breasts so brazenly on display, wobbling beneath her open blouse and raised chemise as she stooped over him. With a sudden shock of delight he watched her hand as it darted to his waist. She was actually unfastening his belt buckle!

It was a most incredible sensation. He had fantasised many times about such a moment, hardly daring to believe that one day it was going to happen.

Georgina had never felt so choked up with lust. Not even when making love with Ellie. Her plump, busy fingers were incredibly nervous as she fumbled open the big iron buckle then started working on the shiny steel fly buttons. Her hands were trembling and shaking. She craved to set eyes on the living mystery which lay within those heavy corduroy trousers. She desired to handle the male sex organ more than she had ever wanted anything in her life before.

The final button. One half of the barrier was gaping open. Beneath lay still more buttons; little, white pearly ones which were holding together the front of bulging flannelette underpants. Her pussy twitched; she was keenly aware of its damp condition. She could feel the heat of his genitals seeping through the pants material. She pulled his trousers down until they were concertinaed at his knees, then she began to unfasten the final obstacle which lay between her and the erotic dream she shared with him.

These buttons were easy. She undid the top one, parted the waistband, gave a little jerk and the rest sprang open by themselves. His erect penis leapt up at her in all its potent glory, making her gasp. So very, very big. It was enormous, this thing called a cock, or a dick, or a prick, or a willy. She had not properly realised its size, not even by laying her hand on it above the trousers, or by feeling it pressing into her groin. It was almost as long as a stick of Deal rock and nearly twice as round – and nearly as hard, she discovered as she wrapped her fist around it and felt its pulsing heat.

There was one wonderful secret yet to uncover – that of the hefty bulge which remained tucked into the crotch of Thomas's underpants. Pulling the pants down his muscular hairy thighs, she reversed them until their waistband met the top of his trousers. Testicles. Bollocks. Balls. They were surrounded by a thick tangle of springy pubic hair, but almost bald themselves. They seemed to be a sort of delicate mauve in colour, a pair of juice-filled, fat damsons.

With her pussy getting wetter by the second, Georgina handled the balls. She discovered that Thomas's scrotum

was as soft and pliable as his cock was hard. He groaned.
He gasped. He sighed. She wanted to look at his face at
that moment, to observe what effect her wonderfully dirty
behaviour was having on him, but she could not seem to
tear her gaze away from his hypnotic set of ready-for-
action, male equipment. Without having to be instructed
how – it was in her as instinctively as a young bird knows
how to fly or a fish to swim – she slowly moved her fist up
and down his cock, stretching and pulling its soft skin,
masturbating him.

He was leching on her handwork through her jiggling
tits, whose nipples were bumping on and brushing his shirt
front, with eyes gone very wide and smoky. He bit his inner
lip. Relax, he told himself. Control yourself, Thomas,
don't for Christ's sake shoot your load, don't come, don't
spoil it. In his several years of playing with himself he had
never approached a climax so swiftly.

'Stop it, Georgina. Stop that right now,' he moaned. 'No
more or I fear I'll . . .'

'You'll what?' She stilled her hand. Finally, she raised
her slack-mouthed face to stare at him.

'You know. I'll make a, make a . . . mess.'

She produced a wicked, shameless grin. 'You'll come,
don't you mean, you naughty boy? All of your spunk will
come pouring out of your balls.'

'Yes. God.'

He really wished she wouldn't talk like that. He was having quite enough trouble fighting back an orgasm without
her exciting him even more with dirty words spilling from
those pretty lips. Taking hold of her hand he unprised the
fingers and removed it from his cock. The need to ejaculate
began to recede.

'My turn,' he muttered. His hand found its way beneath
her skirt and began to slip up the smooth, warmly inviting,
chubby inside of her thigh. 'I want to see it, this time. Now
that you've seen mine.'

'All right. Then take down my drawers, why don't you,
you bad boy.'

She clambered impatiently to her bare knees, by his side,

facing him. Feeling totally wanton, unbelievably daring, she raised her skirt all the way up to her tits to offer him a close-up view of her baggy cotton school knickers which were almost the same shade of navy as the skirt.

He was greedily eager to feast his eyes upon that which he, like her with boys, had only previously observed on baby girls. Hooking his thumbs into the sides of her knickers he dragged them in one swift movement to halfway down her thighs. He gazed open-mouthed on the fuzzily blonde-haired, fleshy pussy which was revealed in all its naked glory. His cock throbbed. The need to come surged back. He struggled to control himself.

'Kiss it, do,' begged Georgina.

He looked up at her face in astonishment. '*Kiss* it?' he echoed. ·

'Please.' She nearly added, 'My girlfriend does, and I do it to her, but she thought better of it.

'Well, all right. Bloody hell!' His mouth closed in. He kissed. He, humble stable lad Thomas Farley, now actually had his lips pressed into the hairy flesh of a rich girl's cunnie and it tasted sweeter than home-made apple pie with cream.

How at that moment she craved for him to do to her what Ellie did. To nibble and suck on her little clit, to lick between her legs, to slip his tongue inside her. But, brazen as she had been so far, Georgina failed to summon up the courage to instruct the boy in the gentle art of cunnilingus. He would either do it or he would not.

And, of course, he did not. Another, risqué idea entered her head, refusing to budge.

'Just look at what our headmistress did to my bum,' she said. She turned around, pulled the back of her skirt up high and bent slightly forwards.

'Golly,' he said, his eyes popping. 'She gave you a proper striping, didn't she? Why was that then?'

'Your fault. Collecting your note made me late for Music. You might kiss my poor bottom better if you wish.'

Running his lips over the rosy, bruised buttocks whilst with his hands hooked around the top of her thighs, he

19

groped Georgina's pussy with the fingers of both hands causing Thomas to pant with lust. He had never been driven to such dizzy heights of horniness, neither had he been quite so acutely aware of his cock, which was pleading for satisfaction. Shit, the randy wench had been leading him on a storm and no mistake. Was it possible she would ...? Did he dare ask her?

His aching libido summoned the courage for him. He dragged the audacious words from his mouth. 'I want to do you,' he muttered, into the crack of her behind. Two of his fingertips thrust into her pussy. 'I want to do you good and proper.'

The consuming fires of lust had every bit as powerful a hold on her as they had upon him. The moment she had been awaiting and praying for ever since the dawn of awareness of her sexuality had finally arrived.

'Then – do me, Tom,' she breathed.

Doubling her skirt under her sore bottom, she sank back into the straw. She stripped her knickers down from her knees and off, and with them scrunched in a ball and clutched fiercely in one hand she opened wide her legs in blatant invitation.

So incredibly excited was Master Thomas, so enormously aroused, he once again feared he was going to spill his semen before reaching the coveted goal. Doing battle with his libido, he climbed clumsily on top of her, his knees between hers, his weight crushing her down into the straw. Gasping, with Thomas's hard-on jabbing between her thigh tops, Georgina was obliged to struggle with the boy at that very moment she had been desiring more than anything. Forcing him by the shoulders up and off her, she had him support himself on his hands.

He shoved. His cock-head banged into her to slide fruitlessly across the cushiony softness of her vulva and ram itself between the lower swell of her buttocks. Believing it was lodged in her pussy, he began to jerk his behind.

'For Christ's sake, Tom,' she exclaimed in frustration. 'Here. I'll have to show you how to do it.'

Heaving his belly off her with her own and then sinking

her bottom into the straw so that his cock was poised and pointing at her bush, she used the fingers of both hands to open wide her pussy lips. 'Put it in there,' she told him. 'But carefully.'

Meanwhile, the day being an exceptionally fine one, having enjoyed an early lunch, Lord Brexford had taken the unusual decision of walking it off. His stroll had brought him close to the stables. He would have passed on by and gone into the wood but for the fact that he caught guttural sounds of young voices coming from where there should have been only his horses. Filled with curiosity, he made his way stealthily inside the stables.

Thomas had put it in there, and he had heaved. But once again, because he had let go of it too soon and had shoved at an awkward angle, the glans had slipped out and he had pushed his cock between the fat of Georgina's thigh tops until its head had met straw.

'You hold it there this time,' he panted, raising his bottom for another attempt.

That was the very moment when Jeremy Brexford peeped around the stall door. He froze. His jaw set itself in a tight line. His eyes narrowed to slits. His loins clenched. He had found himself presented with a superb view of his stable lad's white, hairless buttocks luridly framed by the boy's lowered breeches and rucked-up shirt and poised for action. Georgina's black-plimsolled feet with their little white ankle socks were crossed behind the backs of Thomas's knees, her skirt piled at her waist. Brexford could clearly see the boy's heavy, dangling scrotum and the tip of Georgina's index finger curled around the base of the shaft of his cock as she positioned it for entry.

His lordship could hardly believe his good fortune on stumbling on such a salacious scene. Incurable voyeur by nature, Brexford hardly dared draw breath lest his presence be discovered.

'Now,' grunted Georgina, when Thomas's fat cock helmet was fitted nicely in place between her fleshy pussy lips. 'Push. But not too hard, there's a dear boy.' As he did so, his glans sinking between her labia at last, she experienced a little pain. She dragged in her breath in a gasp, and closed her eyes, rolling her head from side to side in the straw. 'Oh. Ouch,' she went. 'Slowly. Slowly, Tom. But don't, don't you dare stop.' Her eyes fluttered open, her gaze fixing on Thomas's gritting teeth. Sensing a shadow behind him, she glanced over his shoulder – and found herself staring directly into the lust-choked eyes of Lord Brexford.

She screamed.

Thomas imagined that he had hurt her badly. He would in any case have ceased his clumsy heaving, since all the unprecedented sexual arousal had pushed him over the top. He was no longer able to hold himself in check. While Georgina was frantically trying to shove him off her, he backed his glans out of her and ejaculated with a loud moan, soaking her pubic bush in sperm and puddling her lower belly.

Georgina struggled out from under Thomas. All her passion had dissolved in the instant of being so shamefully discovered. She was blushing bright crimson as she frantically shoved her feet into her knickers – affording Brexford a perfect view of her soiled pussy as she did so – hauled the drawers up and fumbled down her skirt.

Thomas was unaware that they had been found out. He had collapsed face down into the straw, panting, his head in the crook of an arm as semen continued to seep from his wilting penis.

Self-protectively – for to have been caught deliberately spying was unthinkable – Jeremy Brexford took it upon himself to adopt an enraged and indignant attitude. 'So, Master Thomas Farley,' he grated. 'So. What unspeakably gross behaviour is this, my lad? And in my stables, by God!'

It was Thomas's turn to freeze. He went utterly still, paralysed for long, frightened moments. Then, slowly and fearfully, he raised his head and turned his terrified eyes on his lord and master. There was nothing to be said, even assuming he could speak at such a dreadful moment.

'Pull up your breeches this instant, boy,' thundered

Brexford. 'Your appearance is utterly lewd and disgusting.'
He glared angrily at Georgina. She was shakily getting to
her feet and brushing straw off her rumpled skirt. So flus-
tered was she that she had omitted to lower her chemise.
Her fat tits were milkily wobbling. As Brexford's eyes fixed
on them, greed lurking behind the fabricated anger, she
hastily dragged her chemise down and, continuing to blush
fiercely, she began to fumble her blouse buttons closed
with jittery fingers.

Lord Brexford moderated his tone, though he still contrived to sound incensed. 'You are from Chalmers
Finishing School, young lady, are you not?' he said, his
eyes travelling keenly over Georgina's uniform.

She could only shake her head dumbly in embarrassed
dismay as she stared shamefacedly at the mess of golden
straw piled around her feet. As if in mockery of her plight,
Napoleon whinnied, long and loud. Another horse
answered it.

Thomas somehow found his tongue. 'P – please, my
lord –' he stuttered.

'You will shut your mouth, Thomas. You will speak
only when it is required of you.'

My *lord*? thought Georgina, Shit, *no*. She was in even
more trouble, then, than she had imagined. Horribly aware
of the stickiness at her crotch and belly, she felt most soiled
and deeply humiliated.

'You fail to speak up for yourself, girl, but I see that you
are indeed from Miss Claire Petty's excellent establishment,' said Brexford coldly. 'A young lady of fine breeding
allowing such vulgar intimacy? Worse – a girl of your class
with a *stable* lad? The situation is beyond countenance.
When your headmistress gets to hear of this dreadful scan-
dal she will expel you on the spot.'

Georgina gasped. 'Oh, please, sir, no, sir,' she wailed,
tears welling. 'Don't for pity's sake tell Miss Petty.'

Thomas was miserably attending to the job of fastening
his flies. 'It weren't her fault, Lord Brexford,' he chival-
rously muttered. 'I led her on a treat, I did.'

'No doubt. No doubt, wretched youth. But I believe I

23

just told you to remain silent.' Brexford's tone of voice moderated slightly. 'What is your name, wench?'

'Geo . . . Georgina, my lord.' Her eyes remained rooted amongst the straw.

'Georgina *what*?' My, but she was pretty, he was thinking. Lusciously plump, too. And as for his tantalising glimpse of that sweet pussy . . . Jeremy Brexford's devious brain was going busily to work.

'Please, sir, Georgina Tennant, sir. But you won't tell Miss –'

He interrupted her. 'What have you to say for yourself, Miss Tennant?'

Her gaze crept up as far as his cavalry-twill-covered knees. 'I, I promise I won't come here again. Nothing like this will ever occur again. But, do you see, if you were to tell Miss Petty . . . Oh, my God. Please, my lord, if you do, my father, my father . . .' She was unable to finish. She was in genuine anguish, tears were streaming down her cheeks.

Brexford realised with secret glee that he had this pulchritudinous lass entirely at his mercy. He could do what he will with her, provided that he guaranteed not to tell Claire Petty about her tumble with his lad. Naturally, he *would* make it his business to let the lustful headmistress know; she would revel in the knowledge; but she would not of course enlighten and sack Georgina, or inform her father. Lord Brexford and Miss Petty could both take carnal advantage of this delicious situation.

'But you have to be punished, you do understand that, don't you, wench? Such utterly deplorable behaviour cannot be condoned. It merits the most severe chastisement.'

'But Miss Petty will expel me,' she blubbered. 'My father will kill me.'

'Undoubtedly.' Jeremy Brexford's deviant sexual brain was in top gear as he thoughtfully studied the two of them.

'She's a nice girl, m'lord,' ventured Thomas, at his peril. 'She truly is.'

The manufactured Brexford temper blazed again. 'And you are an unspeakable young varlet,' he snapped. But meanwhile he was raunchily recalling the poised-to-plunge buttocks, the hang of Thomas's heavy balls and the lusty fashion in which the pretty Miss Tennant's legs had been wrapped around his.

'There is no excuse, Thomas,' he went on. 'None whatsoever. Were she a serving girl, a scullery maid, then perhaps. But tupping a young lady of gentle breeding? A girl miles above your station? No, sir. Absolutely not.'

Thomas hung his head in shame. 'No, m'lord.' He truly believed his master's words. The fact that Georgina was forbidden, upper-class flesh from Chalmers had always been in his mind, adding to the excitement.

'Very well, Miss Tennant,' said Brexford, calm once more. 'Having given the matter due thought, I have reluctantly decided on this occasion to be merciful and not to reveal the sordid facts of the matter to Miss Petty.'

A great sigh of relief sobbed through Georgina. She wiped a hand over her damp cheek, then took a handkerchief from her blouse pocket to dry her eyes. 'Oh, thank you, sir,' she mumbled. For the first time since she had seen him watching them she managed for a brief moment to meet his eyes. 'Thank you. Thank you.'

'However, you *will* be punished,' he said sternly. 'Without delay. Both of you. You will follow me into the manor.'

25

Chapter 3

As they approached the grey, grim-looking Gothic pile
with its somewhat eroded flying buttresses and wealth of
stone arched windows, fresh fears began to gnaw in Georgina's belly. The threat of exposure to Miss Petty and her
legendary wrath, and of further caning followed by expulsion, no longer loomed, but lunch-break at Chalmers
would be nearly over and were she not back shortly her absence would inevitably be noticed. Her truancy, if not her
wanton behaviour, would be discovered and she would be
obliged to suffer a beating yet again. But here she was being escorted in the opposite direction to the school – and
to what dire fate?

'Wait here until summoned,' Lord Brexford sternly commanded when they were in the huge arched and domed
hallway with its rather gloomy exhibition of ancestral por-
traits, its heavy oak chests and its small collection of
shining suits of armour.

Georgina Tennant and Thomas Farley, two healthy
lusty teenagers who despite their massively different social
backgrounds had, but a short while before, had their naked
sexual parts pressed together, watched the upright, broad
back until Brexford disappeared through a door. After
glancing nervously at one another, neither one of them
managing to raise the feeblest of rueful smiles, they looked
hurriedly in different directions, their young minds crammed with very different thoughts – Georgina's mainly
concerned with her dread of being late, plus a fear of what
was now to befall her.

However, Thomas was not over-frightened at the prospect of punishment by Lord Brexford and his lady – for surely they would administer it themselves; they always did, and, whilst he had not personally experienced it, he knew that their bark was always more severe than their bite. He was also aware, as were all the members of the thirty-two-strong household, that his master and mistress derived some sort of perverse pleasure from thrashing people. It was whispered that this enjoyment had sexual roots though at his tender age he found it impossible to understand what this implied.

The fact was that, an imminent trouncing notwithstanding, young Thomas Farley was most full of himself. Thomas had seen and touched and kissed all of Georgina's wonderful, secret places. Thomas had had his stable boy's bare cock and balls stroked and fondled by the daughter of a gentleman. Thomas had put it inside her. He had, at long last, *done* it. He glanced shyly at Georgina again, just as she was stealing a peep at him. This time they did not look away from one another.

'What's, what's going to happen to us then, Tom?' Georgina asked tremulously. 'What is he going to do to us?'

'Nothing much. I expect we'll get a bit of a whopping.'

She blanched. 'But you saw my poor bot, the state it's in from yesterday's caning. I'm very sore. I don't think I can take any more.'

'I saw your bum, yes. I kissed and licked it, too.' His cock stirred at the memory. 'Was it good?'

'I don't like to be beaten.' Her hands stole to her backside. She tenderly rubbed it.

'Not that, stupid. The doing you, I mean. I *did* you, remember. Was it good?'

It had most certainly not been good. Well, not the final part at any rate. Before, the leading up, the foreplay, that had been fantastic. But being so shockingly discovered when they were about to go to it had killed the pleasure utterly dead. She was still a virgin, of that she was certain. There had been no blood; he had poked his thing in no more than half an inch or so to bring to her only the slightest discomfort as it dug at her hymen.

'You surely did *not* do me,' she told him, eyes challenging his.

'I did so. It was up you.'

She held her finger and thumb very slightly apart. 'That much only, you twit. Then you went and spilled everywhere. Ugh!' Her knickers were sticky; she would have loved to get them off and wash them and shower herself.

'Oh,' responded Thomas, lamely. The news was not pleasing. Nevertheless he told himself that it had been just as good as a proper poking anyway, even that much. The tip of his prick at least had been inside her, she couldn't take that away from him. 'Well,' he ventured, his young male pride slightly dented, 'we'd have had to stop anyhow, wouldn't we? With him standing there?'

She briefly scowled, then she poked her tongue out at him. Her expression immediately changed; she looked as if she were about to cry again. 'I'm going to be in the most terrible trouble at school,' she moaned. 'I ought to be back there by now, I'm sure. What's the time?'

He consulted his hunter. 'Twenty minutes after two o'clock.'

'Shit.' She fought back her tears. 'Classes started five minutes ago. They'll be missing me already.'

He could not resist a cruel, schoolboy-type remark. 'Then you're going to get a double whopping, looks like.' He grinned. 'Your bum's going to be red raw by the time your headmistress has done with it, I reckon.'

'You are a proper b –, Thomas, you know that? An absolute –' She chopped off the vastly unladylike epithet which was about to emerge from her pretty lips. She coloured, vastly irritated, her fear mounting.

Moments later, Lord Brexford returned, his darkly handsome features expressionlessly covering seething sexual anticipation at what he and Sophronia had conspired together to inflict on the miscreant youngsters. He hooked an imperious finger at them and turned his back.

'Come,' he said.

They followed him through a succession of high-ceilinged, thickly-carpeted corridors past tall, interior window after window and out, near the end of one wing, into a secluded little patio. There, spring sunshine fell limply on a small collection of ancient instruments of torture and castigation. Pausing on the patio's threshold, her plimsolls planted on worn and shiny cobblestones, Georgina glanced nervously around, frowning, at first failing to understand what the implements were.

Lord Brexford crossed to an opposite corner where there stood, side by side, two sets of heavy wooden stocks. In one of them, a prisoner was obliged to sit low to the ground, his neck and wrists trapped in holes between a pair of narrow planks, his ankles trapped between another pair. This confinement was for the purpose of exposing a person to public ridicule and scorn – and a constant pelting with rotten vegetables, eggs and other disagreeable projectiles. The other stocks was a standing version of the same contraption, shaped like a crucifix.

As Brexford opened the padlocks of the low set of stocks with a big, ancient iron key, his wife appeared through a small door behind him. She was disguised in a full black executioner's mask with her hair tucked up inside it, and a shapeless, black ankle-length dress with several rows of black glass beads hanging on its bosom.

'Who's *that*?' Georgina whispered to Thomas. The tiny blonde hairs down her spine were prickling.

'It'll be her ladyship, of course, though she don't want us to know it, does she?' Thomas muttered back.

'Heavens. What's going to happen to us, Tom? They're surely not going to use those awful things?'

Georgina was beginning to understand the implications of the grim objects in front of her: the stocks, the rack, the iron maiden, the whips and thumbscrews, other things which she could not identify but which appeared simply dreadful. The whipping post.

'Us'll be all right. You'll see. I know them. Us'll come to not much harm.'

'Not much . . .? God.'

The imperious Brexford finger was beckoning them again. Side by side, Georgina and Thomas shuffled across the cobblestones towards its owner, both of them looking at nothing but their feet as they did so.

Lady Brexford was holding a leather-handled scourge in one hand and she was threateningly slapping its bunch of foot-long, leather, punishment thongs across her other palm. Dressed as she was in that black, sack-like garment she appeared most intimidating.

'That'll do. That's far enough, you two,' said her husband. The youngsters stopped a short way from him, still concentrating their gazes towards the ground. 'You are both found guilty of indulging in a gross and illicit act of sexual intercourse in my stables. Before I pass sentence, what have you to say for yourselves, if anything?'

Georgina's gaze skidded over the cobblestones then travelled uncertainly from Lord Brexford's dusty brogues up over his person to his stern face. 'If it please your lordship, that's not possible. I'm a virgin,' she said.

He raised an eyebrow. 'I should have hardly thought, from all that I observed, that that can possibly be true, Miss Tennant,' he said. 'Lying merely compounds your sin, and will add to your punishment.'

Pulse beginning to race, she protested, 'Well, it's true, and I swear that it is. We, we were going to do it, and, yes, I did want to do it, but we, we *didn't*, if you see what I mean. We nearly did, that's all.' Her cheeks were slowly turning, as, fearfully embarrassed, she dragged the words out, from pink through every shade of red to scarlet.

'Nearly, eh? Well, well.' Brexford's eyes flickered to Thomas. 'What have you to say about the matter, boy? Does the wench remain a virgin? And stop staring at your boots, they're not going to help you.'

Thomas raised his eyes as far as Brexford's chest. 'It's true, m'lord. Leastwise, I think it is.'

'You think it is. But you don't know. I see. Rather an odd state of affairs, would you not say?'

Lord Brexford's gaze slid sardonically from Thomas to settle back on Georgina. Titillated enormously by the scene he had organised, and by thoughts of what he had in store for his hapless victims, he was vastly enjoying himself.

'Then we have no option but to discover the truth of the matter, have we, missy?' he said. 'Should you be lying, Miss Tennant, your punishment will be that much more severe. If you are not, then it will be a mitigating circumstance which will be taken into account. Nevertheless, whatever the truth you have both acted most wantonly and sleazily and you will be chastised accordingly.' His steely eyes fell once more upon Thomas. 'Particularly you, Master Farley. For daring to dally with an upper-class girl, whether she was willing or not.'

Georgina had not heard much beyond the words 'discover the truth of the matter'. They kept on ringing in her ears. She was quaking, a bundle of nerves. What hideous embarrassment were these people about to inflict upon her? She was not to be long in finding out.

'Come over here to me, girl,' ordered the mask-muffled voice of Lady Brexford.

Georgina failed to move one inch.

'You heard, Miss Tennant. Do as you are bid instantly or it will be the worse for you,' Brexford grunted.

With the greatest of reluctance, her mind a turmoil, Georgina warily approached the lady in black. As soon as the girl reached her, Sophronia dropped to her knees in front of her. Saying nothing, she began to raise the hem of Georgina's dress.

'We shall soon find out if you were telling the truth or not,' she muttered.

The sudden indignity was so shocking that Georgina was unable to move a muscle. Her skirt was rucked all the way up and pinned to her belly. The damp crotch of her knickers was pulled to one side. Lady Brexford's eyes, glinting greenly behind the little slits in her mask, feasted on the pretty, little plump pussy. She opened its lips with her thumbs. She wormed the tip of one of them inside. The only thing which saved Georgina from fainting right away in humiliation was the fact that she had her back to both the males.

'The girl is, indeed, a virgin,' Sophronia revealed, sounding surprised. She let the dress fall and climbed up from her knees.

31

Lord Brexford found the news agreeable. A reluctant virgin on his hands, then. Chalmers seemed to be full of the delightful creatures. 'Very well,' he said. 'You will come over here please, young lady.' He was holding open the upper planks of the stocks.

She went wordlessly to him, heart seemingly trying to thump its way out of her chest.

'Sit on the stool.'

It was a small, three-legged, wooden affair of the kind favoured by milkmaids. Georgina smoothed her skirt beneath her buttocks and parked her behind on the stool. He had her bend double and positioned her neck in the central, semi-circular hole in the bottom plank and her wrists in the smaller ones – an upper arm's length from her neck. He lowered the other plank and locked her in. There was plenty of room for her neck, but the hand holes were tight on her plump wrists.

'Now your feet,' said Lord Brexford. 'Don't worry, this is not going to hurt you.' As he lifted her legs one by one by the lower calves, Georgina had the distinct – and correct – impression that he squeezed them more than was called for, and that his thumbs subjected them to a brief and tender caress. Then she was locked in, helpless, creased forward at the waist, the backs of her knees already getting uncomfortable. As Brexford stood back to inspect his work, her attention was dragged to his eyes; in them there gleamed a strange, indefinable light.

Georgina was facing the whipping post. Thick as a telegraph pole, of old, varnished oak and nine feet high, it had a series of black iron hooks running three feet down from its top. On its lowermost hook there hung a pair of shiny steel shackles.

Brexford turned his attention to the lad. 'It would appear, Thomas, that you enjoy showing off your private parts to young women,' he said. 'That being the case, you may exhibit yourself now. Take off your clothes.'

'But, my lord, I . . .' The lad started to protest, with a blush.

'All of your clothes, Thomas. This instant. Let us cast our eyes on that of which you are so proud.'

Georgina watched in growing personal discomfort as Thomas stripped reluctantly to his underpants, hesitated and was brusquely ordered to remove that garment too. Despite her highly nervous and uncomfortable condition she found herself experiencing a little thrill of excitement as the item of adult male anatomy she had only seen once in her life – and then in its erect state – was revealed in splendid flaccidity. She watched intently as, closing in on Thomas, Lord Brexford grabbed him by the upper arm and marched him to the whipping post. Lifting the shackles down he fastened them to the boy's wrists. Staring silently and sullenly, the naked Thomas showed little fear, but he found himself horribly embarrassed to be thus treated in front of three other people, especially since two of them were of the fair sex.

Brexford forced him to face the whipping post, inches from it. Raising the shackled hands above the boy's head until they were at full stretch, he slipped a central link of their chain over the appropriate hook. Thomas found himself obliged to stand on his toes. Afforded a sideways view of the nude stable lad, so libidinous did Georgina begin to find this sight that, incredibly, her fear started to melt away. No relisher personally of being beaten, she nevertheless discovered the scene of the chained, naked, splendidly endowed young man, faced by a mysterious, hooded woman in black who was apparently about to thrash him, to be extraordinarily arousing. She was astonished to find herself becoming less aware of her shredded nerves and her incommodious, ungainly position and more and more conscious of her pussy. In her childish innocence, she had no way of knowing that she was, apart from by the sight of nude, stretched Thomas, also being sexually affected by being in a type of bondage.

Brexford positioned himself comfortably, leaning against the upright stocks from where he could keep his eyes both on Georgina and the imminent thrashing. He nodded to Sophronia, his mouth curling at the edges into the faintest of smirks. Licking her lips beneath the hood, eyes sparkling, Lady Brexford slowly raised her arm until the scourge, its thongs loosely hanging, was behind her head. She paused, ogling her well-rounded, fleshy target, then swished the scourge through the air. It slapped smack-ingly across a buttock, its ends wrapping themselves around a hip to flick into Thomas's taut belly.

Yelping, Thomas jerked his backside and clenched his buttock muscles. His fat slab of penis and his scrotum jumped. Sophronia sighed, Lord Brexford drew a deep breath through flaring nostrils – and Georgina could not help but drool.

Several thin red lines had appeared on the boy's right buttock and across his hip. Sophronia licked the tips of her fingers and ran their wetness over the marks, making them shine. Thomas's lips trembled. Changing position, Sophronia raised her arm on high once more. She paused, to study closely the lad's face. His eyes were screwed closed, his jaw muscles twitched, as tense as those of his bottom.

The scourge slashed down again with stinging force, this time across the left buttock. Once more, cock and balls jumped with the impact; the boy's circumcised glans brushed up against the post. There was a second loud yelp and a gasp from him as a burning sensation began to in-vade his backside. Lady Brexford, not particularly because she believed in its healing powers, but simply because she got a kick from doing it, applied more spittle.

Georgina had become so engrossed in the scene she had almost forgotten that most probably it was to be her turn next. What she was witness to was unexpectedly but most thoroughly turning her on – just as Ellie's descriptions of her canings had done. Her pussy was getting damper by the second.

Something quite unforeseen was beginning to happen to Thomas, too. He had been cuffed before – on innumerable occasions – he had received hand beatings dozens of times from his mother on his trousered backside. But this was something very different, this naked, public flogging. The scourge lashed across both buttocks on its third, and then its fourth descent. With Sophronia lecherously applying yet more spittle, despite his pain Thomas realised with a start that he was actually beginning to enjoy the red hot glow which was engulfing his behind. As he opened his eyes and his gaze flickered from one to the other of the two unmasked observers who were so intently studying his beating, his embarrassment fell away like a discarded cloak. Here he was, naked in front of the girl he had just all but fucked, and his lustful master, whilst the beautiful young lady of the manor – the sight of whom constantly aroused in him the most libidinous of thoughts – was treating him to a thorough whopping and stroking her spittle-wet fingers on his bare bottom between swipes. And he suddenly began to relish having his genitals on display – besides, he knew full well from swimming naked in the river with his pals in the summer that his equipment, larger than that of any of them, was something to be proud of.

Five, six, seven carefully spaced times, Lady Brexford laid into the fast-reddening behind, enough to hurt but not to split its flesh. The heat seemed to be seeping from the welted area directly into the stable lad's groin. His cock started to stir.

Georgina watched with widening eyes whilst her renegade pussy grew wetter and wetter. Thomas began a regular moaning as the vivid stripes became a complicated network reaching around both hips and tailing off on his belly. He was thrusting his loins jerkily back and forth in almost an attitude of copulation and his cock was fast growing in convulsive little jerks.

Poor, trapped Georgina was experiencing those randy emotions which would normally make treating herself to a hearty frigging imperative. She found the entire experience almost beyond belief, a twist of reality like a passage from that dirty book, *Justine*, which Miss Petty had confiscated from Ellie the previous winter term. As she derived what little masturbative pleasure she could by wiggling and rocking her bottom on the milkmaid's stool, Thomas's cock throbbed all the way up to achieve a hard-on as fine and as strong as the one he had been trying so clumsily to stick into her.

Lord Brexford was possessed of the keenest of noses for

all things sexual. His stable lad's arousal was of course plain to observe, but he was aware solely from the manner in which Sophronia fingered Thomas's buttocks each time she applied spittle to them that his lovely wife was every bit as turned on. And as for Georgina Tennant, why the fetchingly plump young lady's eyes were positively steamy, whilst the fingers of her imprisoned hands were clenching and unclenching, her feet were constantly on the move, her eyes were shining and she was wriggling and squirming on the little stool. She seemed to be almost panting with lust. His lordship, too, was in as horny a condition as the three of them. His cock was begging to be released from the tight confinement of his trousers.

'Enough, Sophie my love,' he commanded. Sophronia, face sweaty beneath the hood, reluctantly lowered her arm. 'Now I believe it's the turn of the wicked wench,' he told her.

Lady Brexford strode with purposeful step to Georgina, the scourge grasped in both hands, as her husband began to free the girl's feet. A twinge of fear revisited Georgina, but her overriding emotion remained that of lust. Going behind her, Brexford took hold of her thighs, planted her knees beneath her skirt on the cobblestones, then removed the stool from between her legs so that she was kneeling doubled forward with her neck and hands still trapped. She tried not to think about what was to happen to her. As she felt her skirt being raised and heaped on her hips, and her drawers lowered half way down her thighs, she kept her eyes rooted on Thomas – whose behaviour had turned gross.

Desperately seeking relief, the boy had pressed his groin into the whipping post. His big hard-on was flattened upwards against the old, smooth wood and his balls were squashed into it. His buttocks tight as iron, he was masturbating himself against the post, his backside pumping and pounding as if he were screwing it. Keenly observing this lewd performance, even as her knickers reached the back of her knees and Lord Brexford ran an appreciative, exploratory hand over her buttocks Georgina found a dirty little rhyme, which had of late been doing the rounds of

Chalmers, running through her head. In days of old, she thought, When knights were bold and women weren't invented, Men fucked holes in telegraph poles and walked away contented.

She wanted to giggle. She wanted to frig herself. She wanted to beg for mercy. She wanted her heart to stop its wild pounding.

'My God, Sophie, will you take a good look at this,' exclaimed Brexford, eyeing Georgina's fat bottom and smoothing a thumb over its bruises.

'It would seem that the girl's had whipping enough,' commented Sophronia.

'Perhaps. Perhaps not.'

'Those marks are very fresh. From yesterday, I'll be bound, if not this very morning.'

Georgina mumbled. 'Yesterday. And I'm still very sore.'

'So you break rules every day, do you, girl?' said Brexford. 'How very perverse of you.' He glanced in Thomas's direction. The lad's masturbatory jerks against the whipping post were getting ever more frantic. 'Master Thomas appears to need a little help,' he observed to his wife. 'And I warrant I know what you would love to do to him, do I not, dear, dirty heart?'

Lord Brexford had recently slightly relaxed the sex rules applying to his wife. Though copulation in vagina or anus was still prohibited to anyone but himself, she was now allowed to fellate whomsoever she pleased.

'*Do* you now?' she said, licking her lips. And *I* warrant I know exactly what you are planning to do to the young lady, she thought. You wicked man.

'Get on with it.'

Without another word, Sophronia dropped the scourge onto the cobblestones. She hurried purposefully back to the whipping post where she got to her knees at Thomas's side. She took the boy by his thighs and turned him to face her, then she pulled her mask up over her ruby painted mouth and offered her pouty lips to his hard-on.

'Try this,' she muttered, to his swollen glans. ' 'Tis softer than wood.'

Thomas had not the faintest idea what she meant. He had never heard of such a thing. When Lady Brexford clamped her lips over the end of his cock and avidly sucked it he gasped in shock as much as in lust.

Lord Brexford had crouched down in front of Georgina, his bulk blocking her view of the whipping-post area. His face was hovering just above hers and his breath – not unpleasant with its faint aroma of after-lunch cigar – was washing over her cheeks as he quietly told her. 'Your bum is in a sad and sorry state already, Miss Petty, I'll be bound. I fear another thrashing may damage it beyond repair; nevertheless I am prepared to administer it, do you understand? However, I shall offer you a choice.' He put his lips close to her ear. 'Just a short while ago, with reference to sexual intercourse, you said that you did want to do it, but had not done so. Is this not so?'

In utter confusion, pussy continuing to ooze, most acutely aware of her ribald sexual display, Georgina could not find words to reply.

'Well? Did you, or did you not? Have the courtesy to answer me, girl.' Anxious for her answer, desperate to free his cock and put it to work in her, Lord Brexford's voice was strained, the tone almost threatening.

'Yes,' Georgina whispered. 'I did.' In the last few moments she had become aware of the slightly warm touch of the spring sunshine on her naked haunches. On top of her visual stimulation by the sight of the naked, whipped Thomas, and from her helplessness at her plight of being trapped in the stocks, she was now beginning to get a thrill from her lewd state of semi-undress. It was all becoming most overwhelming.

'Would you still like to lose your virginity, Georgina?' A hiss.

She nodded, mouth slack, head reeling.

'Take a good look at Thomas. Your almost lover.'

Brexford moved out of her line of vision. Georgina's eyes popped as her gaze fell on the lurid scene in front of her. Thomas had got the idea of a blow-job very quickly. He was heaving his bare bottom in much the same fashion as he had been doing with his genitals crushed against the whipping post, but this time his sturdy prick was jerking in and out between Sophronia's lips whilst she fondled his heavy balls. Unlike Thomas, Georgina had heard of this act – for girls of her age tended to be rather more precocious than boys in such respects, and in any case Ellie had many times related how she had done it to Lord Brexford and to other men in orgies here at the manor. Observing fellatio being expertly performed in the flesh brought a surge to Georgina's massively riding tide of lust. She began rubbing the tops of her inner thighs together, her pussy was contracting, her hands were balled into tight, plump fists.

'And now return your attention to me – your lover-to-be.'

Brexford had got to his feet and was unbuttoning his trousers. Fishing inside his gaping fly, he dragged out a hard-on at least as impressive as that of his stable lad.

'And observe these,' he grunted. He brought out his balls and jiggled them at her in his fingers.

Georgina gasped, her lips slack.

'Well, Miss Tennant. What is to be? It is your choice. Is it to be another thrashing? A report to Claire Petty? Expulsion? Or . . .' He jerked his fist on his cock. 'Or this? Your sweet little cherry?'

She was beginning to pant. She feared that she would faint away with excitement. Mouth gaping, tongue tip poking between her lips, eyes very wide, she sighed, 'That. My, my cherry.' More words spilled from her lips, in a randy whisper.

'Please. Oh, please. Do it to me, my lord.'

Jeremy Brexford almost tripped over in his anxiety to position himself behind her. Uncaring about the cobblestones, he fell heavily to his knees. Parting Georgina's inflamed buttocks with the flats of his hands, he peered lustfully between them, cock hovering. He fingered open her fleshy labia. Pulse racing, he positioned his glans. He gently eased the helmet in until it touched the obstructive little membrane of hymen. Muttering, 'It's going to hurt just a little, but don't worry, it will soon be over,' he began to push.

Georgina cared not a ha'penny piece that it was going to hurt. All girls went through it. This time, she was going all the way. She was going to be free, like Ellie. And what an unbelievably ribald fashion in which to be losing her cherry! Here on her dimply knees, locked in a stocks, watching a hooded, titled lady suck the cock of a stable lad who had almost reached the prize which the lady's peer of the realm husband was now about to take.

With a small grunt of effort, Brexford pushed his hard-on past her hymen.

It hurt, but only marginally. Quickly, the pain was past and Georgina's tight little pussy was crammed in a way that no girlish tongue or fingers could fill it. She squealed once, loudly. Then she began to moan, as if hurting, with each of Brexford's powerful penile thrusts. He was penetrating her all the way until his balls squashed into the plumpness of her upper thighs, withdrawing almost completely to lech momentarily on the sight of the blood and pussy juice smearing his cock as he rapidly climbed the stairway to orgasm, then plunging again.

There was no way that Jeremy Brexford could contain himself for very long after having breeched a young, plump and pretty virgin whose buttocks were red and striped and bruised from a recent caning.

No way could Master Thomas contain himself, either. Not that he had any inclination so to do. As Brexford's seed surged, preparing to erupt from the lord's scrotum, that of his stable lad spurted copiously into his wife's mouth. Thomas could not believe that she was not going to gag and to spit the sperm out, but she did not. On the contrary, she greedily swallowed it down whilst with her hand buried beneath her dress she fingered herself almost, but not quite, to orgasm.

With a lusty shout, the sound echoing and re-echoing around the patio, Georgina came. Then she climaxed almost immediately again, this time with a quiet whimper. Having no desire or intention of impregnating the girl,

Brexford drew out of her. He fisted his cock, and with a series of climactic little jerks upon it he shot stream upon stream of sperm all over those luscious, fat buttocks and over the chubby backs of Georgina's soft, white thighs. When he had done, and was slowly sinking, glassy-eyed, into a squat behind her, his semen was trickling down one of her thighs all the way to the knickers at her knees. Her head was lolling loosely on her imprisoned neck, her eyes were firmly closed, she was heavily panting.

As, some fifteen minutes later, Lord Brexford sent bemused, sated Georgina on her way back to Chalmers – with the fearful threat that should she breathe a word of what had transpired, Miss Petty would be told that she had lost her virginity to Thomas on her back in the stables – and Thomas, dressed once more, bemused himself, left the patio, Sophronia removed her hood.

'I didn't come even once, Jeremy,' she grumbled. 'Everyone else did, but I didn't make it.' Her wet and itchy pussy was giving her hell. 'I want to *come*.'

Brexford's salacious eye alit upon the rack. 'Then come you shall, my sweet,' he said.

Chapter 4

'Flat on your belly, I think, Sophie,' Jeremy Brexford decided aloud. 'That way I shall have access to both your sweet places.'

Lady Brexdford shivered. 'Both places. Yes,' she happily muttered.

The joint, powerful, Brexford libido was in full swing. Sophronia craved sex as a starving woman needs to eat. Her husband, despite having enjoyed an enormous orgasm but a quarter of an hour previously, was more than ready for another carnal session, for he had stuck a new feather in his swordsman's cap with the defloration of a virgin and his loins continued to burn with the recollection.

'What do you have on beneath your dress?' he asked.

She smirked at him. 'One of those pretty little corsets which you like so much.'

'And what else?'

'Nothing at all.'

'Then we shall both sport naked from the waist down.'

Lord Brexford kicked off his brogues so hard that one of them flew half-way across the patio. 'Take down my trousers,' he commanded. After coupling with Georgina he had put his cock away, but he had fastened only one button of his fly.

Wife Sophronia might be – of just over a year – but the constant sexual demands of her exceptionally lusty husband had not served to jade her appetite for him; indeed, if anything, it had sharpened – for Jeremy's sexual imagination was wonderfully fertile, and each revelation of his potent genitalia, often under new and inventive circumstances proved just as fresh and exciting as it had been on the very first occasion.

She undid that lone button. He had on no underpants, his cock lying in hairy shadow behind his gaping flies. Her nimble fingers – their perfectly manicured nails painted almost exactly the same shade of emerald green as her eyes – made short work of unfastening his belt and the restraining button beneath it. The heavy twill trousers dropped of their own accord, the waist and belt bagging around his knees. Sophronia's eyes latched in prurient fascination on his thick pole of a prick, the only one allowed to penetrate her no matter how wild and excessive an orgy the two of them may be involved in. She was permitted to fondle and masturbate, and lately to lick and suck, another man's cock – always provided that her husband was present – she could otherwise excite him with boobs or bottom, and the man was allowed to make free with her person, but on no account was copulation or buggery to take place. On occasion, since Jeremy did not apply the same strict rules to himself, Lady Brexford thought this more than a little unfair, but she went grudgingly along with it. In any case, she had no qualms about watching her husband at it – indeed, one of her most salacious thrills in life was being right there by her side and egging the girl on when her husband was fortunate enough to deflower a young virgin.

'My, my. We must give this dirty thing a wash *tout de suite*,' she muttered. She lifted his limp penis by the glans, between finger and thumb, so that he might clearly see it. It was liberally smeared with dried blood.

'Why?' he asked. 'A fitting enough souvenir, is it not?'

But Lady Brexford did not relish the idea of having a cock soiled in such a manner inside her, and she told him so.

'Very well,' he said. 'Clean it off for me.'

She pulled his trousers down to his feet, and he stepped out of them. He walked in his grey wool socks, stained cock proudly swaying, with her to a granite wall where a small ornamental fountain trickled. The water fell from the open mouth of a sculpture of a leaping fish. Sophronia had him stand over the fish and she commenced to wash off the blood.

The patio was contained within the gloomy east wing of the manor house. The wing, unlived in for fifty years and seldom visited, was thick with dust. However, this afternoon, Meg, a nubile, young chambermaid – one of several members of the large household to have been the recipient of a bare bottom thrashing from Lord Brexford – had been dispatched into the wing by orders of the butler. She was in search of a longcase clock to replace the one in her mistress's bedroom which had irreparably broken down. She had just found the clock. Tall and handsome, it was standing close to a grimy window in an otherwise almost bare, one-time guest bedroom.

Meg's instructions had been first to wind up the longcase to make sure it worked, and assuming that it did to hump it all the way through the manor to Lady Brexford's bedroom. She was vastly irritated at having been lumbered with this unwelcome task since the clock was heavy and awkward and there were plenty of strong and capable men amongst the staff to do the job.

Bloody men, Meg was thinking, as she inserted a key in one of the two holes in the elegant clockface and began to turn it. Always on top, the selfish buggers, always shoving us women around and giving us the hardest work. Bloody men.

Her eyes fell, through the dirty window, on moving shadows in what was referred to by the household as the black museum courtyard. Pausing in her winding, she stuck her buttonish little nose close to the window. She cleaned a patch of dust from the glass. The window was grubby on the outside, too, but not so much so that she could not make out the clear shape of what could only be her master's strong back. Wearing just a waistcoat, a shirt whose tails appeared to be tucked up under his coat, and a pair of socks, he was facing the fountain. Beside him, her forearm disappearing in front of him in the region of his groin, was Lady Brexford, dressed in black.

Meg quietly gasped. For heaven's sake – was Lord Brexford having a pee in the fountain whilst his wife held it for him? Cripes, this took the biscuit!

That was the moment when the last trace of blood had been washed from Jeremy's cock. The gentle ministrations of Sophronia's fair hand had caused his erection to be well on the rise again. He turned away from the fountain, unknowingly offering Meg a full frontal view of himself. Above him, the chambermaid's light blue eyes bulged. Her mistress had her hand wrapped firmly around her master's big penis and she was lovingly stroking it! And, God save us, with her free hand she was pulling down the zip which ran from the back of her shapeless dress – why on earth was she attired in such an awful garment – to below its waist.

The dress opened and fell in a heap around Lady Brexford's delicate feet. Beneath it, she was wearing a white whalebone corselet with pretty little pale pink and blue bows weaved into it, one of the very items of underclothing which Meg had put into her wardrobe that same morning. The corselet uplifted her breasts so that half her nipples were on erotic display, and it raunchily framed her sensual haunches. And the voluptuous lady, like her husband, had on no lower underclothing to cover the shame of her private parts.

As the couple moved together towards the rack, the reddish hue in Sophronia's hair – both of her head and of her pussy – glinted in the sunlight.

'On your belly, Sophie,' murmured Brexford, his voice low and thick with lust, when they reached the ancient torture machine. Meg could not hear his words, though she could very well see that he had achieved almost a full cock-stand, and it was most obvious that he was about to spend that hard-on on his wife.

As her mistress began to clamber onto the insidious contraption which had been designed to stretch a person until either they confessed to whatever they were accused of or their arms and legs were torn from their sockets, Meg, oblivious to her duties with the longcase clock, rushed from the room to hurry excitedly all the way through the wing to the main section of the house. She was in urgent search of Bertram, assistant to the cook – and her not-so-secret lover. A bloody man.

Meanwhile, Georgina, having torn down through the wood belonging to the Deal Manor estate and having arrived, flushed and out of breath, to within sight of Chalmers was dismayed to observe that there was a flurry of activity beyond the grounds of the school which in no way corresponded with the normal day's curriculum. Dozens of girls were spread out all the way around the school, hunting through long grass and bushes. On the English Channel side of the establishment, looking like miniature dolls from where Georgina was hurrying down, but plainly visible, more pupils were scouring the cliff edge, and peering over it down to the lonely beach.

Filled with dread, Georgina realised that it was her absence which must have inspired this operation. They were searching for her. She slowed to a walk, but her mind raced. As she got nearer she started to hear the sound of her name being called out repeatedly on all sides.

The first girl to spot her and to come running towards her, arms waving, was one of her dorm-mates – dowdy, bespectacled Pru. 'There you are, Georgie!' Prudence called out as she approached her. 'Where the devil have you been, you silly twit? The whole school's searching for you.' She spotted the ripped skirt. 'What *happened* to you?'

Georgina's athletic mind had been struggling to work out some sort of excuse. It found one. A rather desperate one.

'It was ghastly. Horrific,' she panted. 'I had a bad tummy – you know that. I went out for some fresh air. There was, there was this frightful *man* in the grounds. He took hold of me and he, he dragged me away, up to the wood. I, I fought with him. I fought like a tiger, for I simply had to get away from him. He was going to rape me. God!'

Prudence squinted at her, her eyes distorted through her heavy-lensed spectacles. 'Pull the other one, Georgie,' she said, pouring scorn on Georgina's words. 'It's got bells on.'

46

'What?'

'He chucked you over the fence did he, this man? He picked you up bodily and chucked you over the fence?'

'Of course not, stupid. He dragged me through the main gates. He, he was a beast. A *beast*.'

'In full view of the dining-room, right? He dragged you through the gates and not one of us saw it. Hah!' Prudence said. She grinned wickedly. 'You've been up at the manor, haven't you, you dirty cow? You've been with that stable lad. Don't think I don't know about *him*.'

Georgina's shoulders sagged. 'Oh, shit.'

'Exactly what you're going to be in, you daft date, you.' They began walking towards Chalmers, Prudence waving and shouting the news that Georgina had been found. 'Petters won't fall for your stupid story in a zillion years,' she pronounced. 'You'd better think of something else, and p.d.q. What are you going to tell her?'

'I don't know,' Georgina said, miserably. 'God, what shall I do?'

'She's going to stripe your bum again, and how. Oh, boy!'

Whilst this little drama was being enacted, up at the manor Lord Brexford had produced a moth-eaten, maroon velvet cushion from a room in the deserted wing and he had used it to hump up Lady Brexford's pelvis from the planked surface of the rack. Having strapped her wrists and one ankle onto the ends of the ropes which went over pulleys and ratchets on all four corners of the rack, he was busy engaged in buckling the fourth strap around Sophronia's other ankle. He pulled it tight. The ropes were lying slackly on the smooth wooden boards above her head and below her feet. With his hard-on wobbly and aching for more action, he began to turn the pulleys.

'Wowww!' went Bertram. Meg had rushed him from the kitchen and all the way through the manor and the two of them had just arrived at the window by the side of the longcase clock. 'I knew they were pervs but . . . hell's bells.' He licked his lips, eyes glued to the kinky scene.

'How are you enjoying it, dearest?' asked Jeremy throatily. 'I don't believe I've ever done this to you before, have I?'

'No. And I like it. Pull me tighter, do,' muttered Lady Brexford. She was not simply liking it – she was adoring it. It was far more than the fact of being stretched and helpless as she was – an intriguing variety of bondage – it was the being bare from the waist down with her bottom raised on high on a cushion and her pussy so lewdly exposed to her husband's gaze. It was the nervous thrill at what was about to befall her – most especially a supposed beating and the promised buggery. It was the vivid mental picture of the lewdery which already transpired on this sunny afternoon. It was the lingering taste of a stable lad's sperm in her mouth. It was the overwhelming need for orgasm.

'Tighter,' she pleaded. 'Stretch me right out.'

He wound up the ropes until there was a slight cracking noise from one of her joints, like somebody cracking a finger. Changing her tune, she begged him to stop. She was as extended as much as she could comfortably bear, as if she were the object of a gentle tug of war. Her cheek was resting on the shiny old wood. She was able only to move her head, hands and feet – and her bottom which was gently and pleasurably rocking on its pillow.

Her husband crabbed his hand between her lower buttocks and hooked two fingers into her pussy, discovering it to be sopping wet.

'You are indeed enjoying yourself, I find, my lady,' he observed. He glowered at her, playing the game to the full. 'This is *supposed* to be punishment,' he grated.

'So punish me, why don't you.'

Fetching the scourge from where it lay where she had let it fall on the cobblestones beside the stocks, he stomped to her with it held diagonally across his chest and slashed a back-handed blow – just hard enough, as if swatting a fly – across her behind. He followed through, swishing the scourge in the opposite direction, and then he repeated the action over and over again – forehand, backhand, forehand, backhand, forehand, backhand. When her buttocks – very quickly – were glowing brightly red, he climbed up onto his knees between her spread legs, still holding the scourge, panting, wracked with lust. Lowering himself onto her back, he angled his cock-head between her pussy lips and shoved the whole length of his hard-on into her.

'Jesus Christ,' muttered Bertram. His cook's trousers were tenting. 'What filthy minds their lordships have got, and that's the truth.'

Straying to the loose, elasticated top of Bertram's trousers, Meg's hand slipped down inside it and beneath a thin pair of underpants to lustily grab his cock. 'Filthy mind yourself,' she observed. 'So what's this, then? Not excited by what them's up to by any chance, are we?'

'I can't help it, can I? It was you as brought me here.'

'And what them's doing has caused *this*, dirty bugger.' She squeezed, good and hard. She was by his side, not looking at him, her wide eyes lustfully rooted on the rack. Her other hand dived down inside Bertram's pants to find and fondle his balls. 'Will you stick it in me, then? Will you be a-poking me?'

He gasped. 'You really think we . . .?'

'Go *on*. Right here. While we watch them go at it.'

Releasing Bertram's cock and balls, Meg reached up with both hands beneath her chambermaid's skirt and yanked her plain white knickers down to her knees. Hitching the skirt up behind, she tucked it into her belt. Then she half bent over, resting the flats of her bare forearms on the shelf below the window and her chin on the back of a hand to offer herself to him.

'Lower your trousers, Bertie. Fuck me. Do me, please? Now?' she asked him urgently.

Meg had never in her short sexual life been so blatant; such was the dramatic effect of first-time voyeurism on her. She was cleaning a fresh circle on the window in front of her nose, her bared white buttocks wobbling a little as a big, black tuft of pubic hair below them dragged Bertram's attention from the courtyard rut.

'We shouldn't, we shouldn't,' mumbled Bertram excitedly

– meanwhile preparing to do it. Together, he shoved his trousers and underpants down his hairy thighs. Closing in on Meg, he rubbed his fat prick helmet down her soft and pinky bottom cleft to slot it into her vulva. Putting his hands over the backs of her forearms on the window shelf, he heaved his cock deep inside her slippery pussy. He raised his eyes to take in the salacious scene below him in the courtyard.

Sophronia had already come. She was again approaching orgasm as Jeremy fucked her hard enough to cause the old stretching torture machine – not torturing today but providing a pleasure centre – to creak and wobble beneath them. Suddenly, his heavings stilled. He withdrew his cock.

'I'm going to poke it into your bum,' he panted. 'Ready?'

She groaned her eager assent.

Climbing off the rack whilst, unbeknown to him, two of his servants were lustily humping as they watched from behind a grimy window, Lord Brexford went in search of lubricant. Despite having been breeched on numerous occasions, his wife's bottom hole was as tiny and tight as a virgin's pussy. His eye fell on a can of oil which had been recently used to grease the stocks padlocks. That would have to do – he could hardly go wandering through the house in his present state of arousal looking for petroleum jelly. Taking the tin to the rack, he poured some on his finger and applied it to Sophronia's pink and puckered bottom hole. The oil was thin, pale yellow and very slippery. It smelt vaguely of lemon.

He tipped out some more, directly between Sophronia's buttocks, then pushed two fingers well inside her anus, rotating them, causing her to squirm and squeak in delight. Then he turned his attentions on himself, lubricating his cock.

'Dirty sod's going to bugger her. Dirty sod. Dirty sod,' panted Meg, unbearably excited as Bertram's impressively sized prick poled faster and faster inside her. In his rising lust, Bertram almost ripped open the buttons of Meg's blouse in his eagerness to grab her wobbling tits in both

50

hands and squeeze and fondle them. His trousers fell to his ankles, his underpants to his knees.

'Happen I'll bugger you,' he groaned.

'Happen you sodding won't.'

Below them, most carefully for he knew it always caused her some hurt at first, Jeremy squeezed his glans between Sophronia's welted, stinging buttocks and into her bottom hole. He paused – though filled with a massive need to plunge – then he pushed a fraction further, stretching the sphincter. He paused once more as she gasped through gritted teeth.

'Aiiieeee,' she went, lifting her head.

'Is it hurting too much?'

'It's hurting. But never mind. Do it. Just *do* it.'

The sphincter gave. She squealed with the sweet pain.

'Shall I stop?' asked Brexford, anxiously.

There was going to be no question of that, for as the pain receded, the forbidden act began to bring Sophronia's pleasure wonderfully dirty.

'Stick it all the way in. Bugger me. Bugger me, darling,' she gasped.

From their position at the window, Meg and Bertram could not actually see the details of the anal penetration; but they greedily ogled their master's nude buttocks as they jerked up and down with ever increasing urgency while he sodomised their tightly stretched mistress. And they could clearly see his heavy scrotum bouncing and flapping.

The faster that Lord Brexford's backside pounded, the faster bucked and heaved that of his second cook, his heavily loaded balls swinging and knocking into Lady Brexford's chambermaid's clitoris.

Jeremy loved to fuck arse. But he had little staying power therein. The bumhole gripped so tightly. Buggery was – in Sophronia's mind as well as his – such a ribald and beautifully smutty act that it invariably brought his sperm surging most rapidly from his scrotum. Despite his so recent orgasm, that happened as usual this time. He shouted hoarsely as, the sphincter gripping his shaft far tighter than contracting vaginal muscles could ever contrive to, he flooded the inside of Lady Brexford's lovely bottom.

Bertram, shagging pantingly away, very close himself to climax, was grunting the words, 'Let me bugger you, Meg, let me bugger you, Meg,' whilst the chambermaid, experiencing a delightful string of little climaxes, kept moaning, 'No, no, no.'

But this was only a sort of salacious game. Moments later, the second cook erupted inside Meg's pussy in a long series of powerful gushes, his whole body shuddering, his thigh muscles rock solid. For the final spurt, he backed out his cock. His attention was distracted from the courtyard – where his master had rolled sideways off Lady Brexford and, breathing heavily, was unfastening her hands – by what he had in mind.

Fisting his cock most fiercely, Bertram let fly his last load. He directed it at Meg's soft, white buttocks, watching goatishly as his semen splashed over them and dribbled down between their cheeks.

Another piquant episode in the history of ribaldry at Deal Manor was closed.

Chapter 5

Claire Petty had poor Georgina grasped firmly by the left ear. It was screwed painfully in her right hand, and the unfortunate girl, squealing, one shoulder hunched up, was being marched along a corridor to the headmistress's study.

Once they were within the dreaded lioness's den, Miss Petty released Georgina to slam and lock the door. Hazel eyes blazing anger, she turned on the girl, a fearsome sight to behold.

'So,' she bridled. 'So. As if it were not transgression enough that yesterday you were late for music, today, you have the temerity to disrupt the entire school – the *entire* school, Miss Tennant – to the extent of obliging me to send a search party out for you. It seems to me that there can be no possible excuse – but no doubt you have conjured up one. Let's hear it, shall we? It had better be very good indeed.'

Georgina was quaking within and without. 'Please, miss, there was, there was this *man*, miss,' she stammered. 'I was feeling a bit sick, taking the air and walking past the fence on the other side of the hockey field when he came from nowhere. He, he grabbed hold of me through the fence and he forced me to climb over it.' She had refined her lie to Prudence, but having got thus far with it she found herself stuck for words. Miss Petty, plump as her charge, with fair, unblemished skin and a comely, attractive appearance when she rid herself of her heavy-lensed spectacles and let down her neatly stacked, chestnut hair, folded her arms across her ample bosom and leant her large posterior back on the edge of her desk. She regarded Georgina with a most dubious eye.

'Tell me more, do. Describe this supposed man.' There was a heavy edge of sarcasm to her words; Miss Petty was not a headmistress for lack of experience in the ways of the world – and she knew instinctively when a girl was lying.

Georgina picked up the material of her dress at the knee and showed it to her. 'You see, I tore my skirt.'

'Climbing over the fence, yes. Pray continue. The man?'

'He dragged me across the field to the wood. It was horrible, miss, hideous. Once we were in the trees his, his hands were all over me. I think he was trying to, to *rape* me.'

How difficult that simple little word was to say to one's headmistress. 'I was fighting with him. I scratched him and then I hit him in the face and, and somehow I managed to get away.'

'You hit him in the face. I believe I asked you to describe him to me. Just what was this face like?'

'He had thick, big black muttonchops, like this.' Hands trembling, she drew imaginary side whiskers on her face. 'And, and a small beard. And these big, bushy eyebrows. And he had a scar on this chin . . . here.' She traced a line near the bottom of her chin.

'I see.' The headmistress's forehead creased into fierce frown lines.

Miss Petty left the edge of her green leather-topped desk and crossed to her fireplace. From above the mantelpiece she took down her rattan cane. She fitted her hand threateningly around the comfortably curved handle.

'You *lie*, Miss Tennant,' she thundered.

'No, miss,' Georgina squeaked. 'No. He . . .'

'You lie,' she repeated, an ominous note of calm creeping into her voice. 'You have just the one small tear in your skirt and apart from that your clothing is undamaged and unsoiled. Yet you claim you were fighting with this mutton-chopped, bearded man. You fought with this black-bearded man – whom you were astute enough to notice had a scar *under* his beard – for what had to amount to something like an hour and a half and you are not even scratched.'

The Petty eyes were wandering in speculation over her charge, a rather different light from that of anger intruding in their mockery. She was becoming aroused by the knowledge that she was about to get another look at the gorgeously fat bottom which she had so soundly punished the day before.

'You lie,' she said yet again. 'And you shall pay for it.' Striding to the corner where she kept her brown leather punishment chair, she reversed the well-used piece of Victoriana.

'Come over here, my girl,' she grated.

Georgina flinched. She blanched. She backed away. Her hands flew to her backside. Its soreness, more or less forgotten for the previous two to three hours, returned with a vengeance.

'Please, miss, no, miss' she begged. 'My bum still hurts dreadfully from yesterday. I can't take any more, I really can't.'

'And so should your bum hurt. A boy was it, whom you sneaked out to see? A village boy?' She smacked the cane down onto the cracked leather of the seat. It made a sound like a firework going off. 'Come *here*.'

Georgina shuffled miserably to the chair, tears welling in her eyes.

'Bend yourself all the way over it. Just like yesterday. Hands flat on the seat.'

Wincing already from the pain to come, Georgina doubled herself over the curved back of the hated chair until it was digging into her belly. Miss Petty's nostrils flared. Savouring her actions, she took hold of the navy skirt behind Georgina's dimply knees and slowly drew it up the back of her legs until it rested in an untidy pile on the small of her back. Hooking her thumbs into the waistband of the knickers, she rucked them down so that they were rolled into the underswell of the girl's buttocks. She stood back a pace with a little smile, her eyes narrowing, wetting her full lips as she hornily surveyed the blotchy, striped bottom

55

skin. Laying the cane purposefully across the fat behind, she carefully measured her aim. Georgina's buttocks tightened at the contact. She tried to cringe through the back of the chair.

Miss Petty raised her cane.

Regretfully, she relented; this was going to be too much for the girl to suffer, this backside was as tender as underdone rump steak. Her cane might easily cut the skin and inflict damage requiring medical attention.

'You have a reprieve,' she said, standing back.

Scarcely daring to believe the evidence of her ears, Georgina began to straighten up.

'A partial reprieve, only, Miss Tennant. Stay exactly as you are.'

With a new, exciting idea titillating her overactive libido, Claire Petty went to the fireplace where she hung the cane back in place on its little brass hooks. From a bottom drawer in her desk, she dug out one of a pair of rabbit-fur, thin-soled slippers which she often wore whilst working on a cold winter's day. Yes, she thought. That would do very nicely. Very nicely indeed. Her gaze dwelt on Georgina's rudely exposed backside with the baggy knickers tucked beneath it and emphasising its naked state. A delicious sight! Her pussy enjoyed a couple of little contractions. Unseen by Georgina she briefly, raunchily, touched herself between her legs, scrunching her skirt at the crotch, digging hard. Then, gripping the slipper firmly by its heel, she went to the girl.

'This, then, is your reprieve – soft leather instead of the cane,' she pronounced softly, showing Georgina the slipper, invoking a little whimper from her.

Miss Petty raised her hand bosom height and smacked the leather sole smartly down across a buttock. It produced a flat, slapping sound, like a loud handclap. The soft, bottom flesh trembled. Georgina yelped. Leather banged into skin again. As the slipper began to rise and fall with regular, smarting whacks, the headmistress, satisfied that she was chastising the girl without doing her any further damage, grew steadily more randy. Her pussy began to ooze.

Something extraordinarily untoward, and utterly unexpected, was meanwhile happening to Georgina. The initial blows had made her gasp with pain, they had brought further tears to her eyes. But these smacks were nothing like the sharp and stinging cuts of a cane, and they were invoking in her rump a widely spread, hot sensation which, as the leather sole rained down on her badly abused bottom, became a glowing throb. The heat was fierce – yet suddenly it was becoming friendly, something like heating up her bare backside at an open hearth after coming in from the cold.

In her mind, Georgina now began to picture clearly the salacious events that had taken place in the torture courtyard at Deal Manor. Her crotch tightened in arousal. She suddenly realised, astonished by the revelation, that, as with Ellie and caning, she was starting to achieve sexual enjoyment from the slippering.

After several more slaps, Miss Petty, riding a most libidinous high, decided that the hiding should be extended to encompass the underswell of Georgina's buttocks and the smooth and chubby backs of her thighs. Breathing heavily from far more than exertion, she took hold of the drawers in her free hand and stripped them down to the girl's knees.

The sight which met her prurient gaze caused her to become suddenly very still. She stared in shocked surprise, hardly crediting the evidence of her eyes – for on the insides of both the girl's thighs there were small, pale red smudges. As Georgina wriggled her bottom, waiting for more, wanting more, lusting for the slipper now, she became aware of the headmistress's fingers experimentally touching her between her legs.

It was blood. There was not the slightest doubt about it. And it did not seem to be the right colour to be menstruation blood.

'Are your monthlies due, girl?' Miss Petty asked.

Slow to catch on, Georgina stammered, 'No. Not for another week at least, ma'am.'

Claire Petty's face loomed close to hers as the headmistress bent around her, a hand on the pile of dress at the small of her back. A ray of late afternoon sunlight caught her glasses, making them glint. To Georgina, her expression appeared to be one of rage; but it was not; her face was twisted with a most unhealthy lust.

'You've been with a boy,' she accused, her voice trembling. 'You've been with a *boy*, Miss Tennant, have you not? He's had you and you've lost your virginity, by God.'

Georgina's world came crashing horrifically around her ears. The threat of expulsion was once again upon her. Of disgrace. Even, perhaps, of banishment from the family home. Her words came rushing and tumbling over one another. 'No I wasn't, no, I didn't, I haven't. No, no. I haven't. I haven't. No, please, miss, no.'

'Oh, but you have. You most certainly have.' Straightening up, Miss Petty had Georgina stand. She unzipped the girl's skirt and pulled it down to her feet. She parted her inner thigh tops and stretched the skin. The tell-tale red stain was spread all over the upper insides of her legs. 'Not monthlies, you say. Then what, Miss Tennant?'

Desperate, Georgina blurted, 'It was, it was that man. That awful man. The rapist. The, the fighting with him.'

'How very interesting. And yet you didn't *cry* rape. You merely told an unconvincing lie about an attempted rape. So what have you to say for yourself *now*?'

She should have done so. Of course – she should have claimed she'd been raped by the imaginary stranger, Georgina realised, seeing her way out far too late. Lost for words, she could only whimper.

This new, intriguing eventuality quickly filled Miss Petty's mind with ideas most salacious. With her hand screwing the heel of the slipper almost double, she went slowly back to her desk and perched herself on its edge. She fixed Georgina with a look of utmost dissoluteness – though the stricken girl did not notice it, for she was not meeting her headmistress's eyes, she was pulling up her skirt.

'You will stay exactly as you are,' barked Petters. 'Drop the skirt this instant.'

Dread-choked gaze fixed on it, Georgina let the skirt fall. Her lust had shrunk away; she was now only deeply aware of what a shameless sight she was presenting to her headmistress in her half-mast drawers – and she was desperately afraid.

Claire Petty happened to be possessed of a mind almost as ingeniously depraved as that of Lord Brexford. Finding herself in a similar situation with Georgina as had Brexford earlier, she determined to turn it to her licentious advantage.

'You are aware, of course, that I am very well acquainted with your parents, Miss Tennant?' she said, measuring her words with great care, injecting exactly the right amount of menace in them.

Georgina shivered. Her hands trembled.

'Methodists. High standing, most respected members of the community. Your dear mother does a great deal of voluntary work for the Church. Your fine father sits on the boards of several charitable institutions.' She paused, awaiting a reaction from Georgina whilst her eyes invaded the girl's groin and her own loins drove her on in her lewd intentions.

Georgina's poor head was spinning. She had experienced so many emotions today, so much in such a short time. Now this on top of it all. She moaned. She snivelled. She managed to drag out a few miserable words, whispered at her knicker-covered knees.

'You are going to tell them, aren't you?' she mumbled. 'You are going to tell them, and expel me, and they're going to, they're going to, oh, oh, oh. My father will throw me out on the street. The poorhouse, Miss Petty,' she wailed. Her face was becoming streaked with tears. Her watery eyes cringingly met those of her headmistress. 'Please don't?' she begged. 'Don't tell them?'

'You did lose your virginity today, did you not?'

What was the point of denying it now? 'Yes.' The word was all but inaudible.

There was a lengthy silence as Claire Petty studied Georgina and the girl stared miserably at her knickers. What the headmistress was about to propose she realised was outrageous even by her own dubious moral standards, but her itchy pussy was driving her relentlessly on. The idea was very possibly a most dangerous one, but it was arousing her beyond measure.

At last she said, 'There is but one, and only one, salvation for you, Georgina.' Her voice was less stern. And this was the first time she had ever used the girl's Christian name.

'I'll do anything, miss. Anything at all,' mumbled Georgina, embracing this unexpected ray of hope.

Miss Petty left her desk and closed purposefully in on her. Cupping her hand over the girl's pubis, she slipped the flat of her middle finger between her pussy lips.

'Do you understand me?' she muttered.

Georgina's eyes went as wide as they had ever done in their life. Her mouth dropped open. She swallowed hard. 'No. I, I don't,' she mumbled.

The index finger joined the middle one, and they both slipped inside her pussy. Miss Petty was astounded to find it damp. Her other hand greedily clasped Georgina's breast, kneading it.

'Do you understand *now*, my dear?'

Georgina gaped. 'You can't mean. But you can't. You . . . actually . . . mean . . . you . . .?'

'I want to do with you what you do with your dormmate Ellie Branks.'

Miss Petty had caught them at their lessie business once. She had been paying one of her surprise visits to the dormitories, opening the doors very quietly, hoping to discover some illicit activity or other. When the door to Georgina and Ellie's room had been only fractionally ajar, she had spotted them nude and threshing around in one another's arms. The secret observation had brought to her an exquisite thrill; she had silently watched until the girls had climaxed, then she had stolen away to her study to frig herself. Remembering now how it had been, she jerked her pussy-invading fingers in Georgina.

'How do you . . .?' Georgina began in a whisper, meanwhile unable to believe that her headmistress had two fingers inside her pussy.

Miss Petty interrupted again, her voice husky. 'There is very little I *don't* know about the goings-on in this school, my girl.' Her other hand changed breasts, groping and squeezing. Her fingers penetrated deeper. 'How come you're wet down there between your legs?' she demanded.

Georgina was utterly confused. She was not finding this sexual molestation on the part of a woman she feared in the least arousing. It was totally inconceivable that Petters – strict, formidable, sexless Petters – should be acting this way with her. There had never been the slightest whisper of her touching her charges like that. Nevertheless, Georgina's bottom was warmly glowing from its trouncing, and she was remembering her so recent sexual excitement. She had been offered her way out.

'It was the slippering, miss,' she confessed. 'I can't think why, but it, it thrilled me.'

'Ah-hah.' The headmistress began unfastening the buttons of Georgina's blouse as her fingers continued to move slowly up and down inside her pussy. Georgina, despite her indifference, even aversion, to this sexual assault, was slightly opening and closing her thighs on the invading hand without being exactly conscious of what she was doing.

Miss Petty spilled her long-held secret. 'It thrilled me, too. But I *know* why.' She was breathing heavily, her words delivered slowly and throatily. 'I have the need for someone to, shall we say, sport with occasionally,' she went on. 'You have the opportunity of being this girl – or you can face expulsion and all that that will imply. If you choose sport, and should I ever get the slightest idea in the future that you have told anyone – Miss Branks, for example, and, believe me, I shall find out – you absolutely will be expelled and I shall recommend that your parents have *this* – her fingers left Georgina's again and she took the entire, fat little pussy in her hand and squeezed it as if ringing a sponge – 'examined by a doctor to confirm my reason for expelling you.' She took a very deep breath. Her lustful eyes searched Georgina's face as she undid the final button of her blouse. She lifted the chemise.

'You have your choice.'

Hobson's choice. A nervous lump of excitement arose from the pit of Georgina's belly to the back of her throat. A niggling, perverse urge to fall utterly in with Miss Petty's twisted offer of salvation drove her on.

'Slipper me a little more, please, miss?' she dared, in a whisper.

'Well, *well*. *What* a wayward young lady you are turning out to be and no mistake.'

Taking hold of both of Georgina's heavy breasts in her two hands, Miss Petty pressed them together. She noisily licked and sucked each pale pink nipple. Slipping off her spectacles, she put them on her desk and buried her face in each softly yielding tit. Then, standing back, she unpinned her hair; it tumbled down over her shoulders in thick, curly tresses. She appeared at once far younger and almost pretty. Wearing a puffily rapacious expression on her face, she was miraculously transformed from a fearsome punishment machine to a wanton sexual animal.

Georgina perceived this amazing metamorphosis in astonishment. She quietly gasped.

Once again, Miss Petty's lecherous hand sought out Georgina's pussy. As she gentled it, she murmured, 'Perhaps you will even enjoy our sport, Georgina, who knows? We shall see – I have an idea that you will. You want more bum-whacking, do you? Then have it you shall. As much as you wish. But first . . .' swiftly, clumsily in her eagerness, she began to undress, leaving the clothes where they fell, '. . . I want to be nude.'

Georgina gaped. She felt like treating herself to a painful pinching to make sure she was awake, that this was not some insane dream. In less than half a minute, her headmistress, chubbier even than she, perfectly white and smooth-skinned, was naked before her but for a triple string of multi-coloured glass beads! She was Petters no more. With her big, wobbly, bead-decorated tits, plump belly and heavy, dark brown pubic thatch she was transformed into a Rubensian portrait of feminine lust.

Miss Petty retrieved the slipper from where she had left it on her desk. In so doing, she afforded Georgina a view of fat but nevertheless round and shapely buttocks which trembled enticingly as she walked. Georgina's pussy twitched. Her loins tingled.

'Get yourself comfortably bent over the chair again, Miss Tennant,' commanded the headmistress, her voice quite gentle, if a little strained. Georgina, this time most eagerly, hastened to obey, luridly displaying her throbbing, scarlet bottom. 'I shall beat you only as much as you have appetite for,' Petters continued. 'You must tell me when to stop.'

There was no reason for Georgina to hide her rising lust any more. As the slipper began to slap her buttocks, two of her fingers found their way into her pussy to rock up and down, while the ball of her thumb went to work on her clitoris.

'Yes, wank yourself, you dirty thing,' crooned Miss Petty. Picking up a loose side of the girl's blouse, she doubled it over her back so as to afford herself a fine view of Georgina's tits hanging nudely and wobbling beneath the raised chemise. 'Frig away to your heart's content. I'll stop, when you have come.'

The naked headmistress retargeted the slipper to that area she had had in mind when she had first pulled the drawers down Georgina's thighs to spot the dried blood – the very bottom of the buttocks, the tight crease between them and the thighs, and the backs of the upper thighs. She slapped the slipper home time after time after rollicking time, her raunchy attention divided between the beaten areas and Georgina's tits, which bounced and swung from side to side as her entire body shook with each smacking blow.

Orgasm swooped with the speed of a plunging bird of prey. Georgina wailed it through clenched teeth. Her masturbating fingers stilled in a flood of juices. Her head dropped so that her thick hair cascaded over the brown leather seat which the nails of the clawed and rigid fingers of her other hand were digging into like talons.

The slipper stilled after a final, hearty whack.

Miss Petty's heart was thumping furiously enough to jiggle the plenteous flesh of her upper belly. She was breathing shallowly, and fast, her mouth wide, her lips drooling. The slipper fell from her hand to land on top of her discarded cami-knickers. A further most scandalous, riveting idea entered her ingenious mind. It refused to budge.

Her drooping, lust-choked eyes were drawn, like a pair of ball bearings to a powerful magnet, towards her fireplace. The magnet was her cane.

Georgina, wearing a dopey, dazed expression, was slowly unbending from the chair as, from the corner of her eye, she saw Miss Petty raise her hand to take the bane of Chalmers back down from its hooks.

'Oh, shit, no,' she wailed. 'Surely you don't mean to . . .?'

'Such scurrilous language would normally not go without punishment,' interrupted the headmistress with an oddly twisted, slatternly smile.

'I couldn't bear any more, miss. I really couldn't. It would almost kill me.'

'But I'm not obliging you to. You've jumped to the wrong conclusion. Come over here.'

Hesitantly, weak with the aftermath of what had been an all-consuming orgasm, and with her bottom more aglow than ever before, though not painfully so, Georgina kicked her feet out of the untidy pile of skirt at her ankles and shuffled away from the chair. Her knees were trapped by her knickers.

Miss Petty nodded at the navy drawers. 'Take those off. And all the rest of your clothes.'

Georgina did as she was bidded wearily – and warily, since she remained uncertain about Petters's real intentions with the cane. When she was naked except for her black plimsolls, Miss Petty, who was much the same height as her, took her fiercely by the shoulders, the curved cane handle firmly clutched in one hand, and pulled her into herself. Lustily, she squashed their naked tits and bellies together, trapping the rows of beads between them. She pushed the top of a thigh between Georgina's legs and bent her knees to rub her pussy up and down on the front of Georgina's thigh. Her empty hand found its way down the girl's back to her buttocks to rummage amongst the burning flesh.

Assuming she was now going to be kissed, the notion – the mere idea of which would have faintly repulsed her only fifteen minutes before – actually pleased Georgina. But Miss Petty's mouth did not clash with hers. Breaking the embrace, pushing herself away, she muttered through spittle-flecked lips, 'I want you to cane me, Georgina. To give my bum as good as I gave yours.'

Putting the curved handle of her cane in Georgina's palm, she closed her pudgy fingers over it.

Georgina looked at the thin and whippy length of rattan in shock. Surely Petters could not possibly be serious? But serious she obviously was. She was already doubling herself over her leather-covered desk top. She meant it all right – and how.

Planting her chin on the dull green leather, her eyes drifting to the reproduction of Constable's The Haywain which hung above the hooks for the cane, Claire Petty gripped the far edge of the desk in feverish, shiny white-knuckled fingers. She tensed and wiggled her proffered buttocks – a behind which had only previously been treated to a beating during orgies up at Deal Manor, and that not for quite some time.

'Get on with it. Cane me.' The words spilled from her mouth like molten lava, hot enough to burn Miss Petty's trembling lips.

Staring at her headmistress's big bottom with its appealing clump of pussy hair nestling beneath it, and at the thin dark line of perineum hairs which thickened out between the cheeks over the little hole, Georgina gulped. Then, unmoving but for her Adam's apple, she gulped again. She was almost paralysed with shock.

'*Do* it, girl. Stripe me,' insisted Miss Petty.

Georgina very slowly raised the cane. It felt impossibly

heavy. She was in that sort of dream world where you desperately want to run but you can't because your legs have turned to lead and refuse to move. In a mad dream fantasy land where finishing school young ladies are invited to beat the bare backsides of their strict and forbidding headmistresses. The cane hovered, but it refused to fall.

'If you don't swipe my bum this instant, *I* shall swipe *yours*.' The words were delivered in a snarl which was heavy with sexual tension.

That partially did the trick. Biting her lip, Georgina brought the cane down, closing her eyes in mid-stroke. But the swish was unimpressive, the connection between rattan and rump barely sharp enough to squash a fly – yet it caused Georgina to jump with guilt.

Miss Petty wriggled her buttocks. They were unmarked. 'Hit me, girl. Hit my bum hard, don't kiss it,' she insisted.

Right, thought Georgina, her confidence mounting. You want it so very much, you are going to jolly well get it. She gripped the handle more firmly. She remembered the agony which she and at least half the pupils of the school had been through beneath this sinister instrument of torture whilst bent over that infamous corner chair. Teeth chewing the inside of her lower lip, she raised the cane high above her head. This time, as she took careful aim, she kept her eyes wide open. She let fly.

The cane cut through the air with a sharp whistle. There was a sharp and resounding crack when it bit into Miss Petty's left buttock. Georgina's tricep jerked as the rattan came to an abrupt stop half buried in resilient flesh. Petters uttered a strangled grunt. Her feet bounced off the carpet and thumped down.

Shit, oh shit, now I've gone and torn it, Georgina worried. For a moment, she was unable to move. The cane lay where it had connected, skin reddening around its edges. Miss Petty's fingers were clasping and unclasping on the desk edge, she was rocking her hips.

'I, I'm sorry, I . . .' began Georgina.

'Don't stop, girl. Don't damn well *stop*,' drooled the headmistress.

That single sting had bitten all the way through Miss Petty's backside to delight her sopping pussy. Moreover, the ribald novelty of being so lewdly exposed and vulnerable in front of a naked young pupil, and the iniquitous role reversal, was serving to bring to her undreamt-of-heights of licentiousness.

Reassured, Georgina set to with a vengeance, which was what she now determined to turn this sado-masochistic performance into – a reprisal for herself and all her previously beaten friends. She began to whack most heartily those two great melons of flesh. She swiped and she switched, backhand and forehand, breasts swinging, puppy fat trembling, eyes glinting, speedily turning her headmistress's bottom as bright red as her own, whilst Miss Petty gasped and grunted and groaned, with her boobs crushed into the leather desk top, heedless of the heavy glass beads which were denting into them, her toes wiggling, feet jumping up and down and her hips jerking with each blow in exactly the same way as if they were those of a man in the act of copulation.

When she neither wanted nor could take more, Petters had still not managed to hit the highest of the high spots. Feebly, she ordered Georgina – who was by then most thoroughly turned on by her salacious activity – to stop. Only her fear of Miss Petty's power persuaded her to obey.

'Lick my bum all over. Soothe it,' the headmistress gasped. 'Tongue me, tongue me.'

Dropping to her knees, the cane still clenched tightly in her sweaty fist, feeling most agreeably dirty, Georgina was by now willing to perform almost any licentious act which was demanded of her. She salivated copiously, shaking her head the while, her hair bouncing, all over her Petter's bottom until both buttocks were as shiningly red as two ripe apples.

The jaded Petty eye fell on an unused candle near her face. The trembling hand of authority snatched it from its ornate silver holder to pass it back across the desk to Georgina.

'Like a man's thing,' muttered Miss Petty hoarsely.

'Stick it right up inside me and use it just like a man's thing. The same way that dirty boy must have done it to you today.'

Thus did the plump and comely, picture of sweet innocence, daughter of strict and wealthy methodists bring off the formidable headmistress of her renowned and most expensive finishing school. Thus did young Georgina Tennant, now sex slave to Miss Claire Petty by dint of having most willingly lost her virginity to the wicked Lord Brexford little more than an hour before, masturbate that most sexually complicated lady to orgasm. On her dimply knees on a worn lambswool rug – on the very spot where countless girls had stood trembling in the past as punishment was pronounced upon them – playing with herself yet again as she ogled most lasciviously the fat, angrily striped bottom and the thick bush of pubic hair inches from her nose, Georgina jerked the long, thick, white candle, point and wick first, in and out of Miss Petty's hot and greedy little rabbit of a pussy. Her hand moved with the speed of a boy's in the final stages of a wank until, moaning and muttering at the Constable hay cart over the fireplace, the headmistress came – and she came, and she came.

Much later, early that evening, just after dusk, Georgina and Ellie found the opportunity to have themselves a bit of a kiss and a cuddle.

'Your poor, poor bot,' sympathised Ellie, slipping her hand down inside the back of Georgina's knickers to gently caress the abused backside. 'But why on earth were you so late back, you silly thing? You must have known what the consequences would be.'

'I was busy losing my cherry,' Georgina told her, as casually as she was able. 'So it was worth it, don't you see?'

'Oh, *great*!' enthused Ellie. 'Good for you. Lucky Thomas.'

Georgina remembered Lord Brexford's most serious threat. She was very careful not to tell her girlfriend the truth. Yes, she thought, lucky Thomas – but not quite in the way you imagine. And lucky me. Her mind was so crammed with the extraordinary sexual events of the afternoon that she was having difficulty sorting them out. She had seen a stiff cock in all its glory for the first time, and she had lustfully exhibited her bared pussy to Thomas, who had all but done her. She had been locked in a pair of ancient stocks by Lord Brexford and from there she had observed the naked Thomas getting a hard-on as Lady Brexford flogged him soundly with a scourge. Lady Brexford had fellated Thomas to orgasm – and had swallowed his sperm – as her lord had taken Georgina's cherry whilst she was still trapped in the stocks. Having lost her virginity she had returned to Chalmers so late that there was a search party out for her when she arrived. She had discovered the sexual joy that a bare-arsed slippering could bring, and Miss Petty had uncovered the guilty secret of her lost cherry. She had been coerced into becoming Miss Petty's sexual slave, and then had enjoyed every second of her enslavement. She had – and perhaps this was the most remarkable of all – thoroughly caned the naked headmistress and afterwards frigged her to orgasm with a candle.

She did not regret a single moment of it all – with the exception that she did not dare breathe a word of it. How she would have loved to tell Ellie at that moment.

'Penny for them?' murmured Ellie, kissing and nibbling her ear.

'You would never believe them. You really wouldn't.'

'But you had a good time, despite the larruping?'

Georgina smiled. She fondled Ellie's breast lovingly. She kissed her tenderly on the lips. Her hand crept up beneath her skirt to the heavy-cotton-clad pussy.

'I'm *having* a good time, dear heart,' she murmured.

Chapter 6

In matters sexual, Jeremy Brexford was all but insatiable.
It should surely have been enough for any man in his late
thirties to have an utterly compliant, beautiful wife in her
early twenties entirely at his beck and call, and constantly
to indulge with her in a great variety of wanton sexual
practices, including the occasional orgy. But enough it was
not. For the past nine months, Lord Brexford had been
keeping a young mistress, a lady every bit as acquiescent
and as gorgeous as Sophronia. He had her installed in an
elegant, ninety-year-old town house, designed by John
Nash, in Hyde Park Square, London, a part of his London
estate.

The young woman's name was Charlotte; it pleased him
to address her as Charlie. She was tall and willowy – which
advantage she contrived to emphasise with a most sensuous walk – and her thick and wavy auburn hair was the
colour that Sophronia's would have been had the glint in
it been more pronounced. She had been brought up in the
insalubrious streets of London's East End.

Jeremy indulged his mistress lavishly. He had equipped
her with as large a wardrobe as his wife possessed, he
showered her with expensive gifts and swamped her with
jewellery. The one thing he could not abide about her during their initial frolics together had been her rough manner
of speech and sloppy comportment in general. To the end
of rearranging these aggravations to his satisfaction, during the first six months of their relationship he had paid for
almost daily elocution lessons for her. He had employed a
teacher of the gentle arts, deportment and the social graces.

She was even learning the piano – and proving to be an excellent student.

Jeremy Brexford had performed on Charlotte the near miraculous, Professor Higginsian exercise of transforming a cockney sparrow into a Berkeley Square nightingale. Lately, he had been going up to London to visit this graceful bird in her richly feathered nest as often as he could find a reason.

Lord Brexford needed an excuse to indulge himself with his Charlie. For despite Sophronia's free and easy attitude towards sex, and irrespective of the fact that he often made love to other females in front of her, he felt that it might be dangerous to their married relationship should she discover that he kept a secret mistress. Fortunately, motives to go to London were plentiful, for he had vast real estate holdings in the city – entire streets of luxury town houses apart from the one in which he had settled Charlotte. Conveniently, as far as visiting his mistress was concerned, Sophronia – who far preferred the countryside and her horses to smoky London – seldom wanted to accompany him.

As the rule about his wife being allowed – provided that it was in his presence – to dally in all things salacious with other men apart from vaginal and anal intercourse, so had Brexford a strict rule with his Charlotte. Full penetration by men friends of his was granted in her case, as long as he was involved in the scene; she was, after all, only a mistress, not a wife. However, it was absolutely forbidden for her to have any physical contact with a man beyond a mere handshake, or a modest kiss on the cheek, when Jeremy was home at Deal Manor – as he was most of the time.

Charlotte, born and raised in the squalid neighbourhood of Cable Street, Stepney, had struck gold. She was not about to get herself turfed out from this life of utmost luxury at any price. Even if she should fancy another man when Jeremy was in Deal – and she did, frequently – the risk of being caught with a lover was too great, since her noble lord never announced his visits in advance. Besides, her maid was on his pay roll and as such was not to be trusted. Beyond frequent masturbation – for she was an exceptionally horny young lady – Charlie behaved herself.

Unless he happened to be travelling up to London with Sophronia on one of her rare shopping trips, Lord Brexford did not take his Rolls-Royce motor car. He had not yet troubled to learn to drive, and chauffeurs, like all domestic staff, were given to gossip. Idle tittle-tattle in the servants' quarters about a kept woman in London was bound, sooner or later, to reach the keen ears of his wife. So he went up by train; in any case he found the steam train marginally more comfortable than the new-fangled automobiles which were almost as bumpy on the narrow, rutted roads of Kent as a horse and trap.

It was early on the pleasantly warm evening of the day after the torture courtyard excesses at Deal Manor when Jeremy arrived, by hansom cab from Victoria Station, at his mistress's abode. It had been a warmish spring day and he felt tired and sticky from the journey. Quite often, the first thing he would do upon setting eyes on Charlotte – who had sex appeal to stir the blood of anyone but the feeblest of wimps – was to fall rapaciously upon her. This evening, he fancied taking a bath before indulging in anything else. She coquettishly offered to join him.

'What was that you were singing when I arrived, Charlie darling?' he asked her as, naked, up to their necks in hot, scented water, they soaked together in a big, copper tub. They were sitting face to face. Being a gentleman, Brexford was propped with the awkwardness of the brass taps to contend with at his back.

' "Bird in a Gilded Cage",' she told him. 'It's a very pretty tune, don't you think?' Her large, soulful brown eyes smiled into his as she added, 'Me, really, is it not?' She had – coincidentally since it was a song which indeed might have been written especially for her – been accompanying herself to it on the piano in the drawing-room overlooking the road when he had rung the bell.

'Well, I must say I'm delighted with the progress of my little bird,' he told her. 'When we first met you would have sung something like "Oim on'y a berd in a geelded cige." '

She laughed. 'Don't think I can't still.'

'I'm sure you can.' He smiled at her. 'But kindly don't.'

Brexford studied his mistress with keenly appreciative eye. She looked so unbelievably luscious with her reddish hair – which reached to her waist – piled up in a fluffy white towel to keep it dry, and with her white, perfectly moulded shoulders poking out of the bath water. He could clearly see the pointy pink tips of her breasts just below the surface and, vague and indistinct, deeper down, the intriguing, dark smudge of her pussy hair. Incredibly gorgeous, he thought. And amazingly fuckable.

'It's extraordinary what you've managed to achieve in these past few months,' he said. 'But then I always knew you were intelligent and talented. I can now introduce you into polite society and nobody would believe you aren't to the manor born.'

'But you don't,' slipped from her pretty lips. Whoops, she thought, even as it did, I shouldn't have said that. He hates to be criticised.

For an instant his eyes fractionally hardened, warning her not to repeat the offence. 'No, I don't – and you of course know very well why, so let's hear no more of it.'

'Sorry.'

The eyes turned soft again. His chunky knee appeared above the water as his big toe found her pussy beneath it and wormed its tip in. 'Do that to me, why don't you?'

She closed her thighs on his foot. 'But you haven't got a little mouse.' That was what he liked to call her pussy, her little mouse.

'No. I've got a fat, hungry snake and it's going to bite you.'

Her foot sought out his genitals, its heel digging into his scrotum and its ball flattening his penis up into his belly. She rubbed. 'Don't you mean, I'm going to bite it?' she meaningfully asked him.

'One hopes so.'

His cock was beginning to stir. His toe happily wiggled in the slipperiness between her pussy lips. Their eyes smokily locked. She sat up straight, sending a small wave down

73

the bath, bringing her smallish but lovely tits out of the water, thrusting them coquettishly at him. The prick beneath her titillating foot rapidly grew hard, a muscular slab of intriguing flesh longer than it.

'Are you clean enough now to be dirty?' she asked.

He chuckled. How very much he wanted her all of a sudden. His loins were on fire.

'Ouch,' he went, freeing his dented back from the taps. He had been so intent with his toe-fucking and his growing hard-on, and with her captivating beauty, that he had failed to notice how hard the brass had been digging into him. Climbing onto his knees, he moved awkwardly in on her face, spreading his legs on either side of her thighs. His solid cock hovered, swaying in front of her mouth. He linked his fingers behind the soft pillow of towel at the back of her head.

'I've changed my mind. Don't bite,' he told her.

She chuckled throatily. Her big, soft lips closed over his cockhead as he pulled her face into his groin. He began to rock his hips slowly, thrusting his prick back and forth in her mouth as far as he could without causing her to gag. As she avidly sucked, she made a slurping noise. After a while, he took it out. He wrapped her fingers around it and shoved his balls at her mouth, crushing them against her lips.

'Lick me, my love,' he grunted. 'You know how I adore it.'

Lick she did, with great enthusiasm, all over his scrotum. Then, one at a time – for she could not accommodate both at once – she took his fat balls into her mouth and sucked them whilst her fist jerked up and down on his cock.

After long moments of this, he manoeuvred around, facing the other way to present her his backside. He bent down, hands on her thighs. 'You know what I want you to do now,' he said. 'First wash it squeaky clean. Afterwards I'll do the same to you.'

She adored this particularly interesting, lewd act – both performing it and having it performed on her. Its forbidden nature turned her on even more than did giving Jeremy

74

a blow-job. Soaping a flannel, she rubbed it in the crack of his behind, working up a good lather. Pushing a fingernail of flannel into his bottom hole, she rotated it. She rinsed the soap off, then she moved her head forward to squeeze her tongue up into where the flannel had been, as far as it could reach, as she took hold of his cock and balls.

The wet, eager little tongue stabbing in and out of his bottom hole brought to Jeremy a most salacious delight. He shut his eyes tight and tilted back his head. Except that he was merely panting, and that the light above him came from a spherical gas lamp, he might have been a wolf howling at the moon. However, there was a very definite limit to how much of this scrofulous pleasure Lord Brexford could take without ejaculating. After a minute or so of it, he shuffled himself around and sat down between Charlotte's feet.

'Your turn, Charlie,' he muttered.

She knelt with her upraised buttocks close to Brexford's face, the saturated clump of auburn pubic hair beneath them dripping scented water. He took his time about flanneling the bottom cleft and hole, then he flickered his tongue up and down the crack, along the perineum, and plunged it into her pink little hole. As he tongue-fucked Charlotte's pretty bottom, going right in past the sphincter, he was stabbing two fingers in and out of her pussy.

They were as aroused, there in her big bath, as two people could be without actually climaxing. He was fisting himself beneath the water whilst she moaned. It was going to be a mutual explosion, very soon – but Jeremy was going to make sure it was in the properly appointed place. He slipped his tongue out of her. 'Don't move, Charlie,' he said.

He climbed to his knees behind his mistress, a hand on her hip. Holding his cock, he guided its head into her pussy then rammed it all the way home. From the strangled shout the action produced from her – a noise which raised the maid's knowing eyebrows in the kitchen below – that thick and throbbing prick might have stabbed right into her womb. They were both well aware that this was to be a very quick fuck, no long-drawn-out act of love – and they wanted it no other way.

He went at her with desperate fury, shagging her like an impatient dog who has stolen a turn at the street bitch on heat whilst the other mongrels bark and snap at his heels in an attempt to get him off. His buttocks pounded, his balls swung thumpingly into her thickly haired pubic mound, his head rocked.

The soapy surface of the bath water had become as restless as that of a miniature choppy sea. Little waves tickled Charlotte's madly jiggling tits, they slopped against the edge of the bath, they spilled over to splash on the white tiled floor.

Jeremy came with a massive heave of his hips which almost knocked Charlotte onto her face and sent a tidal wave over her end of the bath to bucket onto the tiles. The maid, with dinner almost prepared, rolled her eyes to the ceiling at the spattering noise and the animal sounds of the two of them moaning and shouting through their orgasms.

They went almost completely still, locked together as far as Brexford's noble balls, gently swaying, relaxed, utterly contented. The bath water flattened. The small storm was over.

'I have been toying with the idea of something rather daring we might experiment with tonight,' Jeremy told Charlotte half an hour later during a candlelit dinner. 'It occurred to me on the way up, in the train. I wasn't completely sure about it, but now I am. My head begins to reel with its possibilities.' He poured his fourth goblet of an excellent Château-Latour '03 and topped up hers.

'Perhaps it's the wine that's making it reel?' she ventured.

'No – you are well aware of my capacity in that direction. But *le vin* frequently seems to encourage such interesting speculation.' He tipped some more of the Château-Latour down his throat, eyeing her thoughtfully over the cut crystal rim of the sparkling goblet.

'Well? What is it, this daring idea?' she asked him

through a delicious mouthful of jugged hare. 'Out with it, you rascal.'

He chuckled. 'Rascal, indeed. I thought to have you play the part of a harlot.'

She gasped. 'But surely you can't mean . . . a common streetwalker?'

'A tart, yes. A whore.'

He expanded at length on his latest, racy inspiration whilst she listened in silence. When he had finished, she decided that she found it most amusing. She had been on the game once, and he knew it, for Lord Brexford had picked her and a girlfriend of hers up in a seedy club in the West End and brought the favours of the two of them together.

'Well. Back to the good old days, then,' she remarked with a lopsided little smile.

'Just for this evening, yes.'

He took her up to her bedroom where he had her zip herself into an eye-catching, crimson satin dress with a daring *décolletage*. She decided that her hair should be left as it was, piled somewhat untidily, but with a cute little red velvet hat perched on top of it, an orange ostrich feather curling down towards her forehead. She overdid her make-up, painting her face in much the same fashion as she used to as a tart. Then they took a hansom to a certain notorious public house, with which they were both familiar, in the East End.

The George and Dragon in Whitechapel was crowded almost to capacity; it was raucous, and cigarette and cigar smoke hung in the air like a smog. As the lord pushed a way for himself and his mistress to the bar, a pianist wearing a battered top hat was thumping an out-of-tune, tinny-sounding piano. Most of the clientele were loudly singing one of the popular drinking songs of the day, 'My Old Man'.

Brexford ordered them two very stiff whiskies. He heartily approved of the fact that Charlotte drank whisky; women who enjoyed liquor, he had observed, were invariably his type. He managed to find a space to sit, their backs to a cracked plaster wall, on a wooden bench with a beer-stained and puddled table in front of them.

'Well, here we are then,' remarked Charlotte, gazing all around with laughing eyes, vastly amused to be back in her one-time environment.

'Here we are indeed.' Jeremy took a long pull on his whisky. He was also happy to be there, for there was something about the atmosphere in places such as this which was good for his disreputable soul. 'We must watch carefully for our opportunity.'

As it happened, the chance they were awaiting presented itself almost immediately. It came in the form of a very tall, thin, angular man who parked himself close to them, standing by a wooden pillar with his pint glass of ale on a shelf surrounding it. He was most elegantly dressed, with expensive, shiny black leather boots and a well-cut frock coat over a fancy waistcoat and a frilly white shirt, a silken cravat with a silver stickpin at his throat. From his hand there dangled an ebony cane with a silver knob. Clearly he was a gentleman, not one of the locals.

The man had a lean and swarthy face with dark side-whiskers which curved dashingly into a neat black moustache, and on his head he was wearing a curly-brimmed fine-furred bowler hat. His eyes were smallish, glinty, with a worldly wise look about them – and they kept flickering over Charlotte. She rather liked what she saw; thinness notwithstanding, the fellow appeared attractively tough.

'There's your punter, I do believe,' said Brexford, as the man's eyes strayed to her and fractionally lingered for at least the twelfth time.

'Not while I'm with you, he won't be,' she said.

'No. You're absolutely right.' He thought for a moment. 'The best thing would be if you and I stage some sort of tiff. But if he doesn't try to pick you up the second I've gone, make rapid tracks out of here. I'll be waiting close by in a cab for you just in case there's any trouble. And I'll have another standing by for the two of you.'

'All right.' Charlotte's pulse quickened. 'How then shall we do it?'

'Hit me.'

'I beg your . . .?'

'Slap my face. Good and hard.'

'My God.' She took a deep breath. 'Ah – now, then?'

'Swear at me first. Loud enough to draw attention.'

Charlotte grasped the idea most clearly. 'You bleedin' no good bastard!' she yelled at him, above the singing. Then she hit him. Heads jerked in their direction as the flat of her hand caught him a stinging blow around the cheek.

His expression turned very angry. 'Why, you miserable, ungrateful scrubber,' he threw at her at the top of his voice, jumping to his feet. 'After all I've done for you. That's the end. We're finished, do you understand? Finished. You just lost your only source of income.'

'You soddin' think I need you? I don't need *you*. Fuck off. Go on – sling your fuckin' 'ook.'

It was a most convincing display. Lord Brexford, eyes blazing, face a mask of rage, left. He shouldered his way roughly through the assembly to storm through the door and out into Whitechapel.

'Excuse me, I could not but help overhearing,' said the stranger, wasting no time in approaching her. His accent was faultless, the voice pleasantly deep. 'Would you perchance allow me to buy you a drink?'

'Don't 'ang about, do you, mister?' said Charlotte. 'Why not? A double Bell's 'n' a splash. Ta.'

As he made his way to the bar, she cast a wary eye all around her. It was as she feared: two women with heavily rouged cheeks, clearly whores, not far away from where Charlotte was sitting, were talking animatedly with one another as they stared at her with hostility written all over their faces. Hastily she looked away from them. As the crowd began boisterously singing 'Maybe it's Because I'm a Londoner', the man returned, bearing Charlotte's whisky and a fresh glass of ale for himself.

'Lively sort of place, is it not?' he observed as he put the drinks down and parked his thin behind next to her on that part of the bench still warm from that of Lord Brexford.

'It's all right.'

'Sorry you had such a nasty fight with your friend,' he said, false concern in his expression.

'No you ain't. Neither am I. Anyhow, 'e weren't a friend was 'e? Just another John.'

'Ah.' He moved in close to her so that their shoulders touched. 'Then you, um, you see, I wasn't sure. I thought perhaps you may have been lovers. Or even husband and wife.'

'You wasn't sure about what?' He really was quite OK, thought Charlotte. He smelt rather nice, too – unlike the pub itself which had the rancid odour of a football team in the locker room immediately after a match, mixed with the rank cocktail of tobacco and ale.

'John is a *fille de nuit* expression for a customer I believe, is it not?' he asked her.

He could not have put the suggestion that she was a whore with more refinement. But for her recent education in the French phrases snootily peppering upper-class British speech she would not even have known what *fille de nuit* meant. 'We're all on the game in 'ere, mate,' she said.

'Yet I'm tolerably certain that I haven't seen you in here before.'

'You 'aven't? Your loss then.'

'Not any more.' He stared meaningfully at her. The fingertips of one of his lean and well-kept hands ventured to brush her knee.

'. . . I've got a funny feeling inside of me . . .' went the raucous voice of the crowd – which just about summed up Charlotte's emotions at that moment. Suddenly, those emotions became more complicated. The pair of tarts who had been talking about her were looming over her from the other side of the table.

'What's your game then, love?' asked one menacingly.

'I beg your pardon?' Without realising it, Charlotte's response to this challenge had been to slip back protectively into educated speech pattern.

'Don't get toffee-nosed with me, doll,' said the woman, glaring angrily. 'You're on our pitch, ain't you? I'd get off it if I was you. Like, sharpish.'

Charlotte shook her head, frowning. 'I haven't the faintest idea what you are talking about. My friend and I are doing not the slightest harm to anyone. Now – please go away.'

The whores stared at one another, somewhat puzzled. The way in which Charlotte spoke belied her appearance. Nevertheless, the other one said, 'You're on our manor, 'n' you're poachin' our punters. Scarper. Else we'll 'ave you thrown out, won't we?'

'Do me a favour, Lucy,' said Charlotte's companion – surprising her with the use of the woman's name. 'You do the scarpering. Piss off, there's a dear?'

'But the cow's –'

'Go *away*. If you ever want to see any more of my money, do like I said, eh? Do like Houdini. Vanish.'

They promptly left, grumbling away to one another.

'I think that perhaps we should also disappear. It might be the wisest course,' he said, eyes probing the crowd. 'But first, will you tell me your name?'

'Charlotte. And I never said nothin' about goin' with you.'

'Mine's Philip.' He smiled at her and briefly touched the back of her hand. 'I have to say I much prefer the other way you speak. Where did you learn it?'

'Never you mind.'

He shrugged. 'Have it your own way. But it's obvious you've spent a lot of time in the company of gentlemen.' Finishing half of his ale, he shoved the glass away from him. 'So let us get down to business. How much do you charge?' he asked.

'That rather depends.'

'On what exactly?'

She swallowed a large slug of whisky; her nerves needed it at this juncture. It burnt her throat, then her belly. 'If you just want a gobble or an 'and job in . . .'

He interrupted her. 'Do me a great favour? Please? Speak the other way?'

It was confusing her, all this chopping and changing. 'If you like. What I was trying to say was, if you had in mind that I should fellate you or masturbate you in a cab or a back alley somewhere, that will be one price. If you want

81

to come home with me to make love as long as you wish, that will be more expensive.'

'Both,' he said, eyes running across her breasts.

'Both what?'

'I want to come home with you and I want to fuck you for as long as suits me. And I would like you to wank and blow me in a cab on the way.'

This blatant talk was exciting her – the more especially so because it was with a complete stranger. She could hardly wait to get his fly undone and to discover how well endowed he was. 'A crown then,' she told him.

'Agreed.' Getting up, he took her by the elbow and helped her to her feet. 'Also,' he murmured, just loud enough for her to hear, '. . . my needs can at times get somewhat complicated.'

That's fine with me, mister, thought Charlotte. Because I'll have Jeremy there to rescue me if the going gets too rough. Peeping Tom Jeremy. 'Bondage and so forth?' she ventured.

'And so forth, yes.'

'The price just went up. Seven shillings and sixpence.'

'Three half crowns it is.' He cast a worried eye around. Regular John in this establishment he might be, but if the pimps decided to get difficult there could be serious trouble. 'Let us then get out of here.'

Several pairs of hostile eyes, both male and female, followed their progress as they made their way to the door, but there was no attempt to molest them. Lord Brexford, as he had promised, was on the other side of Whitechapel, in a hansom cab, its single grey horse standing meekly in front of it. Another, empty, cab was waiting outside the George and Dragon for Charlotte.

The tinkling of the piano and the off-key singing . . . *that I love London toowwn . . .* drifted from the brightly lit pub into the air – which now had a touch of chill to it   as the door opened and Charlotte emerged with Philip in tow. Brexford's features creased into a satisfied, wicked smile. Sticking his head through the open window of his hansom he called out to the driver who was sitting high behind with the reins held loosely in his hands.

'Hyde Park Square, my man – and don't spare the horses,' he told him.

'Hyde Park Square, please,' said Charlotte to their cabbie as she hauled herself up and inside. 'At a walk. We are in no hurry.'

Philip followed her up. He closed the small, curved-topped door. 'That's quite a way off,' he remarked. 'All the way on the other side of the City and the West End.'

As the cabbie cracked his whip, and the horse trotted slowly off, whinnying, she murmured, her hand high on his thigh. 'All the better. You paid me for some sex on the way, did you not?' Leaning out of the window, she repeated her instructions to the cabbie not to hurry. 'My friend wants to see the sights,' she added.

Her 'punter' began to undo the lace front of her bodice with nimble fingers. Feeling outrageously sinful, relishing her role, she took his hand away from her breasts and held out hers. 'Seven shillings and sixpence,' she said. 'In advance, if you please.'

Fishing in a waistcoat pocket, he brought out a silver coin and handed it to her, grinning. 'Half a crown now,' he said. 'Half a crown when we're inside your house. And half a crown before I leave.'

'All right.'

'Now I really *do* want to see those famous sights.'

He closed the curtains, finished unlacing her bodice and handled her tits out. Determined that she should act the part of the whore to the full, Lord Brexford had had her paint her nipples the same scarlet colour as her lips.

'Pretty,' Philip muttered. 'Very pretty indeed.' Kneading her breasts, he ducked his head to them and licked the very tip of each nipple. He picked up the jade necklace which hung upon them, testing its weight. 'This is the real thing,' he said. 'What's more, your clothes are of the finest cut and material. And you have an upper-class accent when you want. I somehow can't figure you out for a half crown whore.'

'I ain't. I'm a seven and a tanner whore, ain't I?' she said brightly.

'With an address as expensive as your clothes.'

As he gentled her tits, smudging their nipple lipstick over them a little in the process, he studied her face closely.

'I believe that you harbour some dark and deep secret, Charlotte,' he told her.

This man Philip, a total stranger until but twenty minutes or so ago, was making her feel most deliciously horny. She searched his pale blue eyes. 'I have many dark secrets,' she breathed.

'I'm sure that you do.' He squeezed her tits together, rolling them inwards so that the nipples almost touched. 'Time to earn your first half crown. I should very much like to have these cushioning my dick. Please get it out.'

He was not wearing a belt. Trying not to appear too eager – she was, after all, acting the part of a hard-bitten prostitute and situations like this were supposed to be as commonplace to her as working on a conveyor belt was to a factory girl – Charlotte unbuttoned his fly. He had on a pair of white silk pants, also buttoned, beneath his trousers. He watched intently as she unfastened them and a thick mass of tangled pubic hair sprang into view.

He lifted his backside. 'Pull them down. Better, take them right off.'

The hansom cab had just passed Aldgate Pump and was heading into Leadenhall Street.

Fascinated by the sudden appearance of a stirring cock which was just beginning to unnestle from its soft and fleshy bed of balls – an uncircumcised cock as long proportionately as its owner was tall, but not so skinny – Charlotte stooped forward to drag trousers and underpants together down Philip's legs, over the gleaming, black half-boots and off. Taking the trousers from her, he put them unhurriedly in their creases, folded them neatly and laid them on the green leather seat at his side. There were two red cushions in the carriage, one at each corner of the seat. He picked them up and dropped them on the floor beneath his feet.

'For your knees,' he said.

Kneeling on them, she leant into his groin. Taking her

tits in both hands, she scooped them around his genitals. Grunting pleasure, he jerked his backside. His cock, its glans pointing up at him through squashed tit flesh, was rising in tiny jerks.

'Suck it all the way up, Charlotte. Gobble me – was that not the vulgar expression you used earlier?'

'Mmmm.' Obediently, she closed her mouth on it. Moments later, it had grown into a solid eight-incher, and it was the full pair of balls her tits were cushioning as her head nodded up and down, the orange feather in her hat jiggling, and her cheeks contracted. Her pussy was beginning to get delightfully wet.

The more to appreciate the sensations which were engulfing her, she closed her eyes. Philip's strong cock, which had tasted slightly salty at first, now had a pleasantly spicy flavour as a little fluid seeped from it. The scrotum felt pleasantly squidgy encased between her breasts. The background sound of the steady clopping of the horse's hooves as it walked at a leisurely pace into Cheapside had an almost aphrodisiacal quality about it. The regular rocking of the carriage on the cobbled road bounced Philip's buttocks on the springy seat, thus enhancing her fellatio and causing the sparse covering of wiry little hairs on the man's balls to scratch her tits teasingly.

Charlotte's horny little pussy was pleading for penetration – but it was hardly the business of a whore to beg to be fucked. Philip was observing the top of her bobbing head with its little feathered hat through slitted eyelids. Jesus, he was thinking, was there anything in this world better than a first-rate blow-job with one's balls cushioned in a lovely pair of tits? Then he remembered what else he had in mind for later, yes, he thought, perhaps there was.

She would have loved to at least slip her hand up under her skirt and into her knickers to frig herself, but Charlotte could not even do that without giving herself away as no whore. She sucked happily on, all the way through Cheapside, Newgate, Holborn Viaduct and High Holborn, constantly expecting him to come at any moment in her mouth, prepared for this interesting eventuality, content for it to happen. But he did not ejaculate, he merely spilled a little more of the spicy-tasting lubrication fluid.

They were being driven along Oxford Street – though they had no way of knowing this without opening the curtain – when he took her head with his hands cradling her ears and pulled her lips off his cock. She had been wanking him as she sucked and she kept a firm grip on it. It was blotchy with her lipstick which was also smeared messily around the corners of her mouth. She sharply jerked her fist up and down.

'Don't you want me to toss you right off?' she softly asked, gazing up at him. She was so close to orgasm herself that she was squeezing and rubbing her thighs hard together. He was breathing shallowly, his mouth agape, the tip of his tongue on his lower lip, his eyes drooping.

He unprised her hand. 'No. That's enough. I want to save it up for later.'

Amazed at his self-control, she vaguely wondered if he was one of those men who had trouble in achieving orgasm. But she doubted that very much; his cock would surely have been on its way down again long before now. She forced herself to relax her thighs – no way was she going to be able to bring herself off like that – at least now now that his prick had left her mouth.

Bending down, he picked up his underpants from the floor. He put his feet through their leg holes and pulled them over his boots and up to his knees. He handed her his folded trousers. 'Put them on, would you? Be careful with them.'

She pulled them up to his pants, then hoisted the pants in place as he raised his buttocks. His erection was like a living tent pole inside them. Raunchily enjoying herself, she eased his trousers all the way up his slim but muscular thighs. Never in her life had she had the experience of dressing a man who sported a hard-on; it was a weird reversal of the norm.

She gave a little giggle. 'I'm never going to be able to close all the buttons,' she observed. 'Not with you in that state.' Having fastened the bottom two, she was having a struggle to get the fly to meet so that she could do up the next one.

'Leave it. Don't touch me any more. My dick will go down in a minute or so.' He seemed to be engaged all of a sudden in a minor battle with himself; his face muscles were tense and twitching, he was clasping and unclasping his hands. He opened the curtain on his side of the carriage and sniffed the crispy air. Then he glanced at her again. 'It might help matters if you lace your boobs back in.'

She tucked her breasts away, did up the laces of her bodice, then, wishing her naughty little pussy would cease its torment, she scrambled off her knees and sank down beside him, pulling back her curtain. They had already passed Oxford Circus and were heading for Marble Arch.

'Nearly home,' she observed. 'Just a few minutes more.' Sticking her head out of the window she called up to the cabman. 'You can have Dobbin trot the rest of the way,' she told him. The man slapped his reins on the horse's haunches.

'Almost there, are we? Good show,' commented Philip. He was doing himself up, having quite a struggle with the buttons. His cock, it seemed, was in decline – but not that much.

At Hyde Park Square at that moment, the maid was letting Lord Brexford in. He had lost his key a month before and he kept forgetting to order a new one. After telling the woman to take herself back to the bed he had disturbed her from, he followed her up the steep staircase and went into Charlotte's bedroom. Adjoining the room there was a small dressing-room. He made his way in there, leaving the light off and the door slightly ajar. Hidden in deep shadow he would be afforded a splendid view of the sexual frollickings shortly to take place. Impatient for those events to begin, he went to the window where he awaited the arrival of Charlotte and Philip.

His vigil was a short one. He had beaten his mistress to her house by a mere seven minutes despite having his cabbie trot the horse most of the way. The hansom came jogging down the street and the cabman drew up his mare beneath a street-lamp outside Charlotte's front door. In the yellowish light of the gas lamp, as Philip helped Charlotte down from the carriage Lord Brexford observed that her lipstick was badly smudged around the mouth and that she was wearing the sort of doey-eyed expression which signified that she was well and truly sexed up. Well and good, thought his lordship. His loins twitched.

'Not such a bad little place for a half-crown lady of the night to be living in,' commented Philip as Charlotte let him into the spacious, tastefully decorated hallway with its thick Persian carpet, splendid pair of matching crystal chandeliers and its imposing marble statue of a standing Indian wearing a be-rubied turban.

'It suits me very well, thank you. So very nicely positioned, too. Of course I have to work hard to keep it up but . . .' she smiled artfully and gave a little shrug '. . . then I happen usually to enjoy my, ah, profession.' The taste of his cock was turning slightly stale in her mouth. 'Would you like a drink?'

'How about we have one in your bedroom.' He walked to the bottom of the stairs.

She took a lighted paraffin lamp from its niche in the mauve flock-papered hall, handed it to him and opened a door by the staircase. 'Perhaps you would fetch a bottle? Then you can take your pick. There's a wine cellar down there. Personally, I fancy champagne.'

When he emerged, bearing a bottle of excellent vintage Dom Perignon, Charlotte was fixing her lips in front of an elaborately gilt-framed mirror. She appeared super cool and perfectly relaxed, a hardened prostitute for whom the business of selling her body was as routine as that of a butcher peddling his meat. Yet her mind was in a turmoil: the real reason for this elaborate charade was upon her – upstairs her kinky lord would be lurking, hidden away, waiting to spy secretly upon her and ogle as she was being used by this fine gentleman in any way which took his fancy.

'The lady keeps an incredibly well-stocked cellar,' observed Philip. 'The plot thickens, as they say. Glasses?'

'Upstairs.'

'Then kindly lead the way, my dear.'

To sustain her role, before starting to lead the way up the narrow staircase, she tugged his sleeve. 'First, my two and a tanner,' she said, flattening her palm at him.

His face split into a chummy grin. He found a silver half-crown piece in his waistcoat pocket and gave it to her. Then, as she planted a foot on the first stair, he glanced at the vintage on the label of the champagne. 'Cheap at the price,' he commented. 'The bubbly alone must be worth all of that.' And indeed it was, it was of the finest.

By the side of Charlotte's king-sized, four-poster bed with its delicate – but seldom closed – lace curtains there stood an elegant, glass-fronted cabinet which was fully stocked with bottles of spirit and shining crystal glasses – Lord Brexford often enjoyed a drink whilst fornicating and he liked to have his liquor close at hand. From it, she took two tulip-shaped champagne glasses.

In the dark dressing-room, through a three-inch crack in the slightly open door, Jeremy Brexford, keenly excited, watched as Philip dextrously stripped the wire from the neck of one of his best bottles of champagne. The man had hardly begun to thumb the cork when it came out with an impressive bang to shoot across the room and thump into one of the dressing-table mirrors. Foam spilled onto the colourful Chinese rug.

Philip filled Charlotte's glass, then his own. She emptied it in one, long, thirsty gulp then smacked her lips, holding it out for more. This crude behaviour, she realised, was hardly the way a true lady would act, but then she was no lady on this dirty night and she did not want to appear like one.

First replenishing her glass, Philip then sipped a little from his. His small eyes, meanwhile, were darting searchingly around the room. His gaze lit on a huge oak wardrobe. Going to it, he opened its double doors, one of them squeaking on its hinges as he did so. They were suspended on their outside edges so that the full-length mirrors on their backs offered Charlotte the facility of inspecting herself from the rear whilst dressing.

'Yes; this, I believe, will do very nicely indeed,' he said.

Charlotte frowned at him. 'It will? For what, pray?'

He peered inside. 'For the bondage. And for some of the so-forth.'

'A *wardrobe*?'

He failed to react to her surprise. Instead, he commenced removing her dresses from the cabinet in groups of three or four and laying them on top of one another on the bed, treating them with care.

'May I ask what on earth you think you are doing?' she asked, swallowing more champagne.

'I'm making some room.'

Making some room. What in the name of God was this character up to, wondered Charlotte. Surely he wasn't planning to lock her in her wardrobe? Her eyes probed the darkness beyond the open dressing-room door. She could just make out the shadowy form of her lover. He was sitting very still on a chair, out of the way of the thin shaft of light which cut into the room from the bedroom, and he had closed the curtains in there so that his shape would not be obvious against the light which had been entering the window from the street-lamp. Had she not known he would be there, she would never have noticed him. In that case, neither would Philip, even were he not quite so intent on whatever it was he was setting up.

'Yes. That should do, I think,' Philip muttered, half to himself. Sliding open one of the drawers which were tucked into a side of the wardrobe, he rummaged through its contents. He closed it and tried another, then another – where he found what he was looking for. Removing from it two pairs of frilly French knickers, he tucked them loosely into one of his jacket pockets.

'Your five bob's worth doesn't get you my clothes thrown in as well,' remarked Charlotte drily.

He chose to ignore the comment. 'Remove your skirt and take down your knickers, please,' he requested her, parking himself on the edge of the bed to watch.

The lump of excitement in the pit of her belly thickened, added to by the knowledge that Lord Brexford was also observing her.

90

'But keep the shoes on,' Philip added. She was wearing sexy, high-heeled, black patent-leather boots which reached the bottoms of her calves.

She undid the buttons and stepped out of her crimson skirt. Without a second's hesitation, she stripped off her lacy cami-knickers. Her long, slender legs were bare. Her bodice with its red net bottom fell just short of her auburn-haired pussy, displaying it most prettily.

'Come over here to me,' said Philip. His voice had gone quiet, his eyes rooted on her loins.

When she reached him, he bent forward so that his face was inches from her groin. All his attention was focused on her pussy. He licked it, a tom-cat at a bowl of cream. His tongue, as it slipped sensuously over her little bud of clitoris, made her shiver in delight. He salivated over the fleshy inside tops of her thighs, where the pubic hairs curled into them.

Then he turned her around. 'Bend over.'

Feeling utterly lewd, thoroughly enjoying the rude exhibitionism, Charlotte complied.

At that moment, Lord Brexford's view was of Philip's back and of Charlotte to just below her knees – for the bed was between himself and them. As his mistress bent down, Brexford's cock began to stir. Slowly and silently, he started to get out of his clothes.

'Open your bottom hole, why don't you?' asked Philip thickly.

'Dirty bugger, ain't you, dearie?' said Charlotte. Flattening her hands on her buttocks, she stretched them apart.

'I am, I am,' he muttered.

He did not touch her little hole, he simply stared lecherously at it, wetting his lips. Peering between her legs, she could see him from the waist down. There was a huge bulge in his trousers, she saw. As she watched, he grasped it and rubbed.

The man ogled Charlotte's private parts for what seemed to her to be almost an eternity. By the time he, somewhat hoarsely, uttered his next command, Jeremy Brexford was naked in the next room and he was sporting a full hard-on which he lovingly caressed.

'Time for you to get yourself in the wardrobe,' muttered Philip.

'Ah – is it really?' she said, very quietly. Feeling just a little wobbly – from more than the effects of alcohol – she first helped herself to more champagne, gulped it down, then she did as he had asked. There was a big drawer in the base of the wardrobe which obliged her to step high up to climb inside.

'On your knees, would you, facing me,' Philip told her. 'Stretch your hands above your head and grab hold of the rail.'

A thick brass pole for hanging clothes on ran horizontally above Charlotte's head. She could comfortably reach it. When her hands were wrapped around it, Philip took the French knickers a pair at a time from his pocket and used them to tie her wrists securely to the pole. Once done, he unlaced her bodice so that her lipstick-smeared tits fell free. Angling the wardrobe doors slightly inwards so that she was afforded a double view of herself in their mirrors, he stood back to admire her.

'A most arousing sight, would you not agree?' he murmured. Next, he picked up her silken cami-knickers from the rug and twisted them into a thin rope. Before she realised what he was about to do, he had stepped forward and, holding the knickers like a strangler's cord, he had forced them between her teeth. As she grunted protest and shook her head, he knotted them behind her head.

'Don't panic, Charlotte, there's a dear,' he said. He stood back from her again. 'It's only a game. Taste good, your drawers, do they? They certainly should do, where they've been.'

The naked Lord Brexford had moved close to the door. He was steadily wanking himself. Charlotte could faintly see his moving hand and his cock in the light from the bedroom. She realised that should this dissolute Philip happen to look in that direction he was likely to notice. But look he did not. He had eyes only for his captive hooker, so fetchingly trussed and gagged with three pairs of her knickers. Without ceasing to ogle her, he took off his

92

jacket, his trousers and his underpants, hanging them over a chair. He left his boots and waistcoat on. His stiff eight inches of prick were poking through his shirt-tails.

Philip's next, shocking action completely changed the tone of the evening in an instant. Staring at Charlotte with piercing eyes as he did so, he picked up his ebony silver-topped cane from where he had left it lying on the dressing-table – and he unsheathed a sword.

Charlotte's eyes bulged. A swordstick – what the *fuck* was this? Her plight so far had amused her and had encouraged feelings most carnal in her. Having within her sight two splendidly erect cocks had added to those feelings. But now they became laced with a sudden – and totally unexpected – shot of fear as, brandishing the thin needle-sharp length of tempered steel, Philip approached her. The sword glinted dully in the gaslight. Had it not been for the fact that her lover was lurking but a few feet away – and that he surely had in his jacket pocket the short-barrelled derringer pistol which he habitually carried in London – Charlotte would have been quaking in terror.

'I imagine that will do, Philip old boy,' said Lord Brexford mildly, stepping into the room. 'You wouldn't want to scare her to death, would you?'

Philip's hellish expression went through a remarkable transformation. Lowering the sword, he produced a grin which was most schoolboyish. It almost split his face in two. 'So there you are, Jeremy,' he said. He glanced pointedly at Brexford's cock. 'And perfectly prepared, I see.'

Relief, mixed with a certain amount of irritation, surged through Charlotte. That unspeakable knave Brexford had set the whole scene up from beginning to end! And as had she in her impersonation, this scurvy Philip had been acting the whole time with his repeated intimations that she didn't seem like a whore. He had known damn well who she was. She would dearly like to cut the balls off the pair of them at that moment. She tried to scream her annoyance – which was already fading away as she began to see the funny side of the situation – through her gag, but it came out only as a strangled grunt.

As Philip sheathed his swordstick with a flourish, Jeremy said, 'This is Lord Antrim, Charlie. A dear old friend of mine. We occasionally meet in the House.'

'Sorry about the sword business,' said Philip. 'It was Jeremy's idea, naturally.' He paused. 'I believe he means the house of ill repute.'

He closed in on her and began undoing her hands. His cock was hovering in its erect state just below her chin – had she not been gagged she might have been tempted to bite it. As soon as she was free she thumped him hard on his chest with the sides of both fists, obliging him to grab her wrists.

'Whoah there, Charlie,' said Brexford. 'It was only an elaborate game. A little fear thrown in with sex to add a touch of spice.'

Her irritation disappeared as she clambered down and out of the wardrobe. Reaching behind her head, she fumbled with the knot of the knickers.

'Leave them where they are,' said Brexford. 'We don't want you hurling foul abuse at us.'

'I shouldn't *mind* that, actually,' contradicted Lord Antrim. 'Amusing to hear a lady using bad language.'

'All right. Then let's hear it.' Going behind Charlotte, Jeremy began untying the knot. The feel of his rock hard cock prodding her buttocks as he did this served to re-kindle her fires of lust. 'Swear at us, Charlie,' he told her, as the knickers came loose. 'As much as you like. Play the filthy-mouthed East End tart.' The cami-knickers dropped onto her shoulder, and he grabbed a handful of tit and pussy. 'Then we two are going to treat you to a fucking you will never forget. You deserve it after putting up with our bit of nonsense so bravely.'

She chuckled throatily. 'You are a wicked whore-son, you know that, Jeremy?' she said. 'You nearly had me fooled there. I was getting scared.'

'As I remarked – a touch of spice. Some extra excitement to prepare you for the night to follow.' He hooked his fingers between her legs to play with her pussy lips. 'How about the dirty language which Philip so wants to hear?'

94

All Charlotte's pent-up lust came surging back. She let fly the dirtiest mouthful of abuse she could dream up – for she certainly wanted some sort of revenge. It was so foul, a product of her East End streetwalker days, that she had both men blanching from the start, and Jeremy quickly asked her to stop it.

She smiled disarmingly and switched from her cockney accent. 'I take it that will suffice, Jeremy darling, Philip, or would you like to hear more of the same?'

'It will *do*, Charlie. My God,' pronounced Jeremy, grinning. 'We should wash your mouth out with soap.'

She grabbed his hard-on. 'And now you're going to treat me to the fucking I'll never forget, no?'

His nostrils flared. 'We are, we are,' he said quietly. Fisting his hard-on, he raised a suggestive eyebrow. 'But first, why don't you . . .?' Raising a suggestive eyebrow, he put a hand on her shoulder and began to encourage her with it down on the rug.

On her pretty knees, scarlet-painted fingernails digging into Jeremy's buttocks, Charlotte took his cock in her mouth and avidly gobbled. From the corner of her raunchy eye she saw that Lord Antrim had removed his silken, fancy waistcoat and was busy unfastening the pearly buttons of his shirt. His cock – much the same impressive size as the one slipping and sliding between her lips – was jiggling above those juicily fat balls whose tiny hairs had so recently been scratching her bared tits in the hansom. No annoyance remained within her; indeed, the dramatically induced touch of fear *may* have added a soupçon of spice to the ribald activities. Jeremy, she reflected, was a genius at such things.

Her lover backed his cock out of her mouth. Turning her around by her shoulders, he had her crawl on hands and knees to the bed where he sat in front of her and again pulled her face onto his genitals.

'Why don't you have your way with her?' he invited his friend. 'You will find she has the most delightfully tight little fanny.'

Antrim needed no further encouragement. Wearing only

95

his gleaming leather boots and his socks, he got to his knees behind Charlotte. He angled his cockhead between her pussy lips and shoved hard. His prick slipped comfortably all the way in, causing Charlotte to moan into Jeremy's cock as the bull-sized balls jogged against her clitoris. Her moan was followed by a long string of little grunts as Philip began to ram determinedly in and out of her with his nude torso hunched over her back and his fine, slender hands groping and kneeding her lipstick-smeared breasts.

The harder Lord Antrim fucked Charlotte, the stronger she sucked Lord Brexford. After a lengthy period of this three-way activity, the two men swapped places, and Charlotte, drowning in a sea of lust, found herself giving Philip Antrim his second blow-job of the evening as her lover plunged his prick in and out of her saturated pussy. At long last, that explosion she had been so craving in the hansom cab hit her. She came gratefully, her fingers digging sharply into Philip's buttocks, gasping into his balls.

Brexford uncoupled. Taking Charlotte gently by the upper arm, he helped her to her feet. She had gone limp as a rag doll, her chin was lolling into her neck, her hands hung slackly at her sides; nevertheless her lover's next words scorched her libido.

'We're moving into your dressing-room, Charlie,' he muttered. 'You are about to enjoy every sort of sandwich.'

She felt – at one and the same moment – like a helpless, feeble little girl and a wickedly wanton woman as these two noble peers of the realm with their massive, wobbling erections – both of the cocks shiny with a mixture of her saliva and her pussy juices – escorted her into the other room. Antrim hooked two fingers into her cunt from behind, his hard-on pressing into her buttocks and sliding upwards to flatten its back into their cleft as Brexford quickly moved around to light two of the lamps. He fractionally opened the curtains so that a sliver of gaslight fell across an upper wall and part of the corniced ceiling.

The clothes in the wardrobe within which Charlotte had just been tied were but a fraction of the expensive collec-

96

tion with which Jeremy had provided her. The majority were hanging in wooden cupboards all around the walls of this dressing-room.

Lord Brexford often made love to Charlotte in here, for one very good and bawdy reason: several large mirrors on chromium stands were placed strategically to enable Charlotte to admire herself from every angle whilst dressing, and apart from those mirrors, one chair and a golden silk-covered chaise-longue liberally spread with cushions, the room was bare. The mirrors served very well for a purpose more interesting than dressing – that of watching themselves whilst making love in the middle of the floor amidst cushions.

Jeremy began throwing multi-coloured cushions from the high-backed chair and the chaise-longue onto the Persian rug.

'Tell me, Philip, in what manner would it please you to serve the needful wench now?' asked Lord Brexford.

'Suppose that I leave the choice to you and your remarkable imagination?' responded Antrim, rolling the back of his hard-on in Charlotte's buttocks.

'Very well.' Brexford thought for a second. 'Make yourself comfortable, Philip. On your back on the floor.'

Antrim ceased his ribald activity with Charlotte's backside and laid down amongst the cushions.

'Sit on him, Charlie. Sit down on his dick.'

Trembling with renewed need, Charlotte straddled Philip, facing him. Taking a firm hold of his hard-on, she guided it inside her and sank down on it. In the mirror in front of her, she was presented with three very different views of the penetration. The one she found the most titillating was from behind; his fat balls, his prick going in her, her white, bouncing buttocks, the scene perfectly on display.

She was ogling this lusty sight, moving her bottom up and down as if post-trotting a horse, when Brexford's hairy legs got in the way of it by moving behind her. He folded her forwards by the shoulders until her forearms were resting on the carpet and her tits flattened into Antrim's thin, hairy chest, her open bodice draping on either side of it.

Her lover lowered his bulky self over her back. Charlotte's view from behind in the mirror in front of her was once again unobstructed. Massively turned on, she watched eagerly as Lord Brexford handled his cock until the glans had squeezed its way into her pussy on top of Antrim's shaft. His buttocks went rigid and the muscles on the backs of his thighs stood out as he gruntingly eased his prick all the way in. Charlotte was overwhelmed with an incredibly horny sensation of slippery, fleshy, pussy-stretching, her cunt beautifully filled. She became almost mesmerised by the reflection of two heaving sets of male buttocks, her bottom between them, as the two cocks slid up and down her, back to back, the balls repeatedly mashing together.

For the second time, she came, whimpering noisily, her eyes glued on the salacious view as she did so.

Lord Brexford began – as he so often was wont to – to dictate the course of the action. As Antrim lay almost unmoving beneath Charlotte with his cock buried to the hilt in her, Brexford's pole plunged up and down against his own. Both of the men had had homosexual experiences at public school, and Antrim still enjoyed giving and taking the occasional poke up the backside – but the closest Brexford would allow himself to get to gay sex these days was what he was indulging in at that moment.

Philip's silken, solid cock flesh crammed in Charlotte's cunt so tightly next to his own felt perfectly delicious to Jeremy. The finest moment of all was each time their balls clashed and mingled when he would wiggle his crotch from side to side in order to take maximum pleasure from the contact. Faster and faster went his pussy juice-lubricated strokes, harder and harder his balls banged and squashed into those of his friend.

So energetic did Brexford become as he approached orgasm with pants and grunts and with guttural swear-words spilling from his slack lips, that Charlotte found herself being rocked so violently between the two rutting men that her head was being flung up and down; her ostrich-feathered hat, a survivor up to then, came adrift and fell off. A part of her hair tumbled down. The sensation of being so thoroughly stuffed and spoiled with cock meat was overwhelmingly salacious. She was feeling most deliciously depraved, and the certain knowledge that the lords were deriving homosexual enjoyment from the intimate contact of their pricks within her was adding to her voluptuousness. Her eyes had been closed for long moments. Now, close to orgasm yet again, she opened them on the image of Lord Brexford's pounding buttocks.

At that moment he straightened his arm. His spine curved backwards as he produced his final, powerful thrust. His balls were mashed into those of Philip as they emptied themselves into Charlotte's pussy. She, meanwhile was leching on the sight of his bottom clenching and unclenching as more and more sperm, a seemingly impossible amount, flooded up inside her. Once more she came, squealing, lifting her booted feet from the floor and jogging them in the air. Replete, with a massive sigh Lord Brexford unplugged his Charlie. He rolled onto his back on the carpet, one arm outflung.

Charlotte remained fully impaled by Philip. His fat and sturdy eight inches, now unaccompanied by those of Lord Brexford, suddenly felt far smaller to her than they actually were. He was panting with lust, but he had not come. Charlotte sensed this, though she felt so saturated inside that she could not be sure.

For a moment she reverted to the cockney whore role she had so enjoyed. 'You spunked or not, mister?' she asked him.

'No,' he gasped, humping his hips up and down.

'Blimey.' She reached between their bellies to fondle his balls. They were damp with Jeremy's semen which was leaking from her. 'Ain't you never going to shoot your wad, then?'

Not quite yet, he wasn't. For the potent dose of homosexual carnality had brought to Lord Antrim an irresistible craving for buggery.

'I'm going to spill it up your bottom,' he growled.

Lifting her off him, he manoeuvred her onto her hands and knees.

Meanwhile, Lord Brexford was oblivious to this imminent change in activity; his arm was hooked behind his head, his eyes were closed, his chest was heavily rising and falling, and his hard-on was being very slow to wilt.

Antrim's prick was so slippery with the cocktail of Brexford's spunk and Charlotte's vaginal secretions that there was going to be little need for additional lubricant. He stretched her bottom hole wide with his thumbs. As he had done earlier in the bedroom, he studied it with a prurient eye. Stuffing two fingers in her pussy, he got them thoroughly wet and then poked them into her back passage. He repeated the action, making sure that her anus was well and truly oiled. Without handling his cock, he moved his hips to angle its bulbous tip into Charlotte's little, pink and puckered hole. She found a perfect reflection of the start to her sodomy and her eyes never left the mirror in question. No stranger to a bum-ball, she enjoyed the exquisitely different sexual sensation it brought to her – not least the feeling of wickedness in indulging in a deed unfairly branded as perverted.

All of Antrim's concentration was centred on Charlotte's beautifully moulded, perfectly white set of buttocks. Imagining that they belonged to an adolescent boy, he began his assault on her tight little bottom hole.

She gritted her teeth. The only part of being buggered she did not relish was the initial moment of pain; the cock was of an impressive size, her anus was tiny. Happily, the mixture of sexual juices smeared inside her and over Philip Antrim's prick worked just as well as any grease or jelly. She gave one little yelp, then her sphincter was breached. The bawdy pleasure began.

Charlotte's sharp little cry and intake of breath caused Lord Brexford to open his eyes. From where he was lying he could not clearly see exactly what Antrim was up to: he had only a front view of Charlotte's strained, lust-filled expression and her swaying tits. But her yelp gave him a shrewd idea. Besides, he knew his friend's vices only too well since he shared most of them with him. He sat up and humped himself over the rug on his behind until he was afforded a close-up of the sodomy. By this time, Lord Antrim's cock was buried deeply in Charlotte's bottom hole and his balls were dangling over her pussy.

Philip was gloating on the progress of his buggery. Fascinated as always by the sight of his cock stuffed all the way up a backside, he withdrew it with teasing slowness, pausing when only his glans were still embedded. He jogged the purple helmet in fast, tiny jerks, exciting Charlotte's sphincter, making her gasp and moan.

As much a lover of this most carnal activity as his friend, and a most enthusiastic voyeur, Brexford made a fist around his prick – which was on the rise again without ever having completely relaxed. He wanked and ogled as Antrim heaved his hips once more, penetrating Charlotte's bum up to his balls. With the buggery hotting up, Jeremy's cock hardened.

Clambering to his knees, he walked on them until his genitals were hovering close to Charlotte's face. Its taut expression of ecstasy suggested pain. Her lipstick was smeared messily all around her mouth, her mascara was smudged and running, and apart from the rebel tress, several more strands of hair had escaped from her chignon to trail over her shoulders. She appeared every inch the woman of the night whom she had been impersonating and this fact served to further inflame her lover. Massaging his cock, with it pointing up at his chin, he thrust his jiggling balls at her mouth.

'Lick them, Charlie, there's a good girl,' he growled.

Whilst her bottom was enjoying a most vigorous poling, Charlotte coated Brexford's scrotum with her spittle. His grip changed so that he was only wanking his cockhead with two fingers. Like that he offered her mouth the thick back of his prick. She trailed her tongue lasciviously up and down it, making it as wet as his balls.

Contriving himself beneath her, Brexford raised his backside on two red velvet cushions so that his hard-on was so flattened beneath Charlotte's pussy that the glans poked into Antrim's balls each time the man's cock was rammed fully home. Jeremy savoured this second homosexual contact for a minute or so, observing it through Charlotte's wobbling tits. Then he angled his prickhead into her vulva and heartily shoved.

Filled in both holes by large and sturdy cocks, double fucked yet again, Charlotte was positively choked up with lust. With her head lolling around and her eyes rolling, she was catching reflections of the debauched threesome rut from various angles. More and more of her hair was tumbling down around her shoulders, her fingers were clamped into a cushion, her teeth were bared, she was drumming the pointed toes of her boots onto the rug. She came again with a long-drawn-out wail – and yet another climax was hard on the heels of that one.

Philip Antrim was at last letting himself completely go. In all, including in the hansom cab, he had sported a hard-on during this riotously sexual evening without actually ejaculating for something close to an hour and a half. Now, still harbouring the notion that this smooth, beautifully rounded, naked bottom belonged to a teenage lad – and further titillated by the libidinous clash of scrotums as he heaved his prick in and out of Charlotte's bum hole and Lord Brexford heartily fucked her pussy – he felt orgasm most powerfully sweeping over him.

For long moments the three were one ravenous, sexual beast as semen flowed and pussy juice oozed and buttocks climatically heaved. From somewhere Lord Brexford had drawn on a reserve of sperm, Antrim was letting fly his semen like water from a hose, and Charlotte was almost fainting away with the dizzy height of her final climax – for her it was the most libido-wrenching of all of them as she felt both her bottom hole and her cunt flooded at the same time. The rest of her chignon came tumbling down. She shrieked with ecstatic delight.

The sexual beast broke slowly apart. The utterly satiated trio sprawled in attitudes which might have been those of violent death over the rug and the cushions. The room resembled a battleground where three people had fucked themselves to oblivion. The only sound in the air, for long moments, was that of heavy breathing. Then, from somewhere in the street came the raucous shriek of a mating cat.

Much later, when Lord Antrim was dressed to leave, Charlotte, not having bothered to do anything about her lewdly dishevelled state of dress and with her hair a tangled mess, accompanied him down the stairs. At the front door she held out her hand, an expectant look on her face.

'You 'aven't forgot you owe me two and a tanner, dearie, 'ave you?' she asked him.

Grinning weakly, he took a silver half-crown piece from his waistcoat pocket. He first tested its weight in his hand, then he slotted the coin into her pussy.

Chapter 7

As spring advanced, the days grew progressively warmer. Three days later it was so unusually hot for the time of the year that Miss Petty allowed the girls the special treat of a visit to the beach. The entire complement of pupils, clad in their regulation, thin wool, grey and black striped bathing suits – shapeless, one-piece creations which modestly reached to their knees and elbows and buttoned all the way up to their necks – filed down the steep steps which were hewn into the cliff to the sandy beach.

The normally rough, often raging English Channel was as calm as a village pond, its surface shimmering under a cloudless sky. The beach, washed clean and flat by an ebbing tide, presented a vista of golden delight.

But, glorious weather notwithstanding, it was still only spring and the sea was most chilly. There was much hilarity, screaming and larking around as the girls vied with one another to be first to duck their shoulders. In fact, few of them could actually swim; the gym teacher was about to give lessons.

Ellie and Georgina were among those who were able to swim. There were rivers running through both their parents' estates and they had been taught at an early age for fear of them falling in and drowning.

Most bathing attire of the day was incommodious, and that of the Chalmers girls particularly so. The suits clung wetly and uncomfortably to the skin for a long time after a dip, making the girls feel cold even though the sun was hot. Having enjoyed their swim, whilst most of the rest of the girls were jumping up and down and flapping their arms to get warm, Ellie and Georgina elected to go off for a run – which quickly took them around the edge of the cove and out of sight. They arrived at a long, flat stretch of beach which was seldom visited by anyone except in summer.

Puffing, they slowed to a walk. This happened to be the first time they had been alone together since the afternoon of Georgina's extraordinary sexual initiations and they had therefore had no opportunity to discuss one another's guilty secrets – something they enjoyed doing as often as possible.

The one thing Georgina was terrified to disclose was her sexual enslavement to Miss Petty. But when Ellie asked her about Thomas and what it had been like to lose her virginity, she decided to confide in her despite Lord Brexford's threat.

'Actually it wasn't Thomas who did me at all,' she said, with a cheeky little smile. 'Bet you can't guess who it was.'

'So it was some other boy,' said Ellie, shrugging. 'How should I know?'

'It wasn't a boy. It was a man. It was Lord Brexford.'

Ellie gasped. She took her girlfriend by the arm and shook it, stopping their walk, staring in astonishment at her. 'You amaze me,' she said. 'You're having me on, you dummy.'

'No I'm not. Cross my heart and hope to die if I am. I swear it was him.'

She recounted the entire story of the wicked manner in which she had been coerced by Jeremy Brexford and how fantastically she had enjoyed all that had transpired in the torture courtyard.

'. . . so you see, now he's taken both our cherries, the dirtyman,' Georgina concluded, with a devil-may-care grin.

'Good golly,' exclaimed Ellie. 'And from what you told me, from now on you're obliged to let him do whatever he wishes with you, otherwise he's going to tell Petters that he caught you being had by Thomas? Is that right?'

'Yes.' She tossed her head. 'But see if I care – I can't wait to go there again.'

Of course, the threat of exposure no longer actually hung over Georgina's head since Miss Petty knew that Georgina had been deflowered even if she was unaware that it was Brexford himself who had done the dirty deed. But since she craved so much to cavort more up at the manor Georgina was more than happy to continue to pretend that the danger still existed. Lying to Ellie left a sour taste in her mouth, but she felt she had no option.

'So now we're both Lord Brexford's slaves,' she said.

'*I'm* not a slave,' Ellie objected. 'Why am I a slave, just because you are?'

'You go up there often enough. You've done heaps of very naughty things. You've told me all about them.'

'Only because I want to. He can't make me, can he, even if he can you?'

'Hah. You're bad, bad, Ellie Branks, you know that?'

Ellie cheerfully smiled. 'And now, so are you, my precious.'

They fell into one another's arms, groping, French-kissing hungrily, pressing their damply clad bodies together. Then, hand in hand, they continued on their walk.

In the distance, rounding the far end of the cove, a horse and rider appeared. The horse was being ridden at a fast gallop, a cloud of sand being kicked up behind it.

Jeremy Brexford was standing on his stirrups, leaning over the heavily muscled neck of Napoleon, savouring to the full the heady thrill of the beach gallop also loved by the steed. Jeremy was hatless, enjoying the warmth of the sun on his face and the wind in his hair as the horse's hooves beat out a tattoo on the harsh sand.

He did not notice the stripily clad female figures ahead of him until he was almost upon them, then he had such difficulty in stopping the excited stallion that he was a hundred yards past the girls before he managed the feat of pulling him up. He turned the snorting, whinnying horse around. Ellie and the plump Georgina, no less, he observed to himself – together on an otherwise deserted beach, by God. He trotted Napoleon up to them, wondering as he did so how to handle the situation and in what manner he might profit from such an unexpected opportunity. Reining the sixteen-and-a-half-hands animal in, he smiled a greeting down at the girls.

'A very good afternoon to you both,' he said.

The pulses of both girls sped up as they were confronted with the handsome man who had turned their sexual fantasies into reality. He was looking so terrifically macho atop his big, sweaty Arab steed. They had an advantage over him, but neither one of them realised this; it was that they were aware of each other's sexual activities with the lord, but there was no way he could have known that fact.

'Good afternoon, Lord Brexford,' Georgina responded coyly.

Ellie grinned saucily up at him. 'Hi there, Jeremy,' she said. 'What a surprise.'

Georgina blinked at her friend in surprise as Brexford swung a leg over his steed and dismounted. She had found Ellie's greeting most audacious, despite the fact that she repeatedly romped naked with the man.

Napoleon still wanted to gallop; he was dancing around in sweaty agitation, his master clinging tightly to the reins with his leather-gloved hands close to the animal's twitching ears. 'What are you girls doing down here?' he asked them. 'Shouldn't you be at school?'

Ellie nodded to the west. 'The whole school's back there, on the next beach.'

'Ah. Lovely day for it.'

He ran his eye briefly, searchingly, over them both. Lovely day for it indeed. The bathing costumes might be shapeless, but he was well aware that what lay beneath them was most definitely not. His loins stirred. It was a great stroke of luck to have encountered them both here together, but he had yet to form a clear plan of what he intended to do about it. His gaze swept up and down the beach; not a soul in sight. So much the better.

'Now, let me see,' he offered, his mind racing. 'Of course, we have all met before, have we not? Your name is Ellie, and you are Georgina Tennant, are you not? I know your father, Georgina.'

That was news to her. He knew her father – and yet that had done nothing to dissuade the man from having his evil way with her.

Napoleon tried to rear up on his back legs and he fought him down. 'Excited,' he said. 'Hates to be stopped in mid gallop. But then I could hardly have ridden on past two such pretty wenches, could I?'

Ellie, knowing just how very lecherous Lord Brexford invariably was, now realised his slight difficulty. Keen for a bit of shenanigan with him on this lovely afternoon – as she was willing to bet her favourite pony he was with them – she solved his problem for him.

'Why are you being so guarded, Jeremy?' she said brightly. 'We all three know very well that I've met you several times. In bed, with Lady Brexford.'

Her boldness should perhaps not have amazed him, but it did. It had after all been he himself with the help of Sophronia who had encouraged it in her. He failed to reply to that highly charged comment for several seconds, as libidinous ideas tumbled through his mind. Then he said, 'It would appear then that you two are intimate friends who divulge to each other your innermost secrets. Is that not so?'

'We tell each other everything,' said Ellie. 'For instance, I know that three days ago you took Georgie's cherry.'

Georgina gasped. Now she was for it.

'You were urged to keep utterly quiet about that event, Georgina,' said Brexford, in mock sternness. In fact he was delighted at the way things seemed to be progressing.

'I, I'm, I'm sorry, my lord, I really am,' stammered Georgina. 'I swear I only told Ellie and she won't breathe a word to a soul – will you, Ellie?'

Ellie shook her head, a twisted little smile glued to her lips.

'It's all right. You are forgiven on this occasion,' said Brexford, staring through her bathing costume. His little difficulty, he realised, was surmounted. He would have his way with the pair of them. He led his horse to the base of the cliff. There was a cave there and an outcrop of rock over which he looped the reins of the now slightly, but not much, calmer steed. The girls watched him silently, unmoving. Ellie was becoming horny for the sight of his cock – the only one in her young life so far – which had not pleasured her for more than three weeks. Georgina found herself nervously experiencing similar stirrings.

'Why don't you two come over here with me?' asked Brexford. 'Let us go into the cave. Explore a little.'

'We don't have very long,' Ellie pointed out as they went into the shadowy interior with him. 'If we're away for much longer someone's bound to come looking for us.'

'Then we shan't pussyfoot around, shall we? Sex is on my mind. Hopefully, it is on both of yours. I suggest we confine the exploring to that of one another. By the way, on the agreeable subject of sex, I know something about you two that you're not aware I know. You're lovers. You eat each other's pussies and so forth.'

Ellie gasped. 'How could you possibly know that?' She gaped accusingly at Georgina. 'You must have told him.'

'No, she didn't,' said Brexford. 'You see, I have a telescope. I've watched the two of you in each other's arms in your dormitory. You really should bother to close your curtains, you know.' He took a deep breath, his fine nostrils flaring as his eyes wandered pruriently over them. 'Well ...' he murmured, 'since you so enjoy eating your sexual parts, you can eat this, on your pretty knees.' Unbuttoning his tight, fawn-coloured breeches he pushed them down, together with his underpants, to the tops of his boots. Holding up the front of his shirt with the flat of his forearm, he leant back expectantly against the wall of the cave.

Both girls goggled. Lord Brexford's familiar, thick cock was three-quarters up already and rising in tiny jerks.

'Come *on*, gamahuche me,' he insisted. 'You first, Ellie.'

Kneeling in the soft sand – which was slightly damp because the tide came all the way into the cave – in front of him, Ellie zealously flickered the tip of her tongue over Brexford's glans in the way in which Lady Brexford had taught her, then she sucked his cock deeply into her mouth whilst he clumsily unfastened the buttons down the front of her still wet bathing suit. With Georgina looking on randily – though she was very slightly in shock – he pulled Ellie's top down to free her breasts.

'Take your swimming costume off, why don't you, Georgina?' Brexford ventured as Ellie gobbled greedily away.

Fingers trembling, heart thumping, she hurried to oblige.

'Come here,' he told her, when she was nude. 'Let me see how that thrashed bottom of yours is getting on.'

She went to him and turned her back on him, standing next to her fellating girlfriend, watching her bobbing head. Her backside had calmed down, but – even after three days – the marks of her beatings were plain to see. 'Miss Petty slippered me for being late that day I was with you,' she said. She was beginning to feel deliciously wanton. 'And guess what? I enjoyed it.'

'Like *this*?' He whacked a buttock smartly with the gloved palm of his hand. His cock jerked between Ellie's lips as the leather connected with an echoey slap. The flat flesh quivered.

'*Aaiieee!*' went Georgina. Her hand flew to the offended area at the same moment as Brexford's cracked heartily into the other buttock, and she squealed again.

'You can have as much of that as you wish – just as soon as you like, in the manor,' he promised her.

The slaps had stung Georgina mightily – but they had been nice, adding to her excitement.

'Your turn now to suck me,' he told her.

She turned hesitantly to face him, her hands planted firmly on both stinging mounds of her bottom, rubbing them. 'But I've never – I mean I don't –'

'Well, then why don't you get on your knees?' he interrupted. He pulled out of Ellie's mouth. 'It's about time you had a lesson or two.'

'Um, all, all right.' Still clutching her buttocks, Georgina doubled her chubby legs into the sand. She stared at the glistening prick and the heavy balls with closed lips, mesmerised by the genitals.

'Go on – suck it, Georgie,' urged Ellie. 'It's lovely. It's just as nice as what we do to each other, only different.'

Lovely indeed it was, Georgina speedily discovered. She took to fellatio like a baby takes to the tit. There was something about having her mouth closed around the most interesting part of the male anatomy which she found feverishly exciting. She was like a child with a strawberry ice lolly on a hot day, or a chocolate addict with her face in a box of Belgium delights. She sucked and licked cock and balls with rampant enthusiasm, her fingertip meanwhile caressing her rigid little clitoris whilst Ellie, her eyes inches from the action, drooled.

Two sweet, tight little pussies grew lustily wet.

'It seems you need no lessons, Georgina,' Lord Brexford grunted. 'How well you do it.' His climax was steadily building. 'And so does Ellie. Why don't you share it?' The two nubile young pupils commenced to add to their grooming as ladies-to-be as they paid most lascivious attentions to the peer's cock and balls, passing his prick back and forth from mouth to mouth and taking it in turns to lick his scrotum.

Thoroughly aroused, not far from orgasm, Brexford had the sudden notion to witness in the flesh that which he had only observed through his telescope.

'Why don't you now sixty-nine one another?' he gasped. 'I want to watch you.'

This was a most welcome suggestion indeed. After a final slurping cock-suck each, they broke away from his groin.

'But we must be quick,' panted Ellie. 'Just a sec.' She darted out of the cave and peered down the beach towards where the school party was, relieved to see that there was no one in sight. Then she hurried back inside, loins on fire. Dragging down her damp swimsuit she stepped out of it. With no hesitation she laid on her back on the damp sand and beckoned to Georgina, her silky, slim white thighs wide apart, inviting, welcoming, her knees raised.

'Come on, Georgie, let's do it. Let's *do* it,' she drooled. Her mouth was full of the spicy taste of Brexford's genitals, her nose with the tangy smell of seaweed.

'On your sides,' said Jeremy, a harsh, hoarse note in his voice. His mind had become filled with the very clear, lubricious idea of how he was going to end this steamy encounter.

He feasted his jaded eyes on them as Georgina lay down and the girls rolled into one another, head to crotch, cushioning their faces deeply between one another's thighs, taking firm hold of one another's buttocks. As hands clutched and groped and heads bobbed whilst tongues busied themselves on clits and inside pussies, Brexford vigorously tossed himself. After a while he lay down on the sand behind Ellie, closing his body into her back, raising his shirt-front so that his belly would be bare against her behind. Angling it in gloved hand, he slotted his cockhead between Ellie's cunt lips, then he pushed determinedly, easing his hard-on all the way up her until his heavy pubic bush was squashed against the underswell of her buttocks.

Georgina was wracked with lust. She now had both male and female genitalia within reach of her busy little tongue and she hungrily licked not only pussy, but balls and, as Lord Brexford withdrew to plunge again, the thick, wet underside of cock.

Struggling to hold himself back from coming, Brexford treated Ellie to a brief, but most hearty fucking. Then he withdrew and got up to change pussies, clumsily stepping over the girls in his half-mast trousers and laying down again behind Georgina to fondle and grope her rosy, striped buttocks before lodging his glans, damp with Ellie's juices, into her labia and slipping his length all the way up her. He considered the tempting idea of entering the little hole in her fat bottom, but decided that that was perhaps going over the top in these early stages of sexual initiation; later perhaps, on another occasion at Deal Manor. Soon, but not today.

As he energetically screwed Georgina whilst Ellie salivated his genitals, Brexford was fiercely groping and squeezing Ellie's lower bottom. His gloved middle finger found her pussy and slid into it next to Georgina's stabbing tongue, wetting the leather with juice, darkening the pale grey. Then he left that place and worked the finger into Ellie's bottom hole. He had only breached her rear end for the first time recently, and he had not been quite sure – despite her groans which might have been either of pleasure or discomfort – if she had enjoyed the sodomy or not; she had, in an oddly guilty fashion.

Orgasm now had an irresistible grip on his scrotum. He unplugged Georgina, grabbed his cock and clambered to his knees behind her back. The girls were moaning as tongues licked and poked, and their climaxes began to steal over them. They were squirming and wriggling in the sand, Georgina's stubby toes were curling as Ellie's buttocks trembled.

With a bellow which echoed and re-echoed around the cave walls, Lord Brexford let fly. He directed the stream of semen at the girls' writhing bodies, to where they were locked bellies to tits. Two commendable ballsful puddled in the small ravine where flesh met flesh. As the final drops dripped over Georgina's side, Brexford slipped his hand down through the sperm and the interlocked flesh to smear his seed over the climaxing, shuddering, groaning girls' tits and bellies. Then he collapsed onto his back, panting and gasping in the aftermath of what had been a most powerful orgasm, big chest heavily rising and falling.

Ellie and Georgina broke lazily apart from one another. Ellie with a long, loud sigh of contentment as she rolled all the way over onto her belly to bury her face in her arms, and Georgina with a satisfied grunt.

'Ugh,' went Ellie, a minute or so later. Having sat up, she was running her hands over her tits and belly; sand was stuck to her with more than salty dampness – it was mingling with Lord Brexford's semen.

Brexford was on his feet, fastening his fly buttons, a wearily amused expression on his face.

'Ugh?' he repeated, watching her, 'I'll have you know that that is sperm of the highest quality, young lady. Aristocratic seed.'

Georgina, flat on her back, glanced down at her plump body, inspecting herself, sliding a hand over her flesh. She

113

giggled. Her front was sand-free and glistening with semen. She massaged some into a tit. 'Nice,' she cooed. 'Gooey, but nice.'

'That's the spirit, Georgina. I must say you're an excellent pupil,' commented Brexford. His trousers attended to, he strode from the cave to where Napoleon, not entirely calm even now, skipping about when he saw him, was tied. He freed the reins from the rocky outcrop. 'The coast is clear, girls,' he called over his shoulder. 'Why don't you have a swim, get yourselves washed off?' Restless, the horse started to move away as he put a foot into the stirrup, and he was obliged to hop awkwardly along at its side before swinging himself up into the saddle. He began to walk his mount down the gentle slope of the beach to the softly lapping water's edge.

'Come on, Georgie. I'll race you in,' said Ellie, clambering to her feet.

But after such a sating session of sex, there was little enthusiasm in their race. They ran slowly, side by side past Lord Brexford who watched their temptingly bouncing tits, and then their trembling bottoms, with gleaming eyes. Such was his rapacity he could have taken them both again almost immediately. Reaching the sea, they splashed on, laughing, until it was at their knees, and then they flopped into the water, gasping at its coldness.

Brexford had a final, lingering, wistful look at them, then he knocked his heels sharply into his horse's flanks to urge him into a canter. By God, he was thinking as he leant forward over the animal's muscular neck, by God he was going to have them next time together, up at the manor. And *how* he was going to have them – together with Sophronia and perhaps a raunchy, well-endowed male friend or two. Just as soon as something could be arranged. Lustful excitement surging through him, he spurred Napoleon into a full gallop.

Moments later, with Brexford already out of sight, Ellie and Georgina emerged, dripping and laughing, from the sea. Their laughter was short-lived: an all-too familiar figure had appeared around the headland and was moving, albeit in the distance, in their direction.

'Crumbs, it's bloody Petters,' observed Ellie. 'Quickly, or we're in big trouble.'

At least a hundred yards of beach separated them from the cave and their bathing suits. This time, their legs flew as they tore towards its entrance. But speed was of no avail; even at the considerable distance between the headmistress and her charges, there was no mistaking the difference between naked female flesh and grey and black striped bathing costumes.

Inside the cave, the girls scrambled into their suits, hurriedly buttoning them to their necks. By the time they emerged into the sunlight, the glowering Miss Petty was almost upon them.

'So,' she growled, as she reached them. 'The general behaviour of you two girls is almost beyond belief. You go running off without permission, and then I find that you both have been acting most shamefully. Swimming in the nude now, is it? Right! You will be most severely caned.'

Chapter 8

Having left Napoleon in the capable hands of Thomas Farley to be untacked, rubbed down and stabled, Lord Brexford found himself – without exactly knowing why, for he had ridden off his lust – going in search of his wife. Many of the old doors in Deal Manor were open in order to allow air to circulate on such a warm day, but when Brexford arrived at Sophronia's bedroom he discovered its door to be closed.

Her voice floated singingly from within when he rapped on the heavy oak. She sounded strange, most odd, almost as if she were someone else. 'Who is it who wants me?' she asked.

When he announced himself, she called out, 'Of course it is you, Jeremy. I knew it would be, it had to be,' and she invited him in.

Lady Brexford was in most peculiar circumstances. She had rolled back a Chinese rug, and in heavy white chalk on the creosoted floorboards she had drawn a large pentacle – a five-pointed star purported, amongst other powers, to be possessed of the magic property of warding off evil spirits. Naked but for three strings of heavy, black-glass beads, and a black garter – a thin, white bone tucked into it – around her right thigh, she lay flat on her back within the inner pentagon, her head raised on a black silk cushion, her hair loose and flowing. Several accoutrements of the art of sorcery were gathered in the point of the pentacle that the top of her head was almost touching. There was a fragile human skull – cracked and with small pieces missing – and a pair of bones, three ornate silver candle-

116

sticks with black, burning candles in them, an open, ancient book of spells, a copper chalice and a silver dagger. Lying on the book there was a small clay doll which Brexford observed with an uncomfortable start had pasted on it his face, cut from a photograph.

The most shocking, striking thing of all was the fact that clasped in Sophronia's black-nailed hands there was the ugly, carved image of a North American Indian shaman – a medicine man. Standing a foot high, it was endowed with a thick and shiny seven-inch penis with which Lady Brexford, her knees up and widely spread, was furiously masturbating, using it as a dildo.

Even as Jeremy had turned to her after quietly closing the door, his wife had climaxed with a quiet moan. Her hand stilled. Now, slowly, she pulled the wooden cock out of her pussy and stood the shaman on the floorboards by her hip. She smiled dopily up at Lord Brexford. The image's proportionately monstrous erection was pointing directly at the book of spells which bore the clay doll with his face on it.

'It worked,' she muttered. 'I knew that it would. You came.'

He gazed pointedly between her open legs. 'I believe it was you who did the coming,' he remarked, intrigued at the scene upon which he had stumbled, beginning once again to feel horny.

'So I did. But whilst I was in my orgiastic state I also made a spell. My spirit then called out in the void to yours and caused you to come looking for me. The spell worked, do you see? My magic gets better every day.'

Lady Brexford's knowledge of the black arts had increased dramatically over the previous six months under the regular instruction of a certain Count Alexis Petrovski and the infamous Aleister Crowley. Jeremy Brexford took it with a pinch of salt, believing it all to be high-flown nonsense, but he was perfectly happy to allow Sophronia to indulge in it – if only because witchcraft and sorcery often entailed the holding of an orgy of one sort or the other.

'But I was looking for you anyway, Sophie,' he pointed

out. 'I wanted to recount to you an amusing little adventure I've just experienced. You will enjoy it hugely, of that I'm sure.' He began to move towards her, the sandy toe of his riding boot crossing a point of the pentacle.

'*No!*' she exclaimed, in genuine alarm, jerking into a sitting position. 'Don't come into the pentacle whatever you do. Let me get out of it first, otherwise you'll break the barrier against evil spirits. You'll be putting me in great danger.' She hurriedly climbed to her feet.

'Come *on*,' he protested. 'There has to be a limit to this damned silliness.'

His deliciously nude wife stepped briskly out of the inner circle towards him, her tits temptingly wobbling. 'Scoff as much as you like, Jeremy,' she said. 'But I absolutely promise you that you came here because my spirit called out to yours.'

Despite his cynicism, a slightly creepy, prickly sensation invaded Lord Brexford's spine. Its tiny hairs stood on end. He realised that, before arriving at her room, he had not been consciously thinking of Sophronia at all. He had been in no great rush to tell her of his erotic caper in the cave – that could wait until later – nor even to see her, for his gallop back to the manor had served to dampen his ardour, yet it seemed he had wandered about the house looking for her in an absent-minded fashion. It was all most odd.

'Balls,' he said quietly, eyes wandering over her nudeness which appeared more than usually interesting because of the black beads and garter and her black-painted fingernails and lips. 'Utter balls, Sophie.'

She produced a slackly wanton smile. 'I wouldn't mind seeing them, right at this moment,' she purred. 'Your balls, I mean.' She touched his lips with the side of a finger, at the same time clutching a handful of his breeches – together with what lay beneath them – at the groin. 'Why don't you get undressed and tell me about this adventure of yours on my bed? For surely that glint in your eye suggests that it was of a sexual nature.'

The desire which had been rearoused within him just before leaving the naked Ellie and Georgina on the beach came flooding back. His cock was rapidly stirring. Simply having her grab it so lecherously, and looking at his wife's bare body whilst recalling his wonderful tussle with the girls, was turning him on. He yanked open his fly buttons and pushed his breeches down.

'Your bum's absolutely smothered in sand,' she noted, as he stepped out of the trousers and turned his back on her to hang them over a chair.

He felt a buttock and bent backwards to peer down over his shoulder. 'I thought I was uncomfortable in the saddle,' he commented with a lazy grin. He stripped off the rest of his clothes and made for the bathroom. 'I'll just have a quick shower.'

'You've been humping someone on the beach, haven't you, you bad man?' she called out as she heard the water running. 'Do you never rest?'

'Perhaps in my coffin,' he shouted back, his voice echoing in the big bathroom. 'But I have no imminent plans in that direction.'

On her big, soft bed he told her about his afternoon's three-way fornication in fine detail, savouring the telling – as she was the hearing of it – while he screwed her slowly and expertly in, for a change, conventional fashion – except perhaps for the fact that she still had a human bone tucked into her black garter.

Neither of them had climaxed when he reached the end of the story. They had grooved themselves into the sort of sexual high sustainable for a lengthy, most agreeable, period of time.

'You, my darling, are a dirty, dirty man,' she whispered in his ear, with one of her heavily ringed hands gripping his balls possessively and the other resting on his taut, steadily rocking backside. 'The magic knew about your tumble with those wenches and it brought you straight home afterwards to me for some more of the same.'

'If you insist, my darling.' His tongue crept into her ear. 'This is magic,' he whispered.

'Yes.'

'Sheer, fucking magic.'

119

He slammed his cock all the way into her twice, very hard, as if driving home a massive nail. Then he reverted to the slow, sensual rhythm. Wrapping her feet around his calves, she let go of his balls to clutch his buttocks with both hands, her black-nailed fingertips meeting in the cleft.

She mashed her lips into his, thrusting her tongue into his mouth, then she broke off the kiss to pant, 'Poke your finger into my bottom hole. And I'll do the same to you.'

For a while they copulated with a finger buried to the second knuckle and jiggling in one another's arse holes.

'Nice. So very, very nice,' he grunted. 'It's so very good with you, Sophie. The best of all.' Nevertheless, his perverse mind reminded him that it was just as good with his Charlie.

'If only you and I could be like this together for ever,' muttered Sophronia. Orgasm was slowly, irrevocably, stealing upon her. 'Then there wouldn't be any need for anybody else.'

'But you forget that it's the other people who provide the spice. The variety. The constant turn-on. Life would soon get boring without them. It's the having other people which makes fucking each other so very special.'

After that perhaps dubious piece of home-spun philosophy, there were no more words. The rutting gathered pace. Very close to climax, Sophronia lustily grabbed a meaty handful of scrotum. Craving for Jeremy to come exactly at the same moment as herself, knowing that what she was about with his balls invariably triggered off his explosion, she squeezed hard enough to cause him a moment's pain.

Together they hit the high spot, with mingled, animalistic grunts and while her heels drummed rapidly into his calves. Together, they stilled.

'Speaking of magic,' Sophronia muttered lazily, shortly afterwards as with her hand beneath her rows of heavy beads she absent-mindedly pinched and rolled a nipple between finger and thumb, 'it seems to me that you haven't been involved in any for quite some while. It's been ages since we indulged in an orgy.'

'No. But I understood you'd just put a spell on me?' He took hold of the bone in her garter and pulled it out to drop it on a bedside table. 'And that's enough for one day.'

'I mean knowingly involved.'

'Oddly enough,' he said, a hand at her damp crotch, fingers gentling her pussy lips, 'I happened to be thinking along those sort of lines on the way home. I was turning over in my mind that it might be an amusing experience to get Ellie and Georgina to take part in some sort of a seance.'

Sophronia pushed herself onto her elbows, eyes sparkling. 'An orgasmic circle, for instance?' she suggested enthusiastically. 'We should comprise the mystic number of seven people, with a black-magic high priest officiating – Alexis Petrovski, most probably.'

'What in hell's an orgasmic circle?' he asked.

Her eyes shining with a strange light and her hand resting lightly on his flaccid, drying penis, she explained her idea to him. She outlined carefully a magic rite purporting to have its origins in the earliest days of paganism, then she finishing by telling him that it should be performed in the open air around midnight on a night of the full moon.

'And when, pray, is the next full moon? Assuming that I go along with the idea.'

She tapped the flat of her fingers rapidly on his cock. 'This wanton thing will go along with it, even if you don't.'

He smiled. 'You are so right. Well – when *is* the full moon?'

'I'm not exactly sure. But shortly. Three or four days' time, I think.'

He thought about it. Then he said, 'I fear Georgina is still a little too naïve to participate in such activity without throwing some sort of a nervous fit. Ellie, yes. Ellie is plucky and game for anything, as you are well aware. Georgina is happily showing remarkable promise, but I feel she needs a little more experience. A certain amount of, shall we say . . .' he paused, searching Sophronia's eyes, 'what shall we say – practice?'

Sophronia took his cock in the palm of her hand and

closed her fist around it, sliding the smooth skin up and down as he continued to pay attention to her pussy. 'One way of putting it. Practice, yes.'

'She, I promise you, is going to develop into a sexual fiend, that girl.'

'One hopes so.' She remembered something. 'It's Friday tomorrow,' she said. 'We're of course having some people from London down for the weekend. What fun it would be for us all to have a little sport with that fat wench. That will give her all the extra experience she needs, I do believe.'

'Not so fat,' objected Jeremy. 'I positively adore her fleshy curves. So much more to grab hold of.'

Sophronia throatily chuckled. 'Right. Nicely rounded, then. Enticingly plump.' She tightened her fist on his prick. 'Why don't you dream up one of your wonderfully dirty ideas for us all? We'll invite the lass for dinner tomorrow evening. Expose her to a thrilling new adventure. Do her the world of good, shouldn't wonder.'

Brexford's cock twitched in her fist. It was swiftly on the rise once more. 'How I would lover to bugger the wench,' he muttered.

'And you know what you are? You are a . . .' She failed to finish the sentence. Instead she produced a lop-sided grin. 'Maybe you should; she is certain to enjoy it. You no doubt will, knowing you. But I was hoping you'd come up with some idea even more exciting than that.'

He stared at her, ingenious mind switching into top gear. The tips of his fingers slipped further inside her pussy. 'Most probably I shall,' he murmured, an idea already beginning to take shape: a wonderfully ribald notion, exceptional even for him.

'Yes, maybe I shall,' he repeated slowly. 'I'm beginnng to get a capital inspiration for a bawdy after-dinner entertainment which should bring our guests marvellous and most horny pleasure.'

His cock had grown gloriously hard. She squeezed and rubbed it affectionately. 'You know, dearest,' she trilled, 'this naughty thing seems to spend far more time up than down.'

Lady Brexford ducked her pretty, black lips to what was probably the most active cock in the entire county of Kent – if not in the country.

Chapter 9

For a second time Claire Petty briefly scanned the note – that had been sealed with red wax bearing the Brexford insignia – which a servant had delivered from Deal Manor early that evening. 'My dear Claire,' she read. 'I happened to chance upon young Ellie Branks with a girlfriend of hers this afternoon whilst I was out for a canter on the beach. Her name as I recall was Georgina. Would you kindly arrange that this girl is sent up to the manor tomorrow in time for dinner. We shall expect her at the hour of six.' It was signed – a spidery, almost illegible scrawl – 'Brexford'.

The headmistress's eyes narrowed. On the beach was it? she thought. When they were nude, I'll be bound. So, the profligate Jeremy fancied the fleshy Georgina now, did he? Not a bad judge at that. Perhaps it was just as well then, under the circumstances, that the girl had parted company with her virginity. But she found the peremptory summons just a trifle inconvenient from her own point of view; having just soundly caned Ellie's bared bottom, Miss Petty had deliberately restrained herself from masturbating after the event, saving that lustful craving until she had finished with Georgina's backside. The wayward wench was due to present herself in her study any second. But should she now cane Georgina with the severity that she had had in mind, the girl would not be able to sit down for days, never mind at Lord Brexford's dinner table the following evening.

She would be obliged to spare her. Very well, she decided, she would use her in other interesting ways, instead.

There was most faint knock on her door, so weak as to

be almost inaudible. 'Enter,' bellowed Miss Petty – one of her most dreaded commands.

Georgina crept inside the lair with utmost timidity, her nerves raw. She hovered nervously on the threshold, shuffling from one foot to the other. Ellie had just taken great relish in telling her that Petters had considered fifteen hearty swipes of the bane of Chalmers a fitting punishment for skinny-dipping, and she had delighted in showing her and their other two dorm-mates her striped and throbbing buttocks; having derived, unbeknown to her headmistress, more than usual exquisite sexual pleasure from the beating, she had brought herself even more by saucily baring her buttocks to her friends. However, this new ordeal was going to be no such a turn-on for Georgina, who really did not believe she could take any more, unless, that was, it were to be with the slipper – and then only gently.

'Close the door if you please, Miss Tennant,' grumbled Miss Petty. 'And turn the key. Do not stand there like a blithering idiot, girl.'

'Please, miss, we were doing no harm to anybody,' stammered Georgina, as with trembling hand she locked the door. 'It was just Ellie and me all on our own and having a bit of a lark.'

'Whilst wickedly exhibiting your nude bodies to anyone who happened to peer over the cliff top or taking a stroll along the beach. That is what you so carelessly describe as having a bit of a lark, is it, you shameless young hussy?'

'But, but nobody at all goes along that part of the beach, or the cliffs,' mumbled Georgina in misery. 'Not until summer, they don't, miss.'

'*Really?*' said Miss Petty with heavy sarcasm. She perused the girl pruriently, her eyes drifting over her breasts and belly and down to her loins. 'Nobody. Not even Lord *Brexford*, I suppose? Tell me, Georgina, did you two happen to be starkers when his lordship rode by?'

Georgina reddened from forehead to neck. How could Petters possibly know that the lord had been there? 'Please, miss, no, miss,' she said. 'He, he stopped his horse and spoke to us when we were having our run.'

'Yes. He spoke to you whilst you were running, did he?' She leant forward, eyes slitting behind her spectacles. 'Come over here to my desk.'

Quaking, Georgina did as she was bidden.

'First, we are going to have an inspection. I need to decide how much more caning your backside can tolerate.' Georgina reached the desk. 'Turn around, lift your skirt up to your waist and drop your drawers,' breathed the headmistress.

Miss Petty leant eagerly forward across her leather desk top, peering intently as Georgina put her back to her, hauled her skirt on high and hooked a thumb into the back of the waistband of her knickers, dragging them slowly down. As Georgina's fat bottom was revealed to her, the headmistress closed her thighs tightly on her right hand, digging two fingers into the crotch of her knickers. It was a wonderfully horny sight, those still glowing, familiar buttocks, their interesting condition all her own work. In her state of rapidly rising lust, she failed to take into account that two largish areas, one on each buttock, were a fresher shade of red than the rest: the prints made by the stinging slaps from Lord Brexford's gloved hand. Her pulse quickened. her fingers pressed harder into her crotch, insisting knicker material between her pussy lips.

'The sea water has probably done it some good,' she observed. 'Your rear end, Miss Tennant, appears to be well on the road to recovery. Nevertheless, I have decided that I shall postpone your caning for the time being for fear of inflicting untoward damage.' Her voice – and her attitude – dramatically changed. The harsh edge of authority disappeared to be substituted by a soft and sexy drawl. 'You can do me a service as a penance, rather than being thrashed,' she said. 'Come here to me, Georgina, do.'

Relief swept over Georgina to be instantly replaced by the beginnings of rising excitement; it was abundantly clear that the 'service' was to be of a sexual nature. She pulled up her knickers, let the skirt fall and moved around the desk.

Miss Petty swivelled her chair to face her slave. She

failed to prevent a catch in her voice as she said, 'Get to your knees. In front of me.'

Georgina crouched down onto the pale cream rug.

'Open your blouse. I would very much like to see your titties,' sighed the headmistress.

Whilst Georgina was unfastening her buttons, Claire Petty sunk back in a slouch into her chair, sliding her buttocks forward to its very edge, making a squeaking sound against the leather with them as she did so, and pulled her skirt up to bunch it high on her waist, revealing to Georgina's fascinated gaze voluminous cotton bloomers. 'Take my drawers down and all the way off,' she muttered, as Georgina's big, pink-tipped breasts trembled free from the open front of her blouse.

Petters braced her arms on the rounded wooden arms of the chair to raise her bottom slightly. Georgina, in sexual weirdland yet again, revelling in it, tucked her fingers beneath the waistband of her headmistress's baggy bloomers and pulled them carefully down the fat legs and off over flat ankle-boots. She stared randily at the thick forest of dark brown pubes thus revealed, which almost, but not quite, buried the fleshy, crinkly pussy lips.

Petters humped and wriggled her buttocks still further forward on the seat of the chair so that she was lying almost flat back in it with half her bottom hanging in space. She opened her thighs wide as she reached for Georgina's tits, grabbing them roughly, pulling the girl into her with them until her nose was almost in her pubis. Then she let go. Lust surging through her twitching loins, looking down at herself with smoking eyes, she parted her pubic bush with her middle fingers and brushed the curly hairs clear of her hard little clitoris with her forefingers. Holding herself lewdly exposed like that, she uttered her next command.

'Lick my clittie, Georgie, there's a dear,' she muttered gutturally.

Georgina obligingly – and enthusiastically – tongued the pinky, hard nub of flesh, the tip of her nose buried amongst wiry little hairs. She had only ever performed this act on Ellie, but she very quickly discovered it to be a wonderfully arousing thrill to be licking between a different pair of female thighs. Her tongue flickered faster.

Keeping her clit cleanly exposed with two fingers of one hand, gently heaving Georgina's head up and down with lascivious movements of her crotch, Miss Petty rummaged amongst Georgina's tits with the other hand. Already fiercely excited by her caning of Ellie, and with her sexual tastebuds then further titillated by ogling Georgina's blushing backside, she was in desperate need of relief.

'Stick two fingers up me. Frig me – good and fast. Frig me, bring me off,' she rasped. As Georgina's fingers began vigorously to slide up and down her wet sheath of pussy, Miss Petty insisted, 'Faster. Faster. *Do* it!' Then she promptly came, explosively, with a noisy gasp followed by a massive sigh, clamping her fat thighs around Georgina's ears, entwining her fingers in her hair to drag her face even tighter between her legs, and jogging her knees feverishly up and down until her orgasm subsided.

This most lubricious activity had brought Georgina right to the heady edge of a climax. But she remained disappointingly unfulfilled. Miss Petty pushed the girl away from herself, picked her bloomers up from the rug, lethargically pulled them over her boots and hauled them up her legs. As she dragged them over her bottom – which was still overhanging the edge of her chair – she sent Georgina around to the other side of her desk. Then she heaved herself back up into a sitting position and turned her chair around.

Taking hold of the note from Lord Brexford she briefly ran her eyes over it once more. Oh, you lucky, lucky young lady, she thought as she did so. It seemed such a long time since she herself had been invited for sex at Deal Manor. Naturally, she was intimately aware of the scandalous goings-on between Brexford and his lady wife, and occasionally some of their friends and the few girls who visited – particularly Ellie; Jeremy Brexford took immense pleasure in recounting them to her in scurrilous detail. But as far as the girls themselves were concerned, her only knowledge of what went on was supposed to be that they were asked to make up the numbers for dinner, and that was all that the evening's entertainment comprised. And nobody at Chalmers, of course, had the slightest inkling that Miss Petty took part in orgies at the manor. Had anyone suggested this, they would never have been believed.

She handed the note to Georgina, who smiled inwardly as she read, 'Her name as I recall was Georgina.' Why, what a cunning devil his lordship was and no mistake! More sex was imminent for her, then. She could hardly wait. Sex, she had discovered in her heady few days of it, was like a drug: the more you had of it, the more you craved.

As she unlocked the door and let herself out of Miss Petty's study, Georgina's plump little pussy was even more on fire than it had been when she was going down on her headmistress. The longish passage took her past the gymnasium where several of the girls were being put through their paces. She hesitated by the open door to the empty changing-room, then slipped inside. This could not wait a moment longer. Going through the room and into a water-closet stall, she locked herself in and sat down on the toilet seat.

Biting her bottom lip, her shoulders sagging, Georgina dragged her skirt up to her belly and humped the pile of material there with her left forearm. She pulled her knickers down over her knees to her ankles and spread wide her legs, staring for long moments at that downy-haired part of her anatomy which was causing her so much trouble of late – and in particular at that moment – before easing the tips of her middle two fingers between its plump lips and stabbing her fingers all the way inside.

A riot of raunchy sexual images seethed through her brain, of cocks hard and soft, of bottoms and thighs and cunts, of slipperings and canings and cock suckings and of pussy eatings, and with her fingers jerking up and down inside her sopping little cunnie as quickly and desperately as they had ever done in her life, thus did that comely girl of such a sweet innocent aspect bring herself to an orgasm so massive that she all but fainted with its overwhelming pleasure.

Chapter 10

It was splendid to be taken the relatively short distance from Chalmers to the manor cosseted on a soft leather seat amongst velvet cushions in the back of a chauffeur-driven automobile, especially when that horseless machine was one of the super-luxury models manufactured in the factory of Charles Rolls and Sir Henry Royce. It had been wonderful seeing hordes of envious, girlish faces peering from the finishing school as she was swept regally up the drive and away. And it was simply great to be wearing the only non-uniform dress she was allowed amongst her personal belongings at Chalmers – a glamorous, black taffeta creation whose voluminous skirt was composed of a cascade of tasselled layers falling from waist to floor.

The only thing about which Georgina was unhappy on that early evening was the fact that she had on not a trace of make-up; it was the duty of mothers at home to inspect their daughters' luggage before packing them off to Chalmers, and face paints and powders and other such fripperies were strictly forbidden. She had her hair piled up attractively in a chignon – Ellie had spent an hour working on it for her – and she felt that the freshly scrubbed schoolgirl look of her face did little justice to the rest of her appearance.

Apart from that one thorn in her side, Georgina was happy, but nervous as a kitten, as she was driven through the twilit wood. The butterflies in her stomach began to flap their wings with greater vigour when the Rolls drew close to the manor house and she saw that there were several motor cars parked on the drive in front of it. She had assumed that the invitation to a dinner party had merely been a ruse to get her once more into the sexual clutches of Lord Brexford and his wife, not that there would actually be more visitors.

Sophronia, clad in a floor-length, dazzling evening dress covered in hand-sewn silver and gold sequins, and with a most daring *décolletage* which almost exposed her nipples, greeted Georgina in the great hallway. The last time Georgina had observed this vision of loveliness, the lady had just climbed up from her knees in the cobble-stoned torture patio after heartily sucking off her stable lad. As Georgina took Lady Brexford's delicate, multi-ringed hand in her own in greeting, she could hardly credit the memory. It seemed so impossible it was as if that early afternoon's entire experience had been no more than a wonderfully erotic dream. Yet here she was, invited to Deal Manor on the strength of her lustful reaction to what had transpired.

As they laughingly surveyed her young guest, Sophronia's green eyes had the merest trace of disapproval in them. 'I must say you look a treat, my dear,' she proclaimed. 'The very picture of teenage innocence.' Her eyes danced over Georgina's face. She shook her head doubtfully. 'Almost too innocent, if you ask my opinion. How would you like it if I made your face up before we go in for dinner? I know that it's prohibited at Chalmers, but you aren't at Chalmers now, are you?'

Georgina produced a delighted smile. After this most welcome suggestion she found herself a little less nervous. She accepted the offer with the greatest enthusiasm.

'You must address me as Sophronia, my sweet,' said Lady Brexford as she took Georgina by the hand and walked her across the hall. She hurried her up the elegantly curved grand staircase, along a slightly gloomy passageway and into her bedroom where she sat her, facing away from its decorative gilt-rimmed mirror, at her dressing-table. Crouching in front of her, she carefully applied a little lipstick of an almost brown shade of red, some face powder and a touch of rouge to her cheeks. She took a great deal of trouble over her eyes, taking at least ten minutes. Then she had Georgina turn around to face the mirror.

Georgina gasped. She gaped. She was transformed; what Sophronia had done so expertly to her face had little to do with her own clumsy efforts at home. In fifteen minutes she had been changed from a shiny-cheeked schoolgirl into a most attractive young lady.

'Bet you didn't know you were so very pretty, did you, my dear?' purred Sophronia as she stood behind her, watching her reflected face.

'Golly. Gosh – no. Wow – I can hardly believe it.' Georgina's eyes caught Lady Brexford's in the mirror. Something compelling in them told her not to look away.

Sophronia wiggled the tip of her tongue suggestively at her reflection. Then she said, her hands resting lightly on Georgina's shoulders, 'Don't for one moment imagine that Jeremy – my husband – is going to be allowed to hog such a lovely creature all to himself.'

At this astonishing remark, Georgina could only manage in response a weakly delivered, 'Oh.'

'You do know that I was the lady in the black mask the other afternoon, don't you?'

Georgina gulped. 'Um – Thomas said it would be you, when we first saw you. I wasn't sure, though.'

'Well, it was me.' She gently massaged Georgina's shoulders. 'I get a very special thrill from times like that. You see, what other people might describe as kinky situations I find enthralling.' She bent her face closer to Georgina's. 'You had a great time, too, unless I am very much mistaken – did you not?'

Georgina managed a nervous little smile. Their eyes remained locked. 'Yes,' she said, very quietly. 'Yes, I did.'

Sophronia planted a soft little kiss on the side of her forehead. Her hands stole around Georgina's bodice and she fondled both breasts. 'Good. That's very good. There is no harm to be done by a little deviation from the sexual norm, and much pleasure to be derived,' she murmured.

'I think I'm beginning to understand,' dared Georgina.

'Marvellous.' Lady Brexford paused, squeezing Georgina's breasts hard together, sending little thrills of delight through the girl. 'By the way, Georgie – I may call you

132

Georgie, mayn't I? – I'm well aware that you like girls,' she confided, with another kiss. 'I've watched you with Ellie in one another's arms, through Jeremy's telescope.'

Wriggling in pleasure at the welcome attentions from so gorgeous a lady, Georgina muttered, 'I know Lord Brexford has seen us. He told me about it.' Her entire life, she thought, seemed to be exposed to just about everyone. She shrugged mentally. So what did that matter, provided that no whisper of her naughty but oh so nice behaviour reached the ears of her parents?

One of Sophronia's fine-boned hands slipped between the buttons of Georgina's high-necked dress to worm its eager way beneath the top of her bodice and grasp a bare breast. She fingered the nipple, tweaking it gently.

'Jeremy told you about the telescope when he was humping the pair of you girls in that cave on the beach, didn't he? You and the lovely Ellie?' she murmured.

Cripes, were there no secrets at all in this lordly mansion? And *that* dirty word on the pretty lips of a real lady! Georgina was getting so choked up with excitement that she could find no reply.

As Sophronia's busy hand shifted from one tit to another, cupping it, lifting it, appreciating its warmth, her lips closed in on Georgina's ear. 'Ellie likes me ever such a lot,' she whispered, then she wriggled her wet tongue inside it, causing Georgina to squirm with delight and to giggle. 'We do lots of lovely sexy things together, Ellie and I. We play with one another's tits like I'm doing to you now, and we eat each other's pussies.' Her other hand dived inside the bodice and she groped and kneeded both breasts. 'Do you like me, Georgie? Do you like me enough to want me to do those beautiful things to you? To perhaps do them to me?'

'Yes. Oh, yes,' gasped Georgina. 'I should certainly like that.'

'Then we shall take our opportunity as soon as it presents itself, shall we not? Later on tonight, I hope.'

Lady Brexford straightened up. Both females experienced a pang of regret as her hands slid out of Georgina's bodice to take the girl by the tips of her fingers and coax her to her feet. 'We must go down now and join the others,' she said. 'We have kept them waiting long enough.' She planted a tiny kiss on the tip of Georgina's nose.

As they slowly descended the sweeping staircase together, Georgina found that her head was reeling. She had only just arrived at the house, and already so much seemed to have happened and been said. What then did the rest of this evening hold in store?

She felt shy and clumsy at first as she was introduced to the dozen elegantly attired male and female dinner guests who were assembled in the huge drawing-room. One of the men, the neatly bearded, baleful-eyed Edwin Smythe-Parker, she had heard of – though not of his prolific sexual reputation. He was an extremely successful, notoriously licentious novelist. Another, the tallest by far – a head taller than even the sizeable Lord Brexford – she found distinctly creepy. Dressed entirely in black, his small dark eyes seemed to pierce all the way into her brain as he shook her hand. He was an aristocrat, Count Alexis Petrovski – Sophronia's principal instructor in the art of witchcraft. The rest of the men failed to make any strong impression on her, for she was still trying to pull herself together, but she found the six women – at least when compared to Lady Brexford – somewhat tartish, if attractive.

Sophronia, wearing a subtly seductive scent, stayed close to Georgina during the pre-dinner cocktails and idle chit-chat – during which the girl, somewhat lost in the company of adult strangers, her finishing-school education notwithstanding, stayed mostly silent. After only a short while they all trooped into the banquet hall for dinner.

The hall was brightly lit with thick, flickering candles. Lord Brexford much preferred the atmosphere created by candles to that of gaslight or paraffin lamps: three huge silver candelabras, each holding dozens of flaming red tapers, were suspended low over a great, oak table with room enough to seat fifty comfortably. There were two massive stone fireplaces heaped high with pine and oak logs which were unlit because this mid-spring had surprised Edwardian England with a period of truly summery weather.

134

As Lord Brexford had them all take seats around one end of the table, Georgina noticed that on another sturdy-looking table near by – the size of an average door – there was a mysterious erection; it was some sort of screen which appeared odd and out of place, its function unfathomable. It was box-shaped, holding a heavy red and gold brocade curtain on a hidden frame, six feet square and three feet broad. The two ends of this curtain were closed over each other on the side of the box which faced the table.

There the thing silently and enigmatically stood, bringing a question to everyone's lips.

'What do you suppose that screen may be hiding from our curious eyes, Georgina?' Count Petrovski, seated opposite her, asked. His voice was deep and husky, the accent foreign, his eyes piercing her gown.

'Oh – do you believe there is something inside it then?' was Georgina's lame and barely more than muttered reply as smartly liveried servants began to set platters of steaming broth on the solid silver plates before them.

Though not overawed with the rich and splendid surroundings – she had been brought up in an equally well-staffed and expensively furnished household – Georgina was finding it hard to come to terms with the strange assembly. Not only were the women most definitely tarts, at least three of them were ill-bred – one only had to listen to their cockney accents to realise that. One of them went by the name of Millie. Another was called Lettice.

'But of course there is something inside, dear girl,' pronounced Petrovski. 'You don't suppose that here before us we have a curtain supported on a frame simply for the *curtain* to be on display, do you? It's hardly a priceless antique.'

'No, I suppose, I suppose not,' stumbled Georgina.

The count then asked Lord Brexford – who was seated at the head of the table and wearing, as were all the men, a black, tail-coated evening suit – the question which had been hovering on everyone's lips.

'What mystery is it that lies beyond the curtain, Jeremy old boy?' he said loudly. All heads turned towards the host, their owners most curious to hear his reply.

'Ah-hah.' Jeremy tapped his nose. 'It is a surprise,' he announced. 'My first of an evening full of them. Like a chocolate liqueur, it is to be unwrapped after dinner, to be savoured with the coffee and brandy.'

A murmur of excited approval ran through the assembly. All had been guests at Deal Manor before, some – like the author and the count – on numerous occasions. They all knew that Lord Brexford's surprises were invariably of a sexual nature; that sort of thing was what they hoped for and expected at Deal.

'What did I tell you, Georgina?' remarked Count Petrovski. 'Perhaps it is some dark, even black, secret.' The solemn manner in which he delivered the words caused her a little shiver. If anyone was dark and black it seemed to be he. Meanwhile, she had noticed that Lord Brexford's eye had been lingering almost exclusively on herself throughout his little speech – almost as if whatever it was that was hidden behind the screen were especially for her benefit.

Throughout the lengthy, magnificent feast of pheasant and duck and succulent roast beef, during which wine flowed copiously, followed by a fine selection of deserts, the conversation, getting louder as the wine was consumed, was often suggestive and blue enough to bring a blush to Georgina's cheeks – making her glad of the powder and rouge – and her eyes kept straying to the screen as her mind struggled to imagine what it might conceal.

When coffee was served, brandy and liqueur glasses filled and all the plates cleared away, Lord Brexford dismissed the servants. He got up, calling for silence. He was just the slightest bit unsteady on his feet as, in the expectant hush, he approached the mysterious screen, everyone's attention rooted upon him.

Georgina was feeling distinctly light in the head, a condition which Sophronia sitting close to her, had done much to promote whilst keeping a watchful eye on the girl to make sure she did not overdo her drinking and pass out or get sick and thereby spoil an essential part of the planned surprise entertainment.

Brexford placed his hand on the place where the heavy brocade doubled over itself. 'The moment has arrived which you have all been waiting for, ladies and gentlemen,' he proclaimed dramatically. 'The unwrapping of the after-dinner chocolate liqueur.'

He pulled apart the flaps of the curtain and shoved the screen backwards in one brisk movement so that it collaps-ed in a heap on the stone floor behind the table. He stood aside.

There was a moment's stunned silence followed by a communal intake of breath and then applause and laugh-ter. The improvised screen had been hiding a young, naked man. The lad was standing, legs wide apart, attached by black leather straps to a sturdy wooden frame of the kind used to support a child's swing. His arms were spread wide as if he were on a cross. His ankles and wrists were strap-ped close to each corner of the frame. Over his head and draping loosely on his shoulders was a fine, black silk bag. The only other item he had on was a thick, chrome-studded belt with leather straps affixed to it and passing down from the front of his hips between the tops of his thighs, and back up behind to rejoin the belt, thus starkly emphasising a commendable set of genitalia.

The most extraordinary thing about this revelation was a wool-thick length of brown elastic knotted around the young man's plump penis and this was extended to a little brass ring in the table top exactly beneath it to stretch the cock directly downwards, the elastic taut.

When the applause and slightly nervous hilarity – and a great amount of feminine giggling, though shock had kept Georgina quiet – died down, Lord Brexford said, 'We are now going to have an interesting little show. What I intend to do is to demonstrate the enormous power of the penis.' He plucked at the elastic. It sung briefly like a bass guitar string as it vibrated. The cock trembled with it, then stilled.

The Brexford eye narrowed on Georgina, who was hav-ing a great struggle to come to terms with what she was seeing. He tapped the young man's cock with the back of a finger as he said to her, 'If it weren't stretched somewhat

137

out of shape you no doubt would have recognised this enticing appendage, Georgina.' With a flourish, he whipped off the young man's head-engulfing silk bag.

Georgina gasped loudly. The back of her hand flew to her mouth. The lad was blindfolded from the tip of his large nose to the top of his forehead, and there was a black rubber ball crammed into his mouth, rubber straps attached to it buckled behind his head, but the facial features and the unruly shock of brown hair were unmistakable to her: it was Thomas Farley, the stable lad, her almost lover.

'Understandably, under its stretched circumstance, you failed to recognise this prick, but I see by your expression that you are very well acquainted with its errant owner,' said Brexford. He smiled flatly. 'Stand up, would you please, Georgina?'

A bundle of nerves which would no doubt have been far worse without the wine within her, Georgina climbed unsteadily to her feet and stood at her place, gently swaying, crimson under her make-up. She tried to avert her eyes from the vision of the lewdly trussed boy, but failed.

'His name is Thomas Farley,' announced Brexford to everybody. 'He was recently caught by myself with his pants down and sexually dallying in the hay in my stables with the fair Georgina. *This*' – he banged the tied cock sharply with the knuckles of one hand – 'was about to penetrate her pussy. Had I not been fortunate enough to chance by at that very moment it most surely would have done. A mere stable lad intent on tupping the daughter of upper-class, highly respectable members of the community, he was, of course, thoroughly thrashed for his affrontery – in front of the girl.' His eyes darted to Georgina, amusement creasing their edges. 'Do you remember what occurred with him, wench, during that lashing? Do you recall what happened to' – he plucked the elastic once more – 'this most impudent member?'

Georgina was experiencing a great deal of humiliation at that moment. She could only shake her head. Words refused to come to her lips, though of course she vividly recollected Thomas getting a hard-on during the beating, and Lady Brexford on her knees in her black hood and sucking him off after it.

'She has lost her tongue, we note,' said Brexford, smiling at her as if in sympathy. 'But, naturally, she remembers. Would you mind coming here, Georgina? It would very much please me – and entertain my guests – if you would agree to take part in my little experiment.'

'All, all right,' she muttered, with no idea of what to expect. She shuffled to him, her worried eyes dancing in nervous little jerks over him and over Thomas, hands clutched in front of her with their fingers intertwining like restless, chubby worms.

When she reached Lord Brexford's side he said to the assembly, 'What happened to the iniquitous Thomas was that whilst my wife was laying into his bared backside with a scourge he had the audacity to achieve a most enormous erection.' He paused. 'Allow me one moment, please.'

Georgina's gaze became glued to the grossly stretched penis as Brexford strode to a corner of the room to open a cupboard. Within, he found a wicker carpet-beater. It was the size of a tennis racket, one of a pair which had once been used to thrash Claire Petty's naked bottom in this very banquet hall. Taking it to Georgina, he pulled her restless hands apart and thrust the handle into her right one.

'Take a firm grip,' he instructed her. 'And don't worry,' he said for her ears only, '. . . it's only a harmless game.' To the rest, he announced, 'This most interesting experiment consists in discovering if the power of the penis is sufficient to overcome the pull of the elastic.'

The table which supported Thomas and his frame was on brass casters. They squeaked as Brexford turned it sideways. Depending on where they were placed at the table, the dinner guests now had a three-quarter view of Thomas's back and buttocks, or his front and genitals, or a sideways glimpse of both rear end and cock and balls with his body cut in half vertically by a wooden post.

'Are you ready, Georgina?' Lord Brexford asked.

'But, but . . . what . . .' Her words trailed off as she

139

stared at the beater in her hand, shaking her head from side to side.

He smiled at her. 'Come, come, now, girl,' he said affably. 'You're not going to be shy about this, surely, are you?'

'But . . .' Georgina found within herself a potent mixture of turbulent emotions: acute embarrassment at being singled out like this in front of all those strange people, reluctant to do what was clearly expected of her and the conflicting emotion of strong sexual stirrings at the arousing sight of this trussed and naked youth who had so nearly taken her cherry.

'Will you please swipe at Thomas's buttocks until I ask you to stop, young lady? Or do you spoil the fun by obliging me to do it myself – and thereby perhaps ruin the experiment? You see, I believe that your fair hand on the delivery end of the carpet beater will add to the lad's arousal.' Lord Brexford pushed Georgina gently around the table by her elbow until she was facing Thomas's back on his left-hand side. She saw that the marks from his scourging at Sophronia's hands, though faded, were still plainly visible.

Brexford lifted her elbow until the beater was swaying by her ear. He let go of her arm. 'Well – will you do it?' he asked her.

She gulped, staring in hypnotic fascination at the naked buttocks, chewing her bottom lip.

'Will you – or will you not? Please make up your mind, we are all waiting.' His tone was unthreatening.

'All right. Here goes,' she whispered, more or less to herself.

But Georgina brought the carpet beater down most feebly. It slapped almost soundlessly into buttock flesh.

'Not like that,' complained Lord Brexford. 'You're just tickling him, not punishing him. You have to try and imagine that his backside is a dusty carpet. Here, let me show you.' Sweeping the wicker implement from her hands, in a continuation of the same movement he slashed it through the air. It cracked noisily into Thomas's bottom, which quivered at the impact, his reddening buttocks going rigid as a stifled groan came from behind the ball gag. Brexford snapped the handle of the beater back into Georgina's hand. 'Like *that*, do you see?' he told her. 'Get the idea?'

Her first abortive effort, then observing Brexford's strident whack and its effect on Thomas, had at last begun to turn her on to the situation. Taking Brexford's advice, she imagined Thomas's rear end to be a carpet and she gave it a good and solid swipe. Fixing her gaze on that interesting area so clearly framed by the black leather belt and the straps which curled around the side of each buttock and down into his upper thighs, Georgina, livening up, brought the beater down again, this time with vigour.

Thomas realised that it was Georgina who was laying the beater into him, and that he was displayed in front of everybody and no longer hidden inside a box screen. Timid, Thomas might have been, but shame he did not feel. Rather, his plight, in a curiously prurient fashion, was beginning to excite him more with each passing second. His feelings were as they had become after a short while of his scourging at the hands of his mistress.

Georgina was warming very much to her task, and swishing the carpet beater into the trembling buttocks with the greatest of gusto, licking her lips, her eyes beginning to shine as the boy's bottom grew redder and redder. His elastic-restrained cock began to stir.

Lord Brexford started to clap his hands each time wicker connected with flesh. The rest of the guests, and Sophronia, joined in. Soon, the sound of the clapping was all but drowning out that of the thrashing. Lust shuddered intensely through Georgina's loins.

The glowing heat in Thomas's buttocks was spreading to his genitals. Defying the elastic, stretching it, his cock rose steadily ceilingwards. By the twelfth bottom smack it was all the way up.

Lord Brexford stayed Georgina's hand. He again pinged the elastic with his thumb and forefinger. This time, its note was higher, and the solid eight inches of stable-lad cock trembled for far longer than before. There was sustained applause, much laughter and ribald cheering from the audience.

Sophronia, much excited, delighted that the first stage of her husband's ingenious, somewhat complicated plans for this evening's debauch had worked to absolute perfection, got to her feet. Considering the condition of the two young people concerned, she was thinking, the second stage should go off like a perfect, dirty dream. Going to Georgina, she prised the carpet beater from the panting girl's fingers. As she did this, Lord Brexford was freeing Thomas's cock of the elastic. This achieved, he stripped the blindfold from the boy's eyes. The black rubber mouth stopper he left in place, simply for the visual effect.

Sophronia laid her hands on Georgina's shoulders and stared into her smouldering eyes. 'You're wet, down there between your legs, I bet. Your little pussy's good and wet, is it not, Georgie?' she said quietly.

'Yes. Oh, yes. God, I'm wet,' whispered Georgina. Her bosom was heavily rising and falling, her hands were clutching and unclutching at her sides.

'Good. That's the way we all want you to be.' She paused. 'Especially Thomas, I imagine by the naughty state of him.' She leant her lips close to Georgina's ear to whisper her next words into it. 'Now, get yourself up on the table with your back to Thomas.'

Pulse madly racing, game for just about anything at all now, Georgina did so.

Lady Brexford was standing below her, staring hungrily up at her. Their eyes steamily locked once again, their only message, pure sex. 'Bend over, dear,' muttered Sophronia, just loud enough for Georgina to hear. 'Bend over, rest your hands on my shoulders and don't move until I say so.'

There was a pregnant hush at the dinner table. Georgina, doubled at the waist and supported on Lady Brexford's elegant shoulders, her eyes probing the woman's *décolletage*, held her breath as she felt her black skirt being drawn up the back of her legs and onto her back. Her bottom, she realised, was but inches away from that magnificent cockstand of Thomas. God! She closed her

142

eyes tight, chewing her lips. Sophronia's gentle, slender thumbs slipped under the elastic of those baggy schoolgirl knickers of Georgina's which the girl realised, uncaring, were in full public view. They peeled them slowly down her plump white thighs to leave them hanging rudely at her knees. Excitement most lustful – mixed with but the merest touch of shame – was thick in Georgina's belly and her breast and her throat, threatening to stifle her. Her wet pussy, desperate for penetration, was going through a series of intriguing little contractions. Solace for it, in the shape of Thomas's big helmeted cock, hovered solidly behind her.

Leering down at the plump pair of exposed buttocks and a tuft of pubic hair just visible low between them, as the dissolute audience held its collective breath, Thomas heaved his loins as far forward as his tightly confined body would allow. His glans slipped under the buttock cleft and brushed pussy lips. Sophronia, unable to see it, fumbled between Georgina's thighs for it. Finding the helmet, then holding it steady in a two-fingered scissors grip, Lady Brexford opened Georgina's pussy with the other hand.

'Thomas's big dick is almost in you, dear,' she muttered. 'If you back up just a little, you'll make it nice and easy for him.'

Georgina pantingly complied, and Sophronia guided the stable lad's prick between her pussy lips, letting go of the glans as it found its way in. Making little, randy grunts, Georgina gradually impaled herself on the stiff and un-moving cock, shuffling backwards until the boy's balls bumped into the underswell of her buttocks as his hard-on was impaled all the way up her.

'Shift back just a little further, Georgie, do. Give him plenty of room to fuck you properly,' Lady Brexford raunchily instructed, loving this business but rather wishing that the stable boy's cock was inside her. A moment later, she said, 'That will do just perfectly. Keep still now – let him do the work.'

'Get to it, Thomas,' Lord Brexford said excitedly. 'Give it to her, my lad.'

Properly fuck, the young man most certainly did. It was

143

an unbelievably arousing way of losing his virginity, in front of all those leering men and women, trussed and gagged and with his behind on fire from its thrashing as he screwed the girl who had administered it, with her knickers at her knees, and her bent over and leaning on the lady of the manor's shoulders.

The lad's taut, strong backside jerked like that of a rutting jack rabbit, his exertions transmitting themselves through Georgina to Sophronia's shoulders which rocked along with the two of them. The atmosphere at the dinner table was beginning to be stifled with sex as the stable boy's big balls flapped while all eyes pigged on the activity. No genitals were unstirring. Hands began to wander greedily over bodies, to fondle and grope, to creep beneath bodices and to open fly buttons; the evening's diversions were now beginning to develop in the direction of a full-blown Brexford orgy.

Georgina was in an unimaginably ecstatic world of ceaseless orgasm, her eyes tightly closed, her fingers digging hard into Sophronia's shoulder flesh as Thomas went through his climactical heaves. The boy was banging his cock into Georgina so hard that Lady Brexford was being almost knocked over backwards with each thrust.

'Pull her off him,' said Brexford urgently to his wife. 'Quickly.' His prick was so hard beneath his tight-crotched trousers that it was beginning to hurt him.

Sophronia dragged Georgina to the table's edge at the moment that Thomas, his cock springing free of her pussy, began to ejaculate. He grunted noisily through the rubber ball as his semen began to surge. His scrotum was full, and this was his very first fuck – and under circumstances most extraordinarily salacious. His initial eruption gushed from his cock like oil from a borehole. It arched high over Georgina's back to hit Sophronia full in the mouth, and as it tailed off it splashed all the way down the back of Georgina's dress to the heap of taffeta skirt at her waist. The second spurt – because he was convulsively jerking his groin and his cock was being flung up and down – caught Georgina low down on the back of a calf and trailed upwards, over the hanging knickers and a thigh to reach her pussy. The third, much diminished, splattered over the bottom knobs of her spine, and the fourth – and last – shot into the top of the cleft in her buttocks and trickled down it.

'So much for the power of elastic. It is easily overcome, as you have seen,' announced Brexford to the immsensely aroused, lustily groping company. He was greatly pleased with the success so far of his bawdy plans. 'It neither restrains a powerful and determined cock, neither does it do a thing to save a pair of knickers from being lowered by a resolute hand.'

Georgina's chin had sagged into the back of one of the hands on Sophronia's shoulders, and her cheek was squashed against that of her hostess. Running her tongue around her semen-soiled lips, Lady Brexford hoisted up the girl's knickers and dropped her skirt into place, staggering under the weight dropping into her.

'You need a rest now, my darling,' she whispered into Georgina's ear – which in reality was an excuse to be alone with her, for she was desperate to get her hands on the girl's fleshy body. 'And we must see to it that your dress is quickly cleaned; there's come all over it. We'll take ourselves off somewhere comfortable.' Helping Georgina down from the table, she hooked an arm around her waist and began slowly to walk her away.

Jeremy Brexford was busily engaged in unstrapping Thomas. Noticing that Sophronia was moving Georgina towards the door he realised what lusty business she must now be up to. He loudly called her back. 'I do hope you have not forgotten what it is I fancy doing with the wench, have you, Sophie?' he asked.

Half-way to the door, Lady Brexford paused. She clutched Georgina's breast and squeezed it. Her lips brushed her cheek. She glanced over her shoulder at her husband. 'Then come upstairs to my bedroom as soon as you wish,' she purred. 'I rather want to watch you whilst you are doing it, dear heart.'

'I'll be there in just a little while,' he responded. 'Prepare her, why don't you.'

The taste of rubber was thick, furry and most disagreeable in Thomas's mouth. As soon as he was free from the frame, he reached behind his head to take it off.

'I think perhaps I should like it if the boy left that on, Jeremy,' said Count Petrovski. The flaxen-haired Millie's pale hand was moving rhythmically inside the count's open fly, but Petrovski's centre of prurient interest was the stable lad – whose cock had only half wilted – and, in particular, Thomas's sore and inflamed buttocks. 'It rather suits him,' the count added, eyes steamily running over the boy.

Brexford stayed Thomas's hand. 'You heard the count,' he said. 'Don't take that gag off.' Well acquainted with Petrovski's predilection for young men, Lord Brexford's intention had nevertheless been to send Thomas packing. That part of the show in which he had been needed was satisfactorily concluded. 'I take it then that you would like to dally with the lad?' he asked Petrovski.

The count extracted Millie's hand from inside his trousers and got up from the table, his hard-on straining sideways beneath his gaping underpants as his trousers began to fall and he was obliged to hold them up with one hand. He closed in on Thomas, looming over him, dwarfing him. Peering around the lad, he flattened his long-fingered hand on his backside. 'With such a muscular, well-rounded and hot bottom, who would not want to spend some time with him?' he murmured.

Thomas gazed up at Petrovski, slack-mouthed and with a wary, yet curious, look in his eye. His rear end, indeed, was most hot; it was burning, his sore buttocks were the colour of ripe tomatoes. The count's hand felt deliciously cool on them.

Perverted and profligate, Lord Brexford might have been, but he was not about to condone homosexual rape – or any other kind of violation – within the ancient walls of his manor house. He spoke to the boy. 'My guests,' he said, 'and my wife are about to take themselves from here into the drawing-room, where an orgy is going to get under way. You are aware exactly what an orgy is, young Farley?'

Thomas nodded as Petrovski's hand stroked and patted his behind, his fingertips with their long and slightly pointed nails intruding deeply into its crack.

'Good. These people are going to have sex together, and I understand that Count Petrovski wishes that you join in with the proceedings. Personally I have no objection. As far as you are concerned, it means that you will have the fortunate opportunity to do to one or more of the young ladies present that which you just did to Miss Tennant. However, it is also apparent that the count will want to do something similar to you.' He paused, pursing his lips. 'Do you understand what I mean?'

Wide-eyed, the boy nodded again. Buggery then. The sinister count was intent in sticking his dick up his bum-hole. It was supposed to be dirty, it was against the law of the land, that Thomas knew. Beyond that, he did not think too deeply.

'Well, it's entirely in your hands, my boy,' said Brexford. 'Leave now or I will not be responsible for the consequences.'

Thomas hesitated, eyes darting around the banquet hall. He made a gesture to intimate that he wanted to remove the rubber ball.

'Let the lad take it off, then,' said Petrovski, leering because it appeared that he was going to have his way. He wanted Thomas at that moment more than anyone else in the room. His hand became a little more eager in its buttock fondling.

'Please could I have a drink, m'lord?' were Thomas's first words. 'I'm fair parched, I am.'

'Help yourself,' said Brexford. Thomas upended a half-full bottle of champagne into a glass and drank it down thirstily and noisily.

'You may have as much of that bubbly as you desire,' said Petrovski, '. . . provided, that is, you come with us into the drawing-room.' The black ruglike back of his spare hand brushed against the boy's drooping, but not yet flaccid, cock, making it swing. 'Well – do you dare to join us?'

Thomas's eyes roved over the shameful scene at the

dinner table, where two of the young ladies had their tits out, one was laying back with her knickers at her ankles as a male head rocked between her legs, and the only female who was not playing with a cock was sucking one.

'Please, sir, yes, sir. I'll come in there with you all right,' he said, sounding almost eager.

Count Petrovski's eyes narrowed, his black nostrils flared and his long, thin nose twitched. His hand was groping and squeezing, rather than stroking, the burning buttocks, the tips of his fingers running lightly up and down Thomas's bottom cleft, touching its hole. 'Good boy,' he breathed. 'Good boy.'

With various bits and pieces of clothing in wild disarray, and several sexual appendages on rude display, the company trooped, most of them somewhat drunkenly, out of the banquet hall, across the great hall and into the drawing-room, Edwin Smythe-Parker taken by Millie who led him by his fully erect cock.

Lord Brexford, meanwhile, hard-on unabated, hurried up the grand staircase. Orgies he had had in plenty, and he loved them. But they could be organised whenever he pleased, whilst first-time sexual events were something to be greatly savoured and enjoyed whenever the opportunity to do so arose – and one awaited him right at this moment, Georgina unaware that she was to be the object of it – in Lady Brexford's bedroom.

Sophronia had wasted no time. Within the space of a very few minutes she had managed to wind up her gramophone, insert a new steel needle into its pick-up head, put on a 78 r.p.m. record, get both herself and Georgina entirely nude, and have Meg collect Georgina's gown for a rapid hand-clean. As Lord Brexford opened the door slightly scratchy strains from Beethoven's Romance for Violin and Orchestra coming from the huge horn of the gramophone met his ears, and the naked, slender back and delightful buttocks of his young wife his eyes. Sophronia and Georgina pinned beneath her on her green silk bedspread, and she was enthusiastically kissing her. Georgina's dimpled knees were widespread, poking up on either side of Sophronia's legs and jerking sensuously as her fat inner thighs embraced the woman's hips. The girl was responding with remarkable enthusiasm to Sophronia's eager but gentle bottom rocking.

Brexford quietly closed and locked the door. As he did so, the music came to an end halfway through the piece. There was a regular, irritating clicking sound as the heavy needle went around and around in the end of the groove.

'Turn the record over, do, Jeremy,' Lady Brexford mumbled without looking at him. Craving to untrap his cock, Brexford found himself instead flipping the record and winding the machine's handle, grumbling to himself that these new-fangled inventions might bring music into one's house, but only in three-minute sections, with a definite lack of clarity and a hollow sound, and they demanded a lot of work.

Lilting violin music filled the room as, eyes feasting upon the female crotch to crotch mutual masturbation, Lord Brexford finally brought his throbbing hard-on out into the air. He stripped off his evening clothes and draped them over a chair, removed his shoes and socks, and left his white silk underpants on the carpet. Then he clambered onto his wife's big bed, got on his side next to the nude lesbian lovers and, propped on an elbow, lazily wanking, closely watched their every action. As her lips mashed into Sophronia's and their tongues wetly mingled, Georgina observed her ladyship's husband watching them. The fact that he had joined them, naked – and with that magnificent cock-stand – added to her lusty pleasure.

Georgina's hazel eyes were misty with sexual arousal. Sophronia had taken the girl's hair down; it was fetchingly spread all over the pink satin pillow. Brexford ogled, and tossed himself until the music again came to an end, then, the loud clicking of the needle annoying him, he got up and switched off the gramophone.

The only sounds in the room were the regular tick of the longcase clock – the same one that Meg had persuaded Bertram the second cook to help her lug from the deserted wing days earlier – and Georgina and Sophronia's little mewls and heavy breathing as their pubises mingled and their crotches writhed.

149

Lady Brexford's little, snowy-white behind began to jerk faster. Leching on the sight from the foot of the bed, Jeremy massaged his prick more vigorously. Crouching down, he encouraged his wife to open her thighs a little in order to afford himself a splendid view of both pussies. The young ladies each slipped a hand down between their squashed-together bellies and began urgently finger-fucking one another towards orgasm.

Brexford now craved to be directly involved in the love-making. Crawling up the bed until he was behind their heads, he knelt there and lifted Sophronia's face off Georgina's and offered his cock to his wife's mouth. Her lips, wet with her and Georgina's mingled spittle, slid welcomingly over the familiar, solid prick.

Finding herself with Lord Brexford's heavy, hairy scrotum jiggling just above the tip of her nose as she was presented with an extreme close-up of Sophronia gluttonously gobbling the cock which had so recently relieved her of her virginity, Georgina was so filled with lechery that she came in an instant. Shuddering from head to toe, loudly groaning, she heaved her crotch so violently that she almost threw Sophronia off her.

Sophronia climaxed but a few seconds later, her husband's cock deep in her mouth. Observing her buttocks suddenly tauten, jerk three times, then relax and go still, perfectly aware of what this denoted, Brexford backed his hard-on out from between her lips. With a great sigh of contentment, Lady Brexford rolled off Georgina to flatten herself on her back on the bedspread. Her husband stretched himself out on the girl's other side from her, firmly stroking his hard-on, his hand gripping high up on Georgina's thigh, the finger and thumb tips buried in the chubby flesh. The moment he had been so lecherously waiting for was very nearly upon him, and he was savouring the contemplation of how it was going to be.

'I bet you are more than happy that I caught you at it in the stables with Thomas, are you not, Georgina?' Brexford asked, as his hand crabbed itself ever higher up her thighs. His prick was pleading for the specialised penetration he so craved; he was longing to plunge it into Georgina's only remaining virgin place.

She produced the puffily content smile of the sexually sated. The make-up with which she had been so delighted was badly smudged. 'Mmmm,' she went. 'I do believe I truly am.' Her eyes were on his hand as it reached the fork between her thighs and its little finger came to rest amongst her pubic hair. So satiated did she find herself, she had until that moment been gazing at his wanking of himself without the sight doing anything to rearouse her.

'You've learned so very much about how joyful sex can be in such a short while,' murmured Sophronia. She turned her head in order to plant a soft kiss on the girl's shoulder. 'Lucky you. So many lasses of your age would give their right arms for the chance.'

I've learned even more than you know, thought Georgina, recalling her ribaldry with Miss Petty. 'Lucky me, yes,' she muttered. She sighed deeply and smiled again.

Jeremy's pinky strayed further amongst her pussy hairs, its tip touching her labia. He meaningfully caught Sophronia's eyes. 'There is one other thing I should like to teach you, Georgina,' he said. 'An initiation I hope you are going to find quite delightful.'

Sophronia silently mouthed the words 'dirty bugger' at him with a little, twisted smile. But she immediately said softly to Georgina, 'I have a good idea what it might be to which Jeremy refers. If I'm right, you're going to positively love it. I certainly do.'

'What is it then? Do tell,' asked Georgina. She sounded a little less sleepy.

'But don't let us waste time talking about it.' The tip of Brexford's pinky wormed its way into the entrance to her pussy. 'Let us do it.'

'But I don't know that I'm in the mood for more –'

He interrupted her. 'It doesn't matter a whit if you're not particularly sexed up at this moment. You don't have to be. But you can see that I am, and have been for some while, which is what matter. I'll wager you will be too, once I get to it.'

Sophronia was swinging her legs from the bed. As her

feet hit the carpet she told Georgina, 'Roll over onto your belly, there's a dear.' She opened a drawer in a bedside table and hunted within, visited by a little tremble of excitement whilst doing so; she was as keen to be an observer of the projected, salacious act as she knew that Jeremy was to be performing it.

Georgina did as she was asked, pillowing her head in her arms, wriggling herself into a more comfortable position, kicking a foot up and down as she was wont to do when she was contentedly on her belly on her bed reading a book. Brexford's eyes latched greedily onto her fat and blotchy buttocks with their titillating little bruises.

'Why don't you apply it, Sophie?' he said, referring to the petroleum jelly, the lid of a round tin of which his wife was unscrewing.

Georgina was not really thinking about very much at all when Lord Brexford flattened a palm on each of her buttocks and stretched them widely apart in order to open her bottom hole for Sophronia's jelly-smeared fingers. She was still euphorically enjoying the contented, faintly throbbing sensation in her satiated pussy and in her loins.

When a cool, slippery finger began poking and twisting in her anus and her sphincter reacted by suddenly tightening on it as another one tried to join it, her brain came shockingly alive. Surely she thought, with a certain amount of alarm, Lord Brexford was not going to attempt to do to her that which it was whispered at Chalmers that very many public-schoolboys were in the habit of so dirtily performing with one another? She slowly and apprehensively raised and turned her head as Sophronia's finger left her tiny hole and Brexford released her buttocks.

Georgina saw that Sophronia was twisting her greasy hand back and forth around her husband's hard-on as he moved forward on his knees between her own legs. His gaze was hungrily glued onto Georgina's backside and there was a most lustful gleam in his eyes. She experienced a little prickle of fear. Cripes, Lord Brexford was surely not going to shove that enormous thing up her bum, was he? – he would split her in two with it!

152

'Relax, Georgie darling, do,' breathed Sophronia soothingly. 'Everything will be perfectly all right, I can promise you.' Letting Jeremy's cock go, she smoothed her greasy palm over both of Georgina's buttocks. They were still vaguely sore and the attention brought to her bottom an agreeably cool sensation, calming her just a fraction. 'Close your eyes,' Sophronia told her. 'This is going to be really, really nice after a while, that I assure you. Cross my heart it will.' As Georgina's head sunk back into her arms, Sophronia kissed her ear. 'Now, darling – don't worry about a thing.'

She did not simply close her eyes, Georgina clamped them very firmly shut. She steeled herself for whatever sensation was about to invade her, urging herself to relax and let them do what they would with her – telling herself that everything that had happened to her so far in her brand-new sexual world had been marvellous, so why should not this be.

It was Sophronia's turn to splay Georgina's buttocks apart with both hands and open her bottom hole – and she revelled in the action. Her features twisted into a living mask of utmost carnality as her husband's faintly yellow, jelly-coated prick approached the equally yellow, well-lubricated bottom hole.

Lord Brexford positioned his glans with the greatest of care. The first stage of his buggery was no trouble, the swollen helmet slipping with ease into the little, pinky-yellow place. His wife made sure to keep the plump and greasy buttocks well stretched in order to afford herself a perfect view of the initial anal penetration. The pale purple cockhead disappeared entirely.

Georgina squeaked like a stuck pig. She wiggled and she moaned. Her feet, toes tensed and spread, jumped up from the bed. She grimaced into the pillow of her arms, jaw muscles twitching, showing her teeth. She held her breath. Lady Brexford let go of the punishment-blemished moons of flesh and they sprang back on one another to bury two inches of cock with a tremble.

'Raise her bum up a bit,' grunted Brexford, holding himself back for the moment from any deeper entry.

Sophronia worked a pink satin pillow under Georgina's

hips. Then she lay down at the side of the girl, put a comforting arm over her shoulders and tenderly kissed her several times on the cheek. Georgina turned her head towards her and opened her eyes; there was a strained and shrinking look about them.

'Everything's just fine, dear,' murmured Lady Brexford. 'You have to let yourself go with it, and not fight against it, that's all. It's going to hurt a tiny bit for just a moment, then it will be *sooo* lovely, you'll see if it won't.' She glanced at her husband. Clearly, he was holding himself back from lunging only with the greatest of difficulty.

'A little more, then, Jeremy,' she told him as she stroked Georgina's hair. 'Poke it in little by little. Whatever you do be sure not to hurt her.'

But as he did so, Georgina yelped, then she yelped again. It was worse than the stinging cut of a cane, she really did feel at that moment as if her bottom were about to be ripped open. Lord Brexford pulled apart her buttocks to check on the progress of his prick. It was in just past the sphincter, he saw; the wench was well breeched, then, if not yet accustomed to it. He buried his cock a fraction more, lewdly groping the bottom flesh as he did so. His victim yelped once more – but it was less loud and it was destined to be for the final time.

Moments later, a transformation most welcome began in Georgina's sensations down there in her backside. The pain was rapidly receding, to be replaced by a wonderfully filling, enormously stretched feeling. It was rather like that of puffing out her cheeks to full capacity, only in a different area. She quietly moaned.

'There you are, it's getting nicer already, Georgie, is it not? What did I tell you? Now you will see, my darling,' Lady Brexford whispered into her ear. She licked wetly all around the ear's little channels, beginning to pant with excitement into it whilst her husband's cock sunk deeper.

'Touch my cunnie? Please? Frig me?' begged Georgina, as her bottom began to be filled with a heat altogether different from that of a slippering – but in its way just as delicious.

Sophronia slid her hand, as her other one found her own

154

crotch and her fingers probed there, between pelvis and pillow to take hold of Georgina's plump pussy, gripping it as if it were a small and furry ball. Her middle finger eased inside it to the second knuckle and got into rhythm with the two buried within herself.

For the moment, Lord Brexford, with his cock half sunk between the big white buttocks he had been lusting after for so long, did not plunge in deeper. Exceedingly experienced in the matter of sodomy, he knew that, in order to impact pleasure – and not more pain – at that crucial moment he should delay the full penetration which his loins were urging him to carry out. Besides, how much more exquisite the sensation if the girl were moaning in delight rather than sobbing in pain, or yelling for mercy. His well-practised cock teased her bottom hole with a long series of tiny little jerks, it drew almost all the way out, then it stroked slowly, easily, up and down, going just a fraction further in with each successive thrust.

Georgina was being introduced to the delights of buggery by a true expert whilst the gorgeous wife of her initiator kissed her ear and her lips and all the way over one side of her face, and played interestingly stimulating games with her pussy. Only minutes before she had been sated, utterly indifferent to the idea of further sex – at least not in the immediate future – but now her libido had grown miraculous wings and was beginning to soar. By the time Lord Brexford's prick had found its way all the way up her bottom to nestle comfortably in there, unmoving for long, thrilling seconds, and she could feel the soft lumpiness of his balls squashed into the underside of her buttocks, she was panting and gasping into Sophronia's mouth and sensuously wriggling her crammed backside, willing the buried cock to move once more.

All but overcome with lust, Sophronia was jerking two fingers in her pussy as if it were a frantic little cock whilst she did the same to Georgina, all the while lustily rubbing her groin on the swell of the girl's hip and peering down her back at the bum-balling prick.

He would have liked to have held himself back, to have

prolonged his sodomy for far longer, but, having been erect for such a lengthy time, Jeremy realised that this was going to be well nigh impossible. He had observed so much bawdy behaviour down in the dining-room, he had closely watched his wife and Georgina bring themselves off whilst he was being avidly gobbled; he had been turned on to the maximum for what seemed like an eternity without climaxing.

He pulled his cock three-quarters of the way out and then held very still. The dragging sensation alone in the tight little place had been almost enough to bring him off. Grabbing Georgina's buttocks in clawed fingers he stretched them wide again in order to further feast his eyes on his bum-plugging. The sight, not surprisingly, was too much for him.

Letting go of Georgina's bottom, he fell forward, his hands indenting the pink pillows on either side of her elbows, his belly flattening into her upper bottom and the small of her back, and his hot and panting breath washing over her neck. As he humped arse deeply, his own rear end went through a vigorous series of climactic jerks while he flooded Georgina's backside with his come.

He rolled heavily sideways with a massive grunt, his cock plopping out of her to slap once into his belly, tremble, then, as he collapsed onto his back, go still, rigidly pointing at the velvet canopy above the bed.

'Oooooofff,' went Georgina. Her anus was warm and sticky inside, her sphincter was going through little contractions in reaction to the brand-new pleasure she had experienced, her juicy pussy walls were clamped on Sophronia's fast stabbing fingers. She had not quite scaled the magic heights, but she was yet again tremendously turned on – and speedily approaching them.

Sophronia was almost there, too. She coaxed Georgina off her belly and onto her back then, climbing over her, she gently lowered her crotch to her face and her mouth to the girl's wet pussy.

They ate each other with the greed of two tigresses who had not been fed for a week, slurping and slobbering, grun-

156

ting and groaning, their hands tightly wrapped around the upper backs of one another's thighs, rolling first one way – to bump into the drowsily watching Lord Brexford – then the other, and very rapidly coming together in perfect unison.

'Unhappily, Georgina, the time has arrived for you to get dressed and leave the manor,' Brexford said when the three of them had recovered sufficiently from their carnal exertions to begin to move. Sophronia told Meg, through a speaking tube hanging by the head of the bed, to bring Georgina's dress up and to leave it outside the door.

Unhappy, Georgina was surely not. She was pleased to be going home to bed, for an enormous lethargy had fallen upon her. She felt as wrung out, as exhausted, as if she had spent a day trudging through a tropical forest with a heavy pack on her back. She could sense a pulse in her pussy, another in her bottom – and the soreness from their three-day-old thrashing was again evidencing itself in her buttocks. What she was experiencing was the wonderful sensation of having been thoroughly fucked.

When Georgina was dressed, Lord and Lady Brexford – not about to miss out on whatever ribaldry was going on downstairs in the drawing-room despite having indulged themselves so gluttonously – pulled on a thin robe each and went with her down to the great hall where they left her by the drawing-room door to take themselves inside. Georgina caught sight of the carnal activity within as the door opened: naked and semi-naked people were engrossed in various sexual acts in couples and threesomes and more all over the room. Millie, she saw, was naked apart from her black boots and stockings and, on her knees on a Persian rug was straddling Edwin Smythe-Parker who, nude on his back beneath her, was jerking his cock in her pussy. Behind the cockney young lady there knelt another man, busily buggering her, and yet another was on his knees in front of her, thrusting his fat cock back and forth between her lips as her friend Lettice licked his balls.

But Georgina's most vividly shocking impression before the door was closed on her goggling eyes and she went off

– with a certain amount of regret now, despite her extreme lethargy – to where the chauffeured Rolls was awaiting her on the drive, was that of young Thomas Farley: the stable lad, his trousers and pants down but not off, was bent double over the back of a blue-velvet upholstered armchair, a tense and unreadable expression on his face as Count Petrovski did energetically to him that which Lord Brexford had so recently done to her.

Chapter 11

'You do realise that what you have just proposed is extremely dangerous, Sophronia? Should we involve ourselves in such a rite we shall be reaching into the realms of deepest darkness,' observed Count Petrovski as he walked his horse into the stony shallows of a swiftly flowing river.

'Tosh. Absolute balderdash. What are we, man – children?' retored Lord Brexford, following him in on Napoleon.

Petrovski chose to ignore the remark.

'We've had orgies and that sort of stuff before, many times. Nothing much of a mystic, let alone dangerous nature ever actually happened, Alexis,' Sophronia pointed out. She stroked and patted her sweating mare's neck, encouraging the white horse to duck her head to the water, but she did not seem to want to drink.

The three of them had enjoyed a long, brisk canter through tracks in a forest to the north of Deal Manor, and, afterwards, as they took their mounts at a walking pace through a cornfield to the river, they had been discussing Sophronia's suggestion for the night of the full moon.

'Sex – that is what happened,' said Jeremy, a note of sarcasm in his voice. 'Nothing mystic or dangerous about it. Sex most wanton and steamy, which of course is what black magic and so forth is largely an excuse for.' Napoleon was very still under him, his muzzle buried in the fast-flowing, chilly water, making loud snuffling noises as he drank.

Petrovski raised a bushy, black eyebrow. 'Nothing mystic

or dangerous about sex, my friend? Wrong on both counts – but that's another subject. As far as the rites we have performed together in the past are concerned, I grant you that those particular events were staged principally as an excuse for self-indulgence. Under such circumstances nothing much spiritual was likely to materialise. However, what Sophronia wants to set up is frankly much more serious. One would need to take most elaborate precautions to protect oneself from the forces of evil.'

'Stuff and bloody nonsense,' scoffed Brexford.

'Have it your own way. I can only warn you.' Both Petrovski and Brexford's mounts had had their fill and the men began walking them slowly side by side upstream, the shallow water breaking and splashing just above their hooves. Sophronia kept up with them along the bank.

After a while, Lord Brexford said to his friend, 'Explain to me about an orgasmic circle?'

'It is a corruption of a seventh-century Tantric fertility rite,' said Petrovski. 'Its intention is to summon powerful demons. And should it perchance succeed we would all be, as I have said, in great peril.'

Sophronia was wide-eyed. Having recently convinced herself that her powers were growing and that they had enabled her to summon Jeremy to her the other day by using a combination of magic and her mind, she experienced a little stab of fear at the count's words. The fright seemed to communicate itself to her horse, which pranced a little beneath her. She turned the mare full circle to calm her down.

'You really believe that the rite is liable to work, then?' she asked.

'It will have within it all the elements of success. Sex, alone, is a most powerful and' – he stared hard at Lord Brexford, – '*mystic* force, and any force strong in man also tends to sway the universe. There is a most potent supernatural element in sex – you of all people should know that, Jeremy, yet you choose to deny it.'

Brexford grinned broadly. 'I agree that fucking is often something like being caught in the grip of a power outside oneself. I wouldn't go as far as to call it supernatural, though.'

'Well, it is. There are philosophical thoughts to that effect in all cultures. Take Tantrism, for instance; its origins are in Tibet and India. It holds the view that human sex organs are instruments of extreme magic. The sex rite which is at present under discussion is intended to allow the participants therein to transcend the mental and physical and rise to a psychic and spiritual level. If all goes well they should attain a giddy height of physical pleasure but – in Tantrism – that pleasure ought merely be incidental.'

'Incidental?' exclaimed Brexford. 'With *Sophie*? Fat chance!'

She laughed. 'And how about with you involved? The non-believing cynic? The mocker?' She pulled a rueful little face at Petrovski. 'I doubt very much it will work.'

'Oh, but it might, you know. It really might. Enjoy the ceremony as much as you will, disbelieve it if you like, but the physical fact of what you, we, are proposing to do, will be enough to reach out there far into the unknown. Then there are the other elements to consider. It will be the night of the full moon when the human mind is at its most turbulent and impressionable. You will be seven making the circle – seven is a powerfully magic number. And there is the important significance of the signs and symbols we shall be implementing. And don't forget the power of the words of the mantra I will be chanting. In the same way as these things sway humanity, they affect the forces of the universe.' His eyes suddenly blazed with a sinister inner light.

'It's going to be a lot of fun,' Sophronia decided aloud; but there was an edge of doubt to her words.

'And, after all you have learned, you still insist that I set it up?' asked Petrovski.

'Absolutely,' Sophronia decided.

That weird, almost frightening light shone even brighter in the count's eyes. 'Very well,' he said, '. . . it shall be so.' He shrugged. 'You have been warned.'

Lord Brexford abruptly changed the subject. He was

becoming bored with it. Besides, one of his quirky, carnal ideas had entered his mind and was refusing to budge. 'Ever done it on a horse, old boy?' he asked Petrovski.

Sophronia looked sharply at him, pulse quickening.

For a moment the count, unlike Lady Brexford, failed to understand. 'Done what?' he responded.

'It. Fucked. What else?'

'Are you serious? On a *horse*?'

'It's perfectly feasible. I have.' Brexford glanced meaningfully at his wife. '*We* have.'

'I suppose you mean having her standing and bent into the animal's flanks, and you –'

'Mounted on a horse, the man and the woman – trotting,' interrupted Brexford. 'How would you like to have a go?'

'But I don't see how it's pos–'

'Sophie will show you, if you so wish.' He turned a twisted smile on her. 'Won't you, my darling?'

This was a turn in events she had not in the least expected. But that was Jeremy, always pulling these sort of surprise stunts. She was no stranger to the count's handsome cock; it had been in her hand and her mouth and between her tits on more than one occasion, the last time during the orgy, shortly after its penetration of Thomas's bottom. It was a lengthy – longer by at least an inch than Jeremy's – sturdy truncheon of a prick, full of a singularly vibrant force. A cock to make her pulse race. But she was absolutely not allowed to fuck anyone except her husband – yet here he was proposing that she indulge in copulation on horseback with Count Petrovski.

She treated Jeremy to a perplexed look which somehow managed a mirror rising lust at the same time. 'If you want me to, then I will naturally be happy to,' she said. 'But, what – what about the rules?'

'Exactly. What *about* your rule as far as Sophronia is concerned, Jeremy?' asked Petrovski, well aware of it as were all the regular orgy participants.

'We all know that rules are made to be broken from time to time. This is one of those special occasions.' He paused,

162

running his eyes amusedly over the two of them. 'If you are both game, that is?'

Lady Brexford positively adored Count Petrovski's very commendable staff. Of all the many that she had had carnal experience of – as far as she was allowed – his was the one she had most craved to have inside her. And on several occasions the count had coveted Sophronia's pretty pussy more than he did the backside of a young man. But he had hardly expected to get his opportunity to sink his cock in it on the back of a trotting horse.

'I'm game, of course I am,' said the count, excitement rising. 'So what do we do?'

'There will be nobody around anywhere in this part of the world, there never is except at sowing and harvest time. I suggest you both strip naked from the waist down. Then Sophie will instruct you.'

They dismounted. Sophronia found herself more than usually turned on at the prospect of baring her private parts – especially since it was out here in the open air and without previous warning or even a hint of what was to befall her. Jeremy helped her off with her boots as she watched Petrovski leaning against his horse and heaving off his. He unbuttoned her riding britches and hauled them to reveal a skimpily fetching pair of pink knickers. His nose hovering close to her pussy, he pulled down her knickers. Feeling most lewdly nude, she stepped out of them. She was now wearing only a longish white shirt with a red waistcoat on top of it, a silken stock at her neck. Her husband knotted the shirt around her belly.

'I want to see this most clearly,' he told her, talking into her pussy hair, nuzzling it. 'I'm going to be riding right alongside.'

The count had on a short, black-and-white-check hacking jacket with a cream shirt of the same length beneath it. Jacket and shirt reached half-way down his hips; his heavy length of cock, stirring as he ogled Sophronia's vulgar state of undress, hung completely exposed below them.

'First, get that sizeable thing all the way up in your favourite fashion,' Brexford told his wife, as he straightened up.

Petrovski was standing with his back to his horse. Going to him, Sophronia crouched down in front of him and lapped the head of his prick into her mouth. Her cheeks drew in sharply as she sucked. She fingered the plum-sized, very hairy balls whilst her other hand stole around Petrovski's lean buttocks and into the cleft, squeezing, finding the little hole that from time to time enjoyed a buggering, teasing it.

Within less than a minute, the count was sporting a massive hard-on.

'Admirable. Sophie's mouth never fails to please,' muttered Lord Brexford. 'Get in the saddle, Alexis, and let your feet hang loose,' he instructed, his own cock on the rise.

Petrovski hauled himself up. Sophronia, heart beginning to beat wildly, a salty, spicy prick-taste in her mouth, put a bare foot in a stirrup and swung herself up, her bare leg sweeping over the steed's head, to face him. She wasted no time – nor did she want to. Hooking her other foot in the stirrup on the other side of the horse and balancing herself on the count's shoulders with one hand, she took a firm grip of his erection and fisted its bulbous helmet between her expectant pussy lips. He gasped as she bent at the knees to sink down on the fleshy pole.

'You see – it's easy,' she muttered, supremely gratified to at last have a cock other than her husband's up inside her.

'And now we actually trot?' the count gasped.

'Post-trotting – and your dick is the post,' quipped Brexford, climbing into his saddle. 'The idea is that you sit in, and Sophie will make the usual trotting movements. Blue' – that was the stallion's name – 'will unwittingly do the rest.'

'Let's go,' sighed Sophronia, already rising lustily up and down on this first cock besides Jeremy's which had been allowed her pussy since she and her husband had met. It felt absolutely delicious inside her – warm, muscular, most wonderfully filling.

Lord Brexford urged Napoleon forward, and all three horses, the riderless mare at the rear, broke into a lively trot. Count Petrovski got the hang of this gloriously inventive, if somewhat uncomfortable, way to fuck right away, since there was nothing to do but sit with his nude buttocks glued to the saddle as Sophronia bounced energetically up and down on his hard-on with the motion of the horse.

They stuck to the wide track which ran along the meandering back of the river, Brexford riding by Blue's side with his gaze latched on the copulation. The count's jacket was flying and flapping behind him, and almost all of his nine inches was leaving Sophronia's pussy each time she bounced up, to impale on his balls when she sank down – a most fast, vigorous, steady fuck. Meanwhile Brexford's solid cock was truly beginning to hurt him as he leched on the very first sight of his wife being screwed – and in a fashion most hornily singular – by another man. Or, rather his wife screwing another man with the help of one of the Brexford thoroughbreds. He was obliged to unbutton his riding trousers and to fish out his erection.

Lord Brexford had never before tossed himself off whilst riding, though he had on two heady occasions ejaculated inside Sophronia in the saddle. He discovered it to be incredibly erotic; it was proving to be a form of penis worship to be wanking whilst trotting beside his screwing wife and friend. He knew he was going to come exceedingly quickly.

Orgasm was rushing over the two mounted – in more ways than one – on Blue, as well. With the wind in their hair and the clean smell of the country and the river in their noses, they were bounced by the horse into a mutual, splendidly ecstatic orgasm, seconds before Lord Brexford's semen left his cock in a great gush to stream into the air.

Chapter 12

It was a comfortably warm, rather breezy night. Little puffs of cloud slipped across the brightly starred sky, now and then to curtain the moon foretelling of an imminent weather change. Eight people, bent on conjuring up the supernatural whilst engaged in extremely kinky sex, trooped, shortly after eleven, through the gardens of Deal Manor; to them, the clement weather seemed set to last for at least that night.

Lord Brexford led the way, his black moon shadow, occasionally snuffed out by a flitting cloud, trailing short and stubby behind him. The rest of the group – for most of whom the chief interest in what was to transpire very shortly in the garden centred in the debauchery rather than the sorcery – was composed of Lady Brexford, Georgina, Ellie, the cockney girl Lettice, Count Petrovski, Edwin Smythe-Parker and Philip, Lord Antrim.

The venue selected by Jeremy Brexford for the evening's sport – for he was convinced it was to be no more than that – was a secluded lawn some distance from the manor house and hidden from it by a high and thorny hedge. Sophronia and Alexis Petrovski, had brought down the paraphernalia required for the late-night session that afternoon. On the finely trimmed lawn, which was as smooth as a bowling green, Petrovski had painstakingly whitewashed a pentacle large enough to contain them all. It measured fourteen feet across, its five points were intersected by two parallel circles, and in each of their tips there sat a thick, black, un-used candle inside a cylindrical glass protector. Within the ring formed by the two circles Sophronia had arranged,

166

spaced at regular intervals, a number of silver chalices and little framed paintings of the mystic symbol of the mantra 'Hrim'.

Lettice's was the only comment as they all arrived at the moonlit lawn – and it was perhaps as appropriate as any. 'Blimey,' she mumbled as she shivered at the strange sight.

Midnight was the appointed hour for the key moment of the complicated ceremony of the orgasmic circle; meanwhile there was plenty of time for them to get thoroughly into the mood.

Still harbouring amazement that Miss Petty had consented to Lord Brexford's request that Ellie and Georgina should attend a late-night party, they had wined and dined earlier with the rest. They understood precisely for what creepy, lecherous purpose they were here in the gardens, for it had been discussed at some detail over dinner. Understandably – despite the fact that Ellie herself had been the focal point of an orgy in the cellars of the manor the previous winter – the girls were considerably more nervous than anyone else.

'I suggest that we all remove our clothes without further delay,' said Lord Brexford, stridently. He produced a sardonic grin. 'The witching hour approacheth.'

'Have a care, Jeremy. Have a care with your sarcasm, my friend. Remember my warning. Beelzebub is easily angered by such an attitude,' muttered the count as he undid his trousers.

'Balls,' responded Brexford.

The act of getting nude together seemed to throw off any shackles of nervousness – even those of the Chalmers girls. Everybody pruriently inspected everybody else – and with horny approval, for the four females had extremely sexually desirable bodies and the men were very well-endowed, each of them considerably above the average in genital dimensions.

Petrovski had them all, including himself, form a tight inward-facing circle in the centre of the pentacle. 'To begin with,' he instructed, his deep voice sinisterly quiet, 'we stir our senses with a communal grope. We use our right hands only, like this,' he took hold of Georgina's pussy and fondled it, making her gasp,' and together we move our hands around the circle, each one of us handling the genitals of the other seven.'

After just one feel of each of the other's private parts, changing their fondling, exploring hands alternately from pussy to cock at Petrovski's command, there was no man whose prick had not begun to rise, no woman whose pussy was not dampening. A cool edge had crept into the breeze, but there was enough mounting sexual heat between the naked eight to keep them comfortably warm.

The instructions now grew more complicated, the actions they were required to perform lewder. They were to use both hands, the women to grope a cock and a tit at the same time, the men to fondle a cunt and a tit so that the ladies were being stroked in three sexual places by three different people at one and the same time. The eyes of the finishing-school young ladies, who were facing one another across the circle, locked lasciviously. At that moment, Ellie had hold of Lord Brexford's almost hard organ – her fist jerking on it – and Georgina's left tit, and Georgina was stroking Lord Antrim's rock-solid cock and pinching the rigid nipple of Sophronia's right breast. There was an expression of wanton, carefree abandon on both the girls' faces as they began, like the rest of the members of the salacious circle, to rock their hips involuntarily back and forth and to make soft, lusty noises.

After several minutes of this outrageous behaviour all cocks were well and truly up and all pussies wet. Count Petrovski slipped out of the circle, leaving Ellie and Sophronia next to one another.

'You are now reduced to the magic number of seven,' he said. 'Move in close to one another so that you form an unbroken ring of flesh and individually masturbate – not one another, now – until I give you fresh instructions.' He paused, his eye roving over them and then briefly searching the heavens. 'The time is almost upon us.'

With their shoulders pressed against those of the person on either side of them, they all began vigorously wanking themselves. Petrovski fetched a chalice of red wine thickened with honey into the circle and daubed a palmful over each person's buttocks, staining the nude bottom a rich red. He needed three chalices in all to complete the job, and he then poured the content of the fourth over his thickly black-haired chest and back and smeared the concoction until he was liberally covered in it, his thighs and arms and face not escaping. His huge cock – also liberally stained crimson – rocking and wobbling, he produced a box of matches from his folded pile of clothes and went around lighting each of the five candles. He next fetched a heavy silver object, intricately designed with pagan symbols, which had been lying outside the ring into the inner circle. Planting the pagan object on the lawn, he fell dramatically to his knees before it, clasping his hands together in an attitude of prayer, sinking his chin into his chest.

Every pair of eyes in the circle was roving pruriently around it from wanking hand to wanking hand. It seemed that the participants in this orgy of masturbation could not get enough of leching on the actions of the others. The sight of the rest, doing to themselves what they were each doing, spurred them on; fingers inside pussies stabbed faster and faster, fists jerked ever more fiercely on cocks. The seven had become one utterly carnal ring of flesh which writhed like a pile of worms and moaned with one voice.

Slowly and quietly, Count Petrovski began to chant a mantra, whilst his head lifted and he observed the communal wanking session with hooded, hungry eyes. After a minute or so of this he paused in his chant to issue new instructions.

'Be sure to be very careful not to break the circle whilst you do what I tell you next,' he said. 'I want you all to turn to your right, firmly grasp a buttock of the person in front of you and get down on your knees. Then move backwards on your knees until your face is bent to the bottom you are clutching.'

When each member of the ring had done as Petrovski instructed and was staring at the moon-washed and smeared backside in front of his or her nose, the ring had tripled in circumference and shrunk to a third of its height. Six of the participants looked at a pair of buttocks of the opposite sex, whilst Lady Brexford's nose hovered inches from the blotchily red-stained bottom of Lettice.

It was the count's turn now to masturbate himself, and he did so with great gusto as he grunted his next, gross, instructions. 'You will now plug one another's bottom holes with your tongues,' he said, leering, his fist leaping up and down his immense hard-on. 'This is to be an anal sexual ring much beloved of the divine king. Do not cease this activity until I tell you to. And take care – it is essential at this stage that no one should climax.'

As noses buried in buttock flesh and tongues slid up bottom holes, only Georgina had any trouble in coming to terms with this beastly command. Hesistant, she stared, extremely aroused yet loath to perform what would be for her yet another first, at Edwin Smythe-Parker's big bottom with its thickly black-haired perineum and his bulging, dangling scrotum beneath it.

'Well, Georgina? For what are you waiting?' asked Petrovski harshly. 'The circle has to be entirely closed.'

Taking a deep breath, she poked out her tongue and probed with its tip experimentally amongst the hairs in the crack in the author's behind, her nose stuffed between the muscular cheeks, until she found the little hole. Closing her eyes, she pushed it in, finding the act to be neither agreeable nor repulsive – whilst discovering that Lord Brexford's tongue, deeply probing her backside, was doing things most pleasantly salacious to her.

'Frig one another as well,' the count told them. Then he continued his mantra – and his wanking – words, in a strange and ancient tongue, specifically designed to reach that supernatural power, a monotonous cadence steadily rising in volume.

Of a sudden, the air became a little chillier. A largish cloud slipped across the moon. The lawn, except for the flickering candlelight eerily illuminating the circle, was steeped in darkness. As seven tongues dipped and plunged in bottom holes and seven hands lustily excited the genitals below those holes, the breeze became stronger and gustier, whipping hair around, lifting and flapping the edges of discarded clothes, whistling through the hawthorn hedge. Somewhere close by, an owl hooted. A dog in far-off kennels began to bark, then another, and another.

As he steadily tossed himself off, and his mantra became so loud that it sounded as if there was a touch of madness in his voice – as, indeed, there probably was – Petrovski's dark, sinister eyes were growing wider and wider. He was no longer paying much attention to the ring but his gaze was searching and stabbing into the darkness beyond the pentacle. It was less than a half a minute before midnight.

His voice gone wobbly, almost shouting, the count issued his final instructions. He had the seven arrange themselves with the men on their backs on the grass and the women on hands and knees, and to mouth one another's genitals – but remaining in a circle.

'Until you come. Until you *come*,' he roared. 'But do not even for one second any of you break the ring. Not even then.'

As the moon reappeared, peeping between thickening cloud and lighting up the pentacle, the count pointed his hard-on at it. Closing his eyes tightly, he began almost to bellow the words of his mantra. The first midnight chime of the church clock, some three miles distant in the village, was brought to the field on the steadily rising wind. As the chimes continued, and orgasm most fierce began to take hold of the members of the scrofulous ring, all the dogs in the kennels began to howl and the horses in the nearby stables to neigh and whinny.

Another cloud covered the moon, with bigger, ominously black, scudding ones on its heels. Something strangely powerful appeared to be manifesting itself in the darkness beyond the pentacle, but such was the power of communal orgasm that nobody noticed – nobody, that is, except Count Petrovski whose fist was flying up and down his cock.

The final midnight chime tolled, its deep echo bouncing off the walls of the mansion. The kneeling Count Petrovski's semen jetted from his balls and arched high in the air to splash onto the grass close to Lord Brexford – who had begun to shoot in Ellie's mouth as his stabbing tongue brought Georgina off. Edwyn Smythe-Parker erupted between Georgina's lips while Sophronia's pussy juices soaked his tongue and Lettice climaxed with Sophronia's tongue poking up her cunt as far as it could reach. Lettice greedily gobbled Lord Antrim to orgasm whilst he did the same to Ellie.

A climax of massive intensity trembled and shuddered around the entire ring.

At once, all the candles died. The wind stopped completely. The clouds ceased their scudding and with a life of their own puffed themselves together until not a star nor a moonbeam pricked through their cover.

All of the domestic animals were going berserk; even a bull bellowing somewhere, and the hens in the coop near the kennels were furiously squawking. As the four women collapsed, satiated, where they had been kneeling and the men grunted and gasped as their final drops of sperm leaked from them, in the deep and awful darkness beyond the pentacle shadows appeared where no shadows had any right to exist. Count Petrovski's eyes glinted in mad triumph as they pierced the terrifying void. The last drips of his semen spilled from his tightly gripped cock.

The air became filled with the clamour of an insanity of noises. Almost drowning the racket of the animals, there was a crazy, terrifying mixture of supernatural sounds – a cackling, dreadful laughter reminiscent of Macbeth's witches, a hooting noise resembling no earthly sound, the clanging of bells, the beating of drums, a succession of horrific screams. The atmosphere turned heavy and humid, pressing in on the pentacle from all sides, suffocating. There was a rank and offensive, goatish stink in it. It tasted sulphurous.

Never had orgasm been forgotten so quickly. The seven climbed shakily to their feet, their faces – even that of Lord Brexford – filled with fear. Ellie and Lettice began to scream, Sophronia to cry. Georgina, chubby features a mask of terror, made a sudden lunge to get out of the pentacle.

Petrovski grabbed her arm just in time. 'You'll *die* out there,' he roared at her. Dropping to her knees she began to blubber, shoulders heaving, tits wobbling.

It got stiflingly hot, as if an invisible fire were raging in the blackness. The insanity continued unabated. It was as if all the evil in the world were trying to break through into the pentacle. The women huddled together, the men helplessly stared around with pale and stricken faces.

Lord Brexford crept agitatedly up to Count Petrovski's side. Fighting to disguise the fear in his voice, failing, he begged him to get rid of whatever horrors he had conjured up. Strange, twisted shadows were leaping and dancing all around the edge of the pentacle.

'Did I not warn you, my friend? Yet you continued to mock, to disbelieve,' sneered Petrovski, a grin most evil contorting his saturnine features. '*He* has come. He's angry and he's out there, and if he breaks into the pentacle, you know where we are all going.'

'Have shot of him, then. For Christ's sake, Alexis.'

The holy name seemed to have a momentary effect. The noises around them merged into a sudden wail as Brexford pronounced it, but then they continued as they had been before.

'I can but try,' said the count. In truth, though he may have thought of himself as being evil, he had not the slightest desire to be dragged into hell. Turning the silver image towards him he knelt before it and began to recite the Lord's prayer. He had the others fall to their knees and join in with him.

Gradually, the awful noises diminished. The heat and stench lessened. The dancing shadows receded. The animals quietened down. The candles relit themselves. As the company reached the end of the prayer and started again at the beginning, streaks of lightning, very close, began to knife into the earth.

In the sudden light from the approaching storm, bright as day, they all caught an unmistakable glimpse of a terrifying, hideous, goat-like, twelve-feet-high, dissolving figure. Then it was dark as pitch again. There was an earth-shaking thunderclap.

It began to pour with rain. The rain did not start, as normal, with a few warning drops and then get steadily heavier; it fell down from the black sky in one great, continuous sheet immediately to drench them all.

'It's all right now,' gasped Petrovski. 'It's all right. We are safe. He's gone.'

They all silently gathered up their clothes. There was no sense in trying to struggle into them, the clothes were soaked all the way through. Naked, saturated and beginning to shake with the cold, the eight – who had indeed succeeded in conjuring up the powers of evil, and maybe the Devil himself with the help of their most orgasmic circle – sprinted back to the manor house.

Chapter 13

'I've thrown away all my witches' things,' Lady Brexford announced during lunch the following day. 'I've even burnt the books. Never, never again!'

Count Petrovski and Lord Antrim had departed, but Edwin Smythe-Parker and Lettice had stayed over at the manor for an extra day.

'No more of that stuff for me, either,' commented Smythe-Parker. 'I've had quite enough, thank you very much.' His hand lit on Lettice's knee. 'What say you, my love?'

'Fair jumped out of me drawers in fright, didn't I? Wild 'orses wouldn't drag me inside that star thing again,' proclaimed the cockney belle.

'But you weren't actually wearing any drawers, dear,' Sophronia pointed out with a grin.

'Well, I would 'ave done if I 'ad of been.'

'I think you are all making much too much of a fuss about what happened,' said Lord Brexford. 'Things were not exactly as they seemed.'

'Oh – so now nothing at all occurred, is that it, Jeremy? Hah! you were in as big a funk as the rest of us,' Sophronia said. She stabbed an accusing finger at him. 'You, my darling, were scared out of your wits.' She washed a piece of tender calf liver down her throat with sweet white wine; nothing seemed to taste quite right to her today – the macabre events of midnight seemed to have upset her metabolism. 'How can you continue to poo-poo the supernatural after all that happened last night?' she added. 'Don't you believe the evidence of your own eyes?'

'No. As a matter of fact I don't. And you shouldn't believe your eyes, either. What happened was, we got ourselves in a bit of a trance induced by Alexis's hypnotic mantra, and we were carried away mentally with all that kinky behaviour. A storm blew up very suddenly – as they are wont to do – and there was a dramatic change in the atmosphere which set all the animals into a panic. The rest was in our collective imagination.'

'Bollocks!' exclaimed Smythe-Parker. 'I am credited with a huge imagination, but I've never dreamed up for any of my books anything as terrifying as what happened. Like it or not, you have to accept the fact that we called up the powers of evil.'

'There's no such thing, my friend. It's a myth, that nonsense about the Devil and so forth.'

'I saw him,' insisted Lettice.

'So did I. We all did,' said Sophronia. 'He was monstrous. Horrible.'

'I saw the same as the rest of you. A twist in the shadows caused by an unusual streak of lightning which, because of the circumstances, we all decided was Old Nick.' But Jeremy Brexford was on very shaky ground, and he knew it. He was by no means sure that he believed what he was saying. He wanted to, desperately, for he was scared that were there a Heaven and a Hell, the latter would be his ultimate destination.

'Well, whatever the real truth is,' said Sophronia, '. . . I'm certainly not going to involve myself in any way in sorcery any more.'

'Planning on giving up orgies as well, are you?' asked Brexford facetiously.

That was quite a different matter. Somehow, she managed to appear demure as she said, with a sweet little smile, 'I rather doubt that, darling.'

'I'm delighted to hear it.' Jeremy's eyes invaded Lettice's *décolletage*. Her frilly, white silk blouse was so low-cut that the dark brown, crinkly tops of the coronas of her nipples were peeping above it. 'I fear that we are all in far too morbid a mood today,' he said to the plump, dusky cleavage.

'I rather think we should endeavour to cheer ourselves up with a little sport this afternoon.'

'I take it by that you don't mean the hunt?' asked Sophronia, knowing full well his words implied yet more sex.

'I know what 'e wants to hunt, don't I?' said Lettice saucily, looking down at her bosom.

Lettice was a dark-skinned young lady of Indian ancestry. She had black and shiny straight hair which, normally worn piled fetchingly on top of her head, today hung to he waist. No whore as such – though she would have entertained few qualms about prostituting herself had circumstances thrust her into the oldest profession – she was a young woman of remarkably easy virtue whose strong good looks had helped her to find her way sexually into the society of the rich and famous, and who profited financially from such company whilst indulging a libidinous appetite of prolific proportions. For the past six months she had enjoyed the fact that the wealthy and talented Smythe-Parker had been keeping her in the lap of luxury, screwing her brains out – and lending her to his friends.

Edwin said, smiling, 'I thought maybe we were in for a bit of a rest, old man. After last night. The old John Thomas has been working overtime lately.'

The remark produced a giggle from Sophronia. 'No chance of that,' she said. 'To my certain knowledge, the longest rest Jeremy's John Thomas has taken since I've known him is about eight hours.'

'So long?' asked Brexford, an expression of mock surprise on his face. 'When was that, my love, I don't seem to remember? Was I perchance ill?'

They all laughed. It seemed that the edge of fear remaining in them after the apparent manifestation of the Prince of Darkness was dissolving away with the prospect of more sex.

The prurient Brexford eye was still plundering Lettice's tits. He was recalling her long-legged nakedness of the previous night and her utterly wanton expression as, opposite him in the tight, orgiastic ring, she had masturbated herself with the utmost vigour.

'You get a very big kick from showing off your beautiful body, don't you, Lettice?' he asked her, knowing full well that she did. 'From publicly exciting that glorious, crinkly-haired pussy of yours?'

'And you're a dirty-minded sod,' she told him.

'Shush wench, do,' admonished Smythe-Parker jokingly. 'You seem to have utterly forgotten your manners – and the fact that you happen to be addressing a peer of the realm.'

She guffawed. 'That about sums 'im up. A bleedin' peer. He pees the same as everybody else, don't 'e?'

Lettice had thus unknowingly given Lord Brexford a capital excuse for proceeding with the ribald idea which had been developing in his mind. Not that he actually needed one, but it would make the game that much more spicy.

'That, slattern, is the grossest of insolence,' he told her sternly. 'You have been unforgivably rude to a member of His Majesty's House of Lords, for which transgression you shall be punished most severely.'

'Here, here,' enthused Smythe-Parker, eyes gleaming. 'She shall be thrashed forthwith.'

'You dare lay a sodding finger on me, either of you, and I'll scream the sodding 'ouse down,' threatened Lettice, getting into the spirit of things.

'Then we shall just have to *gag* you, won't we, dearie?' said Sophronia mildly, with a happy little smile, looking forward to whatever Jeremy had in mind for the girl. 'Sentence has been passed – how are you planning to execute it, my lord?'

Jeremy glanced at the window. Rain was streaming down it so heavily he could hardly see out. The previous night's storm had been violent in the extreme and it had been pouring down all day. 'Ideally,' he said, 'I should like to deal with her whilst she is stretched on the rack in the torture courtyard. But the weather unfortunately makes that proposition out of the question.' He thought for a few moments, his gaze wandering over Lettice, and then Sophronia. Then he said, with a brief and twisted grin, 'Yes. I have a *particularly* interesting idea.' He held out his hand. 'Come along, Lettice. To the whipping post.'

'You leave me alone, you rotten bastard,' grumbled Lettice, playing the game to the full whilst looking forward lustfully to whatever was about to befall her.

'So. Insult upon insult, is it? Slinging dirt at my mother, now. So.' Rising, Brexford took Lettice's arm fiercely by the bare elbow below her puffy sleeve and heaved her to her feet. 'You have been stupid enough to make it even worse for yourself. You will come with me, and Edwin and my dear wife will assist in your chastisement.'

In the huge old kitchens, the scullery maid had just finished washing up the first-course lunch dishes. She was expecting the rest of the dirty plates to be brought to her when in marched Lord and Lady Brexford with their two guests. To the maid's extreme puzzlement, she found herself sent packing; she was told that under no circumstances was she to return until sent for, and to pass the instructions along to the rest of the staff that none of them for the present should enter the kitchens.

'Now,' said Brexford, having loudly banged closed the door – which had no lock. His gaze swept over the full-bellied, black iron stoves and the row upon row of gleaming copper pots and cooking implements which hung against the grey stone walls. 'Yes,' he said, satisfaction in his voice as his eye fell on a scrubbed pine table used chiefly for preparing vegetables. 'That will serve most satisfactorily as our whipping post, I believe.' Going to the table, he smoothed the flat of his hand over its surface, enjoying the feel of the smooth, worn wood as he savoured the notion of the use he was about to put it to.

'Come here, Lettice,' he growled. 'This instant, woman.' She was grumbling away as she did so, but when she was at his side and he told her to bend over the table and try it for size she did so without any show of reluctance.

'If you remove your boots, you'll find it will be just about the perfect height,' he told her.

Lettice complied willingly enough – eagerly, even. She doubled herself over the table again. With her knees only slightly bent, her torso was flattened on the pine surface, with her chin dented on the table's far edge which she gripped in both hands. She was warned not to move. The keen Brexford eye attached itself to some twisted brown-paper fly traps. Hanging from the beamed ceiling, each of them had a number of flys caught on its sticky surface.

'Now, I wonder where they keep . . .?' he muttered to himself, glancing all around the kitchens.

Crossing the heavily worn flagstone floor to some wooden cabinets he began opening and shutting drawers and cupboards until he found what he wanted. He took from a drawer four fresh rolls of fly papers, then he went to Smythe-Parker and handed him two of them. 'These should do a perfect job of securing the wench,' he said. 'You wrap her wrists to the table legs, Edwin, whilst I see to her ankles.'

In the space of a couple of minutes, Lettice was trapped over the vegetable table, firmly bound by the wrists and ankles to the bottoms of its legs, her cheek squashed into the pine where her chin had been. Lord Brexford slipped two hands beneath her to unfasten the pearl buttons of her blouse and unlace and pull apart her bodice. As he fondled her hidden breasts, he said, 'Better for you if your tits are bare against the pine. It will heighten your sensations.'

Lettice smiled. She was all keyed up inside, beginning to feel most horny and prepared and willing for almost anything which Lord Brexford decided was to be done to her.

'Since she is your kept woman,' Brexford told Smythe-Parker, 'it should therefore fall upon you to raise her skirts and lower her knickers to prepare her for her thrashing.'

The author did his duty with great relish. With Lord and Lady Brexford looking on in mounting excitement, he pulled Lettice's full, ankle-length dress and her frilly white petticoats up over her legs to heap them onto her back. Beneath, she had on hand-embroidered, pale blue bloomers which gripped just below her knees with elastic to flare out into three-inch lace hems. Edwin groped and squeezed her buttocks through the bloomers whilst bumping his groin several times suggestively into her bottom, throwing a loaded little smile at his hosts as he did so. Then, making a sexual meal out of it, he eased the long drawers most slowly over the delightfully rounded, slightly dusky bottom until they were hanging, by their knee elastic, inside out from beneath her knees and crumpled over her feet. With her feet spread as wide as the table legs, Lettice was most lewdly exposed, her pale brown pussy lips, pushing their way through a thick mass of the blackest of pubic hairs beneath her buttocks, clearly on show. Briefly, Edwin pawed them. Then he thumbed them apart and humped his crotch into the nude backside.

'For the moment we are supposed to be punishing the lass, remember?' said Brexford. 'Not bringing her pleasure.'

The author backed away from her, the bulge behind his fly most prominent.

For all their benefits, Lettice saucily wriggled her bottom. 'See if I bleedin' care,' she said. 'Do your worst.'

'Care you will, insolent jade,' snapped Brexford. 'You are about to pay most dearly for your earlier impertinence.'

He stalked to where several rows of kitchen implements were hanging over a worn, wooden work-surface. From them, he selected a large, thin spatula of the kind used for lifting omelettes from frying pans. The sides of the spatula's working surface curved from a flat top down into a copper-plated arm which was attached to a comfortably rounded handle. In the business end there were a series of small holes, causing it to whoosh most pleasingly when Lord Brexford slashed it experimentally through the air.

'I suggest you two select your weapons,' he muttered, flexing his as he approached his delectable target with a leer on his face.

Smythe-Parker picked a spatula similar in size to his friend's – except that his had a circular working surface – and Sophronia decided on a light, oblong slab of pinewood with a carved handle, used for slicing bread on; it was deeply etched with knife lines from years of use. Lettice's toes curled as, over her shoulder, she caught sight of the implements.

'Blimey,' she exclaimed 'you ain't planning on murdering me, are you?'

'Hold your tongue, girl and take *this*,' grunted Lord Brexford.

He swished his spatula hard down from shoulder height into her left buttock. It caught the flesh flatly, producing a sharp, slapping noise. Lettice yelped, jerking her feet, making the table rock, her fingers curling around the bottoms of its legs. An indistinct pattern of the spatula's holes appeared on the pale brown buttock.

Brexford ran a hand over the mark then he stood back, a twisted smile on his face. 'We'll take it in turns to thrash the wench,' he said, 'there is no hurry. Let us make it last. Go on, Sophie – whack her a good one.'

But Lady Brexford did not dare wield her breadboard with much more than minimum force; the size and weight of a paddle tennis bat, it was certainly capable of inflicting most severe pain – and that was not the object of the afternoon's sport which was for everybody, Lettice included, to have a good and raunchy time. The thin slice of pine connected across both buttocks with a sound like a wet towel being flapped into a wall. Lettice's entire bottom trembled, the table rocked once more, and she yelped again.

Edwin Smythe-Parker delivered a stinging, but not overly so, cut across his girlfriend's right buttock. This time her cry was minimal. After another complete round of smacks, as her backside began to glow, the girl's yelps ceased altogether to be replaced by little whimpers and moans of excitement. Lettice was starting to enjoy herself, for within her richly libidinous soul there dwelt both an abiding love of pleasure-pain and a constant craving for sexual exhibitionism, the two of which were being wonderfully satisfied at one and the same time on this fine, rainy afternoon. More, she was well aware that this beating was only a preliminary of joys to come. Shortly, certainly, she was going to be treated to – at the very least – a most thorough fucking.

The three of them continued to lay their kitchen implements soundly into Lettice until what had a short while before been an unmarked, dusky bottom was glowing red all over. Lord Brexford, hard-on straining beneath his trousers, called a halt to the punishment. In truth, Lettice was more than a little disappointed – very close to orgasm, she could have happily taken even more.

She waited in tense expectation, pussy sopping wet, for whatever the lustful trio were going to inflict upon her next.

A further, most ribald idea had crept into Lord Brexford's scandalous mind. Lettice turned her head to flatten her other cheek into the table, affording herself a clear view of her favourite peer as he hunted around in the nearby walk-in larder. He emerged bearing two, large glass jars, the content of one of which was dark brown in colour, and that of the other pale yellow. He put the brown one down on a corner of the table and unscrewed the top of the yellow one to dip his fingers inside.

It was honey, and he told Lettice as much as he scooped some out and spread it over her backside with the palm of his hand. 'To soothe your bum,' he said. His carnal inspirations were getting dirtier by the second. As he fingered out more honey and began to work it into the crack of Lettice's bottom, he muttered to Sophronia, 'I'll wager your pussy is by now in extreme need of attention?'

Nostrils flaring, tongue tip flickering to wet her lips, she glanced pointedly from Jeremy's bulging trouser front to the tented fly of Edwin Smythe-Parker. 'It craves relief every bit as much as I see that your pricks do, naturally.'

With sodomy very much on his mind, Jeremy was easing a fingerful of honey up Lettice's little bottom hole. As he rotated his finger inside it, and Lettice squeaked, he told his wife, 'In that case, Sophie darling, lift your skirts, drop your drawers, and we shall have Lettice lick some of this from your cunt.

'My God, what an idea,' said Lady Brexford. Her pulse beginning to gallop, she positioned herself in front of the girl's face. She pulled her skirt up to her belly and pinned it there with a forearm as she lowered her cream silk cami-knickers half-way down her thighs. Her husband slid the glass jar to her across the table. Opening her legs as wide as the knickers would allow, with Edwin gaping most lustily at her actions and Brexford handling himself through his trousers, she scooped three fingers of honey from the jar and smeared it all over her pussy.

'Eat it,' she murmured, humping her pelvis forward into Lettice's face. 'Lick up every little bit.' Raising her head so that her chin was propped on the table's edge, the girl did exactly that, not pausing until the auburny pussy was clean. Bawdily enjoying herself, Sophronia slapped on some more.

'In the name of heaven, Jeremy,' panted Smythe-Parker, 'is there no end to your dirty-minded inventions?' He impatiently unbuttoned the front of his trousers, dragged his hard cock out through his fly and began jerking his fist up and down on it.

'One hopes not,' said Lord Brexford. 'Take this next amusing little stunt, for example. After I've finished it, if you then crave to poke Lettice, you will be advised to drop your trousers all the way down. You will see why in just a few moments. The lovely Miss Lettice is going to appear even more obscenely fuckable than she does at present.'

The brown substance in the other jar was a form of custardy chocolate spread. Jeremy scooped some out and smarmed it in with the honey on Lettice's bottom. When he was satisfied with the sticky, yellowy brown mess he had made, he then began to smear the chocolate spread copiously all over the backs, sides and insides of her legs, working his way from her buttocks and on down past her knees almost to her feet. Finally, he even fingered some inside her pussy.

By the time Brexford ceased his handiwork, the jar was almost empty. Sophronia, quietly panting, had meanwhile been having more and more honey licked from her pussy across the table from him, slowly and sensuously rocking her crotch as Lettice enthusiastically lapped away, her tongue tip frequently leaving the honey-thick pubes to ferret between Lady Brexford's pussy lips, her perfectly straight, small white teeth nibbling from time to time on Sophronia's hard little nub of clitoris.

Jeremy stood back a pace, eyes raunchily running over Lettice's brown-coated flesh. Her chocolate and honey-smeared bare bottom and cunt, and her thickly brown legs appeared far more arousing to him than the soiled flesh of a female mud-wrestler.

'Jesus,' breathed Smythe-Parker, eyes feasting on the sight. Unwilling to control himself for one second more, he shoved his trousers and underpants all the way down his hairy legs, shuffled forward to Lettice with them around his ankles, and rammed his cock all the way into her pussy. His backside commenced a furious bouncing and heaving; he was clearly about to go most quickly over the climactical edge.

'After you, old boy,' said Jeremy in mild, raunchy amusement as, observing this frenetic act of copulation, he busied himself with smearing his hard-on with honey.

Very quickly thereafter, the author came with such a vigorous final slam of his cock that he shifted the table a couple of inches, thereby crushing Lettice's nose into Sophronia's belly.

Edwin remained rigidly impaled in his cockney Lettice for more than a minute, his bottom twitching and jerking as the last drops of sperm leaked from his balls. Uncoupling, he meandered in almost drunken fashion to the nearest chair and sank wearily down onto it. His hips, his lower belly and his pubic bush were sticky with the honey and chocolate mixture, the fronts and outsides of his thighs were patchily brown with chocolate spread.

'So now you know why I wanted you to lower your trousers,' said Lord Brexford, removing his shoes and clambering out of his own. Impatiently – for his need was every bit as pressing as had been Smythe-Parker's – he took his place behind Lettice, but intent on penetrating a different hole. Taking hold of his sticky, yellowish hard-on, he positioned its helmet at the honeyed entrance to Lettice's bottom hole and began to ease it in.

At the other end of the table from her husband, Sophronia had finished with the honey jar. Her pubis was licked clean, and she was holding her pussy lips wide open with the fingers of both hands, her mid-thigh knickers stretched taut enough to split, her crotch bumping and jerking against Lettice's face, and her dress rucked up behind her wrists. Busily lapping and tongue-fucking down there between her ladyship's silken thighs, Lettice groaned as she felt her sphincter being stretched, but she did not pause for one moment in her cunnilingus. She had already come, she was rapidly approaching a second climax and she was not going to allow any temporary pain in her bottom hole to postpone it.

By the time that the Brexford prick was fitted snugly up Lettice's bum, and her flash of pain had transformed to waves of pleasure, Sophronia's crotch was heaving in much the same fashion as if she were sitting astride a man and screwing him. Lettice's tongue dipped and plunged in the auburn-pubed pussy as her head bobbed and the ends of her long black hair jiggled and bounced on the flagstone floor.

The first of the lewdly interlocked threesome to go over the climactical top was Lord Brexford. He roared his orgasm like a bellowing bull. His seed flooded Lettice's bottom as he convulsively jerked his almost fully impaled prick in it, balls jogging against her lower buttock swell whilst they emptied. As he withdrew, the sight of his big cock unplugging the rear end of the girl who was eating her did the trick for Sophronia. She cried out her orgasm to a hanging row of gleaming copper pots, juices seeping over the embedded tongue, knees stretching her half-mast knickers even wider, ripping open a seam in them. Her eyes closed.

Seconds later, humping her groin feverishly to bring herself off by rubbing her clitoris against the smooth pine edge of the table, Lettice came with a wail which was loud enough to penetrate half the house.

The staff of Deal Manor were well accustomed to wild and outrageous sexual noises. It had got so that when Lord and Lady Brexford went away for a few days the ancient pile did not seem the same without the impassioned shouts, the squeals and screams, the grunts and loud moans, and all the other, echoing, orgasmic sounds which accompanied their employers' frequent carnal excesses.

When the scullery girl had breathlessly reported that her master and mistress and their guests had taken over the kitchen at a time when the washing-up should have been finished, shutting themselves in there with orders not to be disturbed, the staff were well aware that it could having nothing to do with cooking. But *sex*? In the kitchen of all places? That was surely taking their abandonment a little too far.

That it had, indeed, been sex, and a riotously abandoned session at that, had been confirmed by the even louder than usual climactic noises. Nevertheless the scullery maid and other kitchen staff were unprepared for the extraordinary mess that the sated four had left the kitchen in when they at long last abandoned it.

The chocolate jar had been knocked from the table as Lettice was being freed, and it had smashed on the floor, almost empty, the shattered glass scattering all over the flagstones. The contents of the honey jar had almost vanished – enough to spread at least a loaf of bread if not two. Half a dozen teacloths, liberally smeared with chocolate spread and honey – and sperm, though the staff were not to know that – were scattered over the floor where Lord Brexford, Lettice and Smythe-Parker had dropped them after cleaning themselves up.

The reasons behind that incredible clutter were most difficult to comprehend – it would take an imagination as vivid as that of their master to work out what deviant behaviour had transpired there.

The biggest conundrum of all was presented by the four fly papers. They had clearly been used for a purpose for which they have never been intended since one of them was rolled around and stuck to the bottom of each leg of the vegetable table, the rolls neatly sliced through, their ends dangling.

Chapter 14

Filled with curiosity about what it was that Lord Brexford had had especially sent down to her, Miss Petty cut through the string of the small, brown-paper parcel. It bore the Brexford seal and had arrived at tea-time hand-delivered from the manor. Within, the headmistress discovered two most perplexing objects. There was a pale yellow silk hood designed to cover the entire head and with eye, nose and mouth holes, and there was a frilly, crimson garter. When she read the accompanying note, she still did not fully understand. She re-read it most carefully.

It had been some while – far too long as far as she was concerned – since Claire Petty had been invited to the manor to participate in an orgy, and the only sex she had indulged in since then had been the solitary sin and, most recently, the lesbian variety with Georgina. The prospect which was so suddenly and unexpectedly presented to her for the following night – apparently a May Day ball with an interesting difference – excited her greatly. What was most puzzling was the fact that, like some Cinderella in reverse, she was requested in the invitation not to appear until midnight. Without a doubt she was to be used in one or another kinky sexual way – and so much the better. She read the note yet again, libido stirring as she did so. She tried on the hood, and with the yellow silk covering her head, she pulled up her skirts, slipped the elasticated garter over her shoe and up her leg and fitted it just above her knee.

The prospect of what it was that Lord Brexford expected of her – and she understood only a part of it – was most daunting. However, nothing could possibly be more shocking than the behaviour she had been subjected to during her very first visit to Deal Manor – and that had culminated with her in writhing, orgiastic ecstacy. Almost of its own accord, as she remembered events most salacious, her hand stole up her thigh to find the crotch of her knickers whilst she tried to visualise what the following night would hold in store for her.

For a while the lascivious headmistress happily frigged herself. But the activity proved to be insufficient to satisfy her. She craved to have sight of and to cane the bottom of one of her girls – and preferably one that she had not set eyes upon before. Recalling that a certain Miss Prudence Brown, a dorm-mate of Georgina and Ellie, had been reported to her for being rude to a mistress that morning – though the rudeness had been trivial, normally no more than a hundred lines' offence – Miss Petty removed the mask and the garter and tinkled her little silver bell impatiently until a prefect knocked on her door and was told to come in. She sent the girl to summon the offender to her office.

Prudence Brown, Pru to her friends, was as slender as Georgina was plump, but not unattractively so. She was two hairs-breadths away from being skinny, with knobbly knees and shoulders and a prominent Adam's apple. She was tall, five feet nine in her socks, and she had a pointy, rather fetching nose, big, soulful brown eyes, long, straight, biscuit-coloured hair, and she wore heavy-lensed, tortoiseshell-framed spectacles. When she arrived on the dreaded threshold of Miss Petty's study she was wearing black gym shoes – and she was quaking in them.

Claire Petty's pussy was damp and twitching, but her sexual arousal was unapparent to the eye. She wore a grim and foreboding expression on her face as she rose from behind her desk. She was anxious to get the preliminaries over and get on with doing her dirty business.

She addressed the poor girl in a voice of thunder. 'It has been reported to me, Prudence Brown,' she said, 'that you had the temerity this morning to reply to a question from a mistress without using the courtesy title of Miss, or her proper name, which is Miss Simpson. You merely, in reply to a question, said "yes". That is impudence. Your explanation?'

'Please, p-please Miss Petty,' stammered the thoroughly cowed girl, lower lip atremble,' that is true, miss. I forgot to say miss, miss. It won't happen again, I promise you. I'm sorry.'

'Sorry *what*?' stormed the headmistress. 'Sorry, *Miss* Petty. Good heavens, girl, you already repeated the offence! What on earth is the matter with you?'

'Sorry Miss, Miss Petty.'

Cripes, thought Prudence, Petters is being absolutely impossible today. She was nervously shuffling her feet and rubbing her sweaty palms on the sides of her skirt. She had been about to change into hockey gear and join in a game and she had only got as far as her shoes when the dire summons was delivered. Now it looked as if she was going to miss the game altogether. But surely Petters was not about to cane her for such a stupid little thing?

She most certainly was. Striding to her fireplace, Miss Petty reached above it for the bane of Chalmers. She decided to dispense with the punishment chair on this occasion, considering it might be an arousing change to cane the girl near the window, where the rays of the late afternoon sunlight would fall across her nude bottom. Just about to instruct Prudence to prepare herself for punishment she had another, most wicked, idea. It would delay the event somewhat, but it would greatly please Lord Brexford – which in turn should pay handsome dividends.

'You are to be caned, Miss Brown,' she calmly informed the girl. She stretched out her hand to the recently installed telephone. 'You are to be caned,' she repeated, 'but first you will wait outside my closed door until I tell you to come back in.'

Trembling even more now that her fate had been so coldly pronounced, Prudence slunk out into the corridor and shut the door.

Miss Petty placed the black, bell-shaped Bakelite listening device to her ear and turned the little chrome handle on its upright stand to get through to the operator in the town of Deal. The girl connected her without trouble to Deal Manor, where she had a brief conversation with Lord Brexford.

After thanking him for his invitation, she informed him that she was about to cane a girl, that she was going to do this in front of her window, and she suggested that he might find it an interesting diversion to observe this amusing event through his telescope.

'Give me fives minutes to get up to the top of the manor,' responded Brexford, in randy enthusiasm. It so happened that the headmistress had interrupted him in one of his frequent, afternoon naughty moods. He was in Sophronia's bedroom, on his knees in front of her as she sat on her dressing-table chair, and he had just removed her knickers, though not her dress. He hung up the telephone and, taking his wife by the hand, pulled her to her feet and hurried her up to his telescope room.

'Enter, please, Miss Brown,' Claire Petty called out stridently, a few minutes later.

Prudence was in a sad state, the waiting had served to further shred her nerves. 'Please, miss, spare me?' she begged. 'I, I'll do you a thousand lines if you like. Miss.'

'Spare you?' Miss Petty grated. 'Certainly not. You are about to receive ten of the very best.' She flexed the cane in both hands, swiped it heartily through the air once, and then again – thus terrorising the poor girl with its whistle – and crossed a rug to the window. 'Come over here to me,' she growled.

Prudence crept silently across the room, a tall, thin, scared mouse.

'Turn yourself around.'

The girl put her back near the window. Miss Petty was by her side on her left.

'Bend down and touch your toes.'

Making the fearsome task less of a strain by bending at the knees, Prudence flattened her fingers on her gym shoes. Her glasses slipped down her nose. Her hair fell over her face. Handful by handful, not hurrying – for the benefit of both herself and the presumably observing Lord Brexford – the headmistress gathered the ankle-length, blue skirt up until it was above the girl's knickers and piled on the small of her back, where she let it rest.

'By golly,' muttered Lord Brexford, eye glued to the telescope in the dusty, top-floor room of the manor which housed it. 'Get me out, Sophie, do.'

Sophronia fumbled undone his fly buttons.

When she felt her headmistress's cool and chubby fingertips slipping inside the waistband of her baggy blue knickers, understanding the drawers were about to be pulled down, Prudence gasped for shame. Blushing, she started to protest.

'Please, miss, surely not on my bare –'

'Shut *up*, Miss Brown,' grated Petters, as she yanked on the knickers, turning them inside out down the girl's thighs. Not only did she find the sight of the previously unogled, exposed, thin buttocks with their curly brown tuft of pussy hair deep down between them most arousing, but the way in which the knickers appeared – baggily hanging around her knees, with the square, white label of their manufacturer on display – further excited her.

'This is going to hurt me just as much as I intend that it does you,' she lied. Raising the cane, she carefully measured her distance.

Jeremy Brexford's view of this could not have been better. His telescope was powerful enough to tell not only the time on Miss Petty's wall clock, but also its make, and he had adjusted its zoom so that the headmistress's study window filled the viewer. The sunlight falling across Prudence's naked backside and bare legs made the picture beautifully clear and colourful. He could make out a tiny mole on the upper swell of the girl's left buttock; it was as if, if he stretched out his hand, he could fondle the slender bottom.

The cane sang through the air to bite with stinging force across Prudence's behind. She howled – and was warned that it would be the worse for her if she failed to remain silent throughout the rest of her ordeal. Biting her juddering lower lip, she fought back her tears and tensed her bottom against the second blow.

The cane did not fall immediately. Miss Petty was intently studying Prudence's left buttock, which had taken most of the slash. A thin, red weal was forming before her eyes. Adjusting her aim as she raised her arm with the intention of producing a similar, satisfying result on the right buttock, she paused with the whippy length of rattan hovering high above her head to glance up towards the manor with a twisted, lustful smile on her face. She swished the cane down again.

Somehow, despite the sharply throbbing pain, Prudence managed to stay quiet. Her embarrassment at being so rudely exposed remained acute as she steeled herself for the next assault.

Brexford allowed Sophronia, who was stroking the solid cock which poked from his flies, a peep through the telescope. Without releasing the prick, she took over the eyepiece and both of his hands slid up her legs beneath her skirt to clutch her naked parts.

Whilst Lady Brexford wanked her lord, she gave a commentary of the action down at Chalmers. 'Claire has raised the cane,' she said excitedly, 'and the wench is wriggling her tight bum. And there it is. Ooo, what a hard whack! It caught her across both cheeks of her arse. She jumped so hard as it landed that her spectacles have fallen off her nose. There are two more red lines. And, I say, what a lovely, thin bot she's got. Must be hurting her like hell, having so little padding.'

Hurt like the very devil, it did. Yes, after the fifth stroke, a happily similar thing began to happen to the virgin Prudence as had occurred with Ellie Branks during her first introduction to a caning; the hot glow was starting to spread into her pussy. It was beginning to dampen – though it was nowhere near as wet as the gluttonous little, furry animal nesting between her assailant's plump thighs. Miss Petty had seldom been closer to coming whilst actually engaged in the act of administering corporal punishment.

Brexford relieved Sophronia of the telescope. Opening her bodice for him so that her tits were swinging free, she pulled his trousers and underpants to his ankles and crouched down on the floor in front of him. Drawing his prick between her lips, she began to suck and to wank him, and to toy with his scrotum and finger his bottom hole. Content in the knowledge that Jeremy was so thoroughly turned on by his voyeurism that she would shortly be the recipient of a most glorious fuck, she was happy to let him keep his telescope to himself until the caning was over and done with.

At the sixth stroke, Prudence Brown was seized with such a tremendous convulsion that it caused her skirt to tumble down, inside out, over her back to the floor, engulfing her head. But the paroxysm was by no means entirely a reaction to the pain; it was the sort of sexual reaction that she might have experienced had she, as the virgin that she was, had an erect cock thrust savagely into her whilst she was bent double; Miss Brown was in the interesting throes of making the startling discovery that a caning was perhaps not such a terrible event after all.

The seventh slash fell almost too hard. Realising that she was getting carried away, Miss Petty paused, gloating on the criss-cross of red marks she had inflicted. Her wet pussy was positively pleading for action. She realised that if she stood slightly more to one side, Prudence, with her skirt tenting over her head to the floor as it was, could not possibly get much more than a glimpse from between her legs of the cane-arm. She hesitated, considering her new, lubricious idea; the recollection that Lord Brexford was watching spurred her on to dare something which she had never before attempted whilst actually caning a girl. Reaching her free hand up beneath her skirt, she worked it beneath a leg of her cami-knickers and thrust two fingers deep into her cunt.

Prudence meanwhile found herself actually looking forward to the next stroke from the cane of Chalmers. She was in an excited mental tormoil, her experience making her crave to do to herself that which Miss Petty, unbeknown to her, was up to next to her. It was of course entirely out of the question – but she made up her mind that she was going to have to treat herself to a jolly good frigging as soon as this punishment was over.

With her fingers vigorously thrusting up and down inside her wet and twitching pussy, Miss Petty striped the tortured buttocks once more.

'Why, would you believe that the shameless woman is wanking herself now?' observed Lord Brexford as he steadily rocked his cock between Sophronia's pretty lips. 'Good grief, if the gal should happen to spot what she's up to, it will be the talk of all Chalmers by nightfall. What say you, Sophie?'

With her mouth crammed full, Lady Brexford was hardly in a position to reply, nor did she wish to pause in her fellatio. She sucked on, with great relish and enthusiasm.

As she inflicted the ninth blow neatly across both buttocks, Miss Petty started to come. She augmented the powerful climax which was sweeping through her by swiping Prudence's bottom three more, frenzied times. Then, thoroughly drained, she pulled her fingers out of her pussy. Her arms flopped lifelessly to her sides, her head drooped and the cane fell from her fingers to clatter onto bare floorboards beneath the window.

Prudence had not the slightest idea that she had been the recipient of two unscheduled slashes. She was riding such a euphoric high that she was craving even more beating. She found herself slightly disappointed when, after an inordinately long pause, during which the air was filled with the sound of Miss Petty's heavy, slightly asthmatic breathing – which she assumed was solely due to her effort in administering the punishment – the strained voice of her headmistress ordered her to straighten up and rearrange her clothing.

'She came,' muttered Brexford. 'By God, I swear the dirty slut came in her knickers.'

Sophronia slipped her lips off his cock. 'Who?' she asked. 'Claire, or the girl?'

'Claire, of course. Didn't I tell you she was frigging

herself? But as a matter of fact, that skinny young wench has a certain look on her face which I seem to know rather well. She's certainly not crying her eyes out. I'll wager she's enjoyed a thrill from her thrashing.'

Sophronia's eyes shone. 'Let us hope she has.' She fisted his prick and squeezed it, hard. 'Fuck me, darling?' she breathed. 'One of those good, hard quickies?'

The invitation was perfectly timed. 'Where would you have me do it?' grunted Brexford, putting his hand over hers on his cock, glancing around the almost bare room.

'Right here, why not?' Opening the window, Sophronia leant out, doubling herself over the dusty sill with one hand gripping the edge of the stone ledge outside the window and her bare tits hanging and wobbling in space as she picked up her skirt behind to offer him her pussy and bottom.

'Shall I bugger you?' he thickly asked her.

'Not this time, no. Fuck my cunt, there's a dear?' She opened her pussy lips for him with index and middle finger. 'Fuck it,' she gasped. 'Quickly. Fuck me.'

Quickly, it most certainly was. With a splendid, sunshine-draped view spread before them – the immaculately tended gardens, the beautiful wood, the distant finishing school on the edge of the cliffs and, beyond Chalmers, the restless, white-flecked English Channel – Lord Brexford, excited beyond measure by what he had been observing through his telescope, screwed his wanton, gorgeous lady wife with such ceaseless vigour that they enjoyed a mutual, explosive orgasm before another minute had passed.

Meanwhile, Prudence Brown, unable to comprehend what extraordinary devil had got into her during her caning – but delighted that it had – was relieving herself of her massive sexual craving in a hiding place where she could be assured of her privacy.

She had crept into a dark broom cupboard and closed the door on herself. Oblivious to the raging throb of her backside – except to the fact that its heat was spurring her on – she was sitting on a wooden crate full of tins of polish with her legs splayed and her knickers at her feet. With a musty, waxy smell thick in her flaring nostrils she was eagerly tossing herself off, three fingers flying up and down her pussy, thumb jerking on her hard clitoris, whilst imagining what it was going to be like the first time she was done by a boy.

Just a few rooms away from masturbating Prudence Brown, her headmistress was back behind her desk. She was seated, sprawled forwards over the leather top with her head cushioned in her arms. Barely recovered from what had been an intensely licentious experience, she was also, like Prudence, wondering what a certain future one was going to be like.

Miss Petty was speculating on what carnal delights might be in store for her at Lord and Lady Brexford's May Day ball.

Chapter 15

Since the fear-filled night of the invocation of the super-natural forces, the weather had been subject to sudden changes and reversals; blustery conditions would invade a seemingly settled, pleasantly summery day, and it would unexpectedly pour down with rain. The evening of the first of May dawned stormy after what had been a lovely day. As Ellie and Georgina were driven up through the wood in Lord Brexford's chauffeured Rolls-Royce, a squally breeze was causing the branches which spilled over either side of the narrow lane to wave around furiously like the arms of a dockside crowd as a passenger liner full of loved ones departed. In the distance, way out over the English Channel, there was the low, continuous rumble of thunder and the sky was flickering with the phosphorescent light of far-off lightning. The smell of rain was heavy in the air, though it was not yet falling.

Miss Petty had postponed informing the two girls about their invitation to the manor until just before the evening meal. Having told them, to their surprise she said that they may be as late back as they liked, for, unbeknownst to them, she too had received an invitation. They were to put on their Sunday best school uniforms.

When the Rolls nosed its way out of the other side of the wood from Chalmers, up ahead of it the crumbly Gothic mansion was ablaze with light. Georgina and Ellie, who only knew they had been invited, but not exactly what the occasion was – except that it was bound to involve sex – saw with slight alarm that the drive was packed with parked automobiles. The alarm turned to dismay when, as they were slowly driven past the wing of the manor which housed the ballroom, they became aware that there were very many dancing couples within, and that they were resplendent in evening wear. Music drifted gaily from the tall narrow windows with their eroded stone, lancet-arch tops, to be snatched away by the breeze.

Here they were, they told one another in confused irritation, going to a ball in outfits they habitually wore for church. It was too annoying, for it was going to be dreadully embarrassing. What on earth had Petters been thinking about?

But their position was not precisely as they had imagined. Arriving inside the cavernous entrance hall, they were asked by the butler to wait. A few minutes later, Lady Brexford joined them. She looked magnificent in a billowing, eggshell blue skirt topped by a black, low-cut blouse embellished with ruffles. With the outfit she had on a matching set of pendant earrings and a triple string of flawless pearls. Her hair was swept high in an impressive bouffant.

Having smothered the cheeks of both of the girls in welcoming kisses, getting between them she linked arms with them and took them upstairs. She marched them through her bedroom and into her dressing-room where they discovered, to their delight and profound relief, that she had suitable clothes for a ball especially prepared and waiting for them.

'Put them on right now, dears,' she told them. 'When you are dressed I'll do your faces for you. You are both going to look absolutely gorgeous for this evening's ball, that I promise you.' She sank down into a small armchair, a prurient little smile crinkling her face as she attentatively watched the two nubile teenagers strip to school knickers and bodices. She told them that their flat, shiny black shoes would have to suffice, but that in any case they would not be on view, since the skirts they were to wear swept the floor.

The outfits, in a similar fashion to that of Sophronia, were in two pieces – unusual for evening wear. The top halves, though different in style from each other's and from hers, were also black. Georgina had a stylish black taffeta skirt to match, not too wide so she felt rather slim in it, and Ellie a pink, flouncy, many-layered affair. By the time Lady Brexford had painstakingly and expertly made up their faces and found diamond and emerald earrings and necklaces to lend them, they were completely transformed into stunning belles of the ball.

Before they went down, Sophronia hugged them to her on either side and kissed their rouged cheeks. Her hand strayed to their breasts and squeezed. 'It is a trifle odd, I know, for us to be wearing two-piece outfits for a ball,' she said, as she walked them slowly down the grand staircase. She proceeded to elaborate on that remark. By the time the three reached the bottom of the stairs, Ellie and Georgina knew the reason they were dressed that way – and it had also been made clear to them, in the sweetest possible way, what variety of brazen behaviour was expected of them later, at a specific hour. Nervous little thrills were jumping through the pair of them as they crossed the hall in the direction of the music.

There were about fifty guests in the ballroom – not a great number considering the capacity of the hall which was at least two hundred, but perfect for what Lord Brexford had planned. The first thing which struck Georgina and Ellie as they began to mingle was the fact that all the women were dressed in two-piece outfits, and all had on black tops. The second was that every one of them was young and most attractive; the oldest could not have been much more than thirty.

The men, on the whole, were far older, many of them of Lord Brexford's mature years. They were attired in tail-coated evening clothes, and they all appeared quite splendidly elegant. Amongst the guests, Georgina and Ellie recognised Lord Antrim, Count Petrovski, Edwin Smythe-Parker and Lettice. The rest, apart from Brexford himself and his wife, were strangers to them. A fact that the Chalmers girls did not know – but might easily have guessed – was that they were in amongst the most profligate, dissolute gathering of London and county society imaginable, a collection of degenerates whose presence their host knew full well would guarantee that the night's debauchery ahead would be a roaring success.

The music was provided by a string sextet. Its members – as specified by Brexford to their London agent for a particularly lurid reason which had nothing to do with their musical abilities, and which furthermore was unbeknown to them or the agent – were young and good-looking. As Georgina and Ellie settled in, relaxing, enjoying the gay atmosphere, the sextet was playing the Lancers. Sixteen couples in slightly ragged formation were briskly stepping out the quadrille. But for the fact that there were no old people present, and all the women were young and lovely and dressed in black tops, this might have been any innocent, country-house get-together.

It was not long before Georgina and Ellie were being whirled around the floor respectively by Smythe-Parker and Lord Antrim in the popular and energetic Gay Gordons. Dancing being considered a most important subject in their finishing school curriculum, the girls performed very well.

The ballroom was ablaze with light from a large number of huge chandeliers. It was electric light, which Lord Brexford had had installed just a month before and only in this hall. He had been doubtful about the change at first, but he had now decided that it was an extremely good idea, for the light from electric bulbs was far brighter than that of gas, paraffin or candles and most suitable for the atmosphere of a ballroom. It made the entire scene seem that much more colourful – though he was convinced that he was going to continue to prefer the old-fashioned forms of illumination in the rest of the house, especially that of candles for dinner.

Dancing, drinking and the nibbling of titbits went on for almost three hours. Smartly liveried servants circulated the entire time with silver trays loaded with glasses of champagne and red and white wine, and a large variety of canapés. There was a small bar with a barman for those who preferred cocktails or spirits.

At precisely ten-thirty, Lord Brexford called a halt to the dancing. He had his staff arrange two rows of high-backed chairs for the guests in front of the raised platform on which sat the sextet, then he sent all the servants out of the ballroom with instructions not to return, not even to intrude their heads around the doors, until summoned. After getting the musicians to move their chairs in a straight line facing the guests, he got up on the platform, turned to the expectant audience and raised a hand for silence.

'It is now time for a very different variety of entertainment from dancing,' he announced. 'We are going to enjoy a little show. We have amongst us a distinguished personage with whom many of you are acquainted, the accomplished Doctor Melvyn Crab. Doctor Crab, as you might know, is a master of the art of hypnotism. He has kindly consented to give us a demonstration, and the musicians have agreed to act as his subjects.' He glanced at a man sitting in the front row. 'If you wouldn't mind, Melvyn, kindly proceed.'

Amidst applause, Crab took Lord Brexford's place. A large, swarthy man with darting, penetrating eyes, curly black side-whiskers and sporting a monacle, he delivered a short speech on hypnotism in which he mentioned L. A. Mesmer, who had perfected the art more than a century before. He next asked the musicians, who had been hovering uncertainly by their instruments, to sit on the chairs, alternating man, woman. There was another smattering of applause. The presentation appeared most academic and proper – as was intended, for the members of the sextet were unsuspecting dupes who believed that they were to assist in a most serious demonstration. Had they known the true, corrupt intentions of Lord Brexford and Doctor Crab, they would surely have snatched up their instruments and rushed pell-mell from the house.

'I shall begin by putting our musical friends one by one into a state of trance, from which they will emerge later, when I command it, with no recollection whatsoever of what has meanwhile happened to them,' the hypnotist told his audience.

202

As he proceeded with this, it looked far too simple, mere fakery, as hypnotism often does – and is. Crab closed fingers and thumb on the temple of the first in line, a heartbreakingly lovely, nicely rounded female cellist who was possessed of a wonderful peaches and cream complexion. Speaking to her softly and persuasively, he opened the gold case of his hunter watch to swing the brilliantly shiny interior of the lid back and forth on its gold chain in front of her eyes whilst repeating the word 'sleep' over and over again in a series of short, commanding sentences. In less than a minute she was gone. She slipped down sideways into her chair, her chin lolling into her ample bosom, her eyes tight shut, her delicate hands dangling loose between her parted legs.

Within the space of five minutes all six musicians were in a similar trance, hunched in various attitudes of sleep into their chairs. With fire glinting in his small eyes, Crab smiled triumphantly and knowingly at his audience. What he was about to have the members of the sextet perform was most disgraceful – he was rarely presented with such an opportunity, but he was a rake and a libertine and as such was raring to do it. He approached the young lady cellist.

'Stand up, please, and open your eyes. You must follow my instructions to the exact letter,' he told her.

Getting to her feet, the young lady directed her glazed eyes to a chandelier without making any indication that she was actually seeing it.

Melvyn Crab again addressed his hushed audience. 'Many of you will most probably be sceptical about the authenticity of mesmerism,' he said. 'You have seen demonstrations and you have harboured the suspicion that the subjects were in league with the hypnotist – and, indeed, I understand your doubts.' He glanced along the line of musicians, pursing his lips. 'Well, the people whom we have here under my control are somewhat special, the highly talented members of an excellent string sextet. As such one would expect them to be sensitive, reserved members of society. Perhaps not every one of them is a paragon of virtue, that I cannot say. But in my judgement they are not voluptuaries – in other words they would be most unlikely to go in for the sort of sexual fun and games which all we gathered here frequently enjoy. I refer of course to orgies and so forth.'

There was a rustle and a lively whispering in the audience. A tense expectation invaded the atmosphere as all present realised that something of more than a little risqué nature was about to transpire.

'Now, I put it to you all,' Crab went on, 'if it were the lovely Lettice, say, standing before me, or the beautiful Lady Brexford, and had they been in league with me and had agreed to be pretending to have been put in a trance, I have no doubt that they would do what I am about to have these musicians get up to with the greatest of relish, such is their – excuse me, ladies – licentious nature. That would be a different matter, and you could feel free to disbelieve. However, I assure you that these people know absolutely nothing of what is to befall them and they will remember not a moment of it afterwards. I doubt if they would willingly fake a trance and then do knowingly what they are about to do for all the tea in China. They are at this moment deep in genuine trances. They are in no way going to be hurt, and, since the events are to be wiped entirely from their memories, they will not be psychologically damaged in the slightest either. And when this little show is over, I guarantee that you will all believe most implicitly in mesmerism.'

Throughout this speech the female cellist had stood perfectly still, her arms straight at her sides, her eyes fixed on the chandelier, appearing not to be listening. Crab said to her quietly, his face close to her ear. 'Would you please tell me your name, young lady?'

'Susanna,' she replied, equally as softly.

'Well, Susanna, you will now kindly disrobe for me. You will remove all of your clothes and you will please put them in a neat pile beside your cello.'

Ellie stifled a gasp with the back of her hand as Georgina whispered, '*What?*'

The command had been quite unthinkable, a gross invasion of personal privacy. Yet, seconds later, without any change in her glazed expression, there the girl was, calmly, as if alone in her bedroom, stripping off before them all and folding the items of clothing before putting them on top of one another at her feet. There was not even the slightest hesitation when she was down to her underwear. She even stepped out of her knee-length, voluminous bloomers first, and afterwards – the final item – her white corset, and, nude, she then started to unclip the gold chain from around her neck.

'No, that will be all, Susanna, you may leave the chain on,' said Crab, his eyes raking over her luscious, white curves with their thin red lines in her belly and sides where the corset had been digging. 'Arrange your clothes in the manner I told you, would you?'

As she took the items to her cello, offering her spellbound, somewhat shocked audience a splendid view of nicely rounded buttocks with a little dimple in either one, and then even offered them a perfect view of her downy-haired pussy as she bent down with her back to them to stack the clothes, Lord Brexford realised something of importance. He left his seat to say quietly to Doctor Crab, 'That platform is most grubby, Melvyn. They should all at least leave their shoes on. You do see why?'

The doctor saw his point immediately; dirty feet later, when and if discovered, would point to the fact that the feet had been bared during the hypnotism – and most assuredly raise other questions in the musicians' minds best left unasked.

Crab told Susanna to put her shoes back on. She did so without a murmur, then he had her take her seat. She sat up very straight and primly on it, legs together, hands curled over her knees, gazing across the ballroom towards the dark windows; rain was trickling down the glass, lightning was getting nearer every second, and there were ceaseless grumbles of thunder.

Before moving on to impart his piquant commands to the next of the young women, Melvyn Crab asked Susanna to open wide her legs and to keep them open – which she did without a murmur, so that she was sitting there with her pussy and its lips perfectly on display for all to ogle.

The audience seemed to be holding a collective breath, so silent were they. The next girl's name was Francesca. Her hair was thick and black and remarkably shiny – and so was that of her bushy pubis which, its display made the more lewd by her black, knee-length, button-up boots, was publicly bared in a very short space of time. The third girl, Nancy, a violinist, was also dark-haired. She was quite chubby, the lines left on her sides and belly by her discarded corset were deeper and redder than those on Susanna – which were already beginning to fade. With Nancy nude but for her shoes and sitting with her plump, curly-haired pussy winking at the audience, it was the turn of the men, not one of whom had opened his eyes during all this salacious business.

The iniquitous Doctor Melvyn Crab had the male musicians rudely expose their genitals, but not undress. Instead, one at a time, he told them to open their eyes, to sit up straight, to unfasten their evening trousers and to pull them, and their pants, down to their ankles, and to leave them hanging there. They were persuaded to sit, like the women, with spread legs; there penises were completely flaccid, cushioned into their scrotums. Knees bumped against knees all the way down the line, the entire genitalia of the hapless sextet was now most obscenely on display.

There was not one member of the lascivious audience who did not by now believe one hundred per cent in the genuineness of Crab's wicked performance. He had been absolutely right in his comments before it had commenced – in that had it been any of them up there with him on the stage they might have been wide awake and secretly co-operating, but surely not these gentle, refined musicians – that was utterly beyond belief. For the Brexford's and their guests – with the exception of Georgina and Ellie who had yet to realise what the average sexual hunger amounted to – were well aware that their extraordinary carnal appetites and proclivities were exactly that: extraordinary, very much beyond the normal, and viewed by any run of the mill members of society who happened to find out about them with – rightly or wrongly – shock and even horror.

Lord Brexford and Doctor Crab had agreed when plotting this corrupt mischief that it was not to go so far as hypnotically induced sexual intercourse. That would be grossly overstepping the mark – and even they had their limits. It would be abusing these innocents to an intolerably outrageous extreme to have the men introduce their members into the ladies' fannies. There was even the possibility that one or other of them, male or female, might be virgins. It would be a type of enforced rape to have them fuck. But there were other sexual high jinks, ultimately harmless, which they could be made to perform in order to inflame their audience thoroughly.

Individually, Crab told the men, 'You are going to be fellated, do you understand? Your penis is going to be sucked by a delectable female mouth. That pleasure will cause you to be extremely excited. You will very rapidly achieve full erection.'

He had them turn their chairs sideways to afford everyone a perfect view. Producing cushions for the girls to kneel on, he instructed them one by one in their duties. A triple, public, blow-job got under way.

Despite their wild enthusiasm for all things connected with sex, and their thirst for more and wider experience and knowledge therein, Ellie and Georgina had at first been stunned and even embarrassed when the girls uncomplainingly stripped themselves nude. These reactions had modified as each set of cock and balls had been revealed to them, and now, as pricks quickly rose and hardened in avidly sucking mouths – and, judging from the pleasure sounds coming from the platform, all the participants were having a whale of a time – the Chalmers girls were becoming just as turned on by the utterly lewd display as were the rest of the observers. It was rather akin to a 'peeping Tom' form of voyeurism – for surely the members of the sextet had no understanding that they were being watched, even supposing that they were consciously aware of what they were doing.

'Enough,' commanded Crab, when all three cocks had been good and hard for two or three minutes. 'Let the cock-sucking now stop.' He and Brexford had further agreed beforehand that ejaculating in mouths, or even over faces or parts of bodies would also, like copulation, be taking the business too far. The hynotist had the girls get to their feet and to offer their pussies to the men for cunnilingus. Tongues were obediently to work, greedily slurping.

Meanwhile, Crab went down behind the chairs to tell each of the girls in turn, 'You are going to enjoy a most splendid orgasm. What is being done to you at this moment is one of your greatest thrills, a delightful pussy tonguing is what you have always craved most in your life. You can feel the orgasm building now in your loins. Building and building and building, do you understand? You must not hold back. You are coming. You are coming, and it is delicious.' He paused, eyes gleaming. 'When you hear me say the word "now" you will come.' He paused again. '*Now.*'

And come they did. All together, almost magically. As the hypnotist uttered the key word, they jiggled their pussies frantically onto the lapping tongues, with their buttocks and tits wobbling away whilst they groaned and sighed their way through climaxes, then they went still. But they failed to sag limply – as is normal in the aftermath of orgasm – they simply stood there as if awaiting the next command as the men continued to pussy-lick until Crab ordered them to stop.

The subsequent order was the final one. They all straightened the chairs and each girl sat on the left of a man. Crab told the men that as soon as their female companions began to stroke their cocks their climaxes would begin. And that was exactly what occurred. The girls vigorously wanked them, and the men came almost immediately, their semen shooting in an arch towards the audience to splash into the dust on the edge of the platform.

'All right. Susanna, Alice, Francesca, release the penises now. Then you will please all sit perfectly still,' said Crab.

He took a large, white handkerchief from his pocket and, crouching down, with it he carefully mopped up the little puddles of sperm. Then, fighting to keep his voice from shaking because what he had induced these people to perform had excited him personally so much he was close to ejaculating in his pants, he once again spoke to his audience.

'In a few moments,' he said, 'when the erections have completely subsided, I am going to have the subjects get dressed. I know you must all be greatly aroused by what you have witnessed, as I must confess I find myself, but it is vital that you do not let this show in any way. The musicians must not get the slightest suspicion that what has transpired here has been anything beyond the usual hypnotic fun and games nonsense.'

Lord Brexford joined him on the platform. 'You should all applaud when these good people are brought out of their trances,' he told his guests. He looked at his watch. 'There is still a short while to go before the hour of midnight, and you all know very well what is scheduled to happen then – at least, you are aware of a significant part of it. We are each one of us, naturally enough in view of what we have just witnessed – and continue to watch – craving at this moment to indulge our sexual appetites. Well, patience, my friends. The waiting will serve to intensify the final pleasure.'

The three penises had returned to their flaccid state. Producing another handkerchief, Doctor Crab cleaned the last traces of semen from thighs and cocks, then he had the sextet get dressed and sit once more. They went about the business of putting their clothes on in as detached and calm a manner in which they had removed them.

'You will awaken the instant that I clap my hands,' Crab proclaimed. 'You will remember nothing at all of what has transpired.' He repeated himself, and then he clapped his hands, loudly, twice. Eyes blinked and cleared. As the audience broke into applause, the members of the sextet threw puzzled looks at one another, made little, amused but sheepish shrugs, and shook their heads slowly from side to side. Clearly, they recalled absolutely zero of their behaviour.

Lord Brexford took a deep breath, then let it slowly out. As sexually aroused as any of his guests, he was nevertheless – amazingly for him – actually experiencing the faintest pangs of guilt as he thanked the musicians for their co-operation and asked them to re-form and to play a little more. He had used them most shamefully. On the other hand, the performance had provided a most lubricious experience for his guests. He forced his doubts from his mind; as Melvyn Crab had observed before the session began, no possible harm would be done – and it surely had not. He reminded himself that the best of the evening's sport was yet to begin.

The music began again with the lively Strauss waltz, 'Roses from the South'. A few couples made half-hearted attempts at dancing, but there was no longer even the faintest trace of gaiety in the ballroom. The prevailing mood was sex, it was hanging thick and heavy in the atmosphere, dictated by throughly aroused loins and panting libidos.

Being obliged to wait until well past her normal bedtime of eleven o'clock before even leaving Chalmers, whilst turning over and over in her mind the possibilities of what might be in store for her at Deal Manor, had played havoc with Claire Petty's nerves. The hood and the garter mystified her without giving her any great cause for concern, for her nerves were not a result of fear, but of the keenest anticipation of wanton sexual abandon.

As Lord Brexford's chauffeured Rolls-Royce bore the headmistress in fine style out through the gates of the finishing school and up towards the wood, she was remembering what had happened to her on her very first visit to the manor, during the winter term. There had been a storm then, just as there was now – it was pouring with rain, lightning was knifing into an angry sea and thunder rumbling – and she had arrived to find the manor house exhibiting only the faintest of light. Shortly thereafter, having been obliged to strip naked in front of the elegantly

210

dressed Brexfords and four other guests, she had had her tits coated in candle wax, she had been subjected to bondage, she had been screwed and buggered, drenched in red wine and soundly flogged with carpet beaters – and she had adored every marvellous, kinky second of it.

The Rolls's windscreen wipers, chocking noisily away, were doing losing battle with the rain. Nevertheless, as the motor car emerged from the wood, Miss Petty could see that the house was ablaze with light.

As had Ellie and Georgina been some hours earlier, Petters was greeted in the great hall by the obsequious butler who asked her to wait there. It was not for long. A few minutes later, Lord and Lady Brexford emerged from the ballroom to greet her with hungry smiles. They hurried her into the drawing-room.

Standing on a colourful Chinese rug in the middle of the enormous room was the same contraption to which Thomas Farley, the stable lad, had been secured naked, but for a belt, and thrashed by Georgina.

'Have a long, strong drink, Claire,' Lord Brexford told her, while Sophronia poured her a goblet of a particularly heady claret. 'Methinks you are going to need it.'

'You did remember to bring the mask and the garter, I trust?' asked Sophronia as she handed her the goblet. She was so filled with sexual tension that her hand trembled and she spilt a little of the wine.

'Indeed I did. But I can't for the life of me imagine what –'

'I should have thought that you would have worked out the reason for the mask for yourself,' interrupted Brexford. 'Two of your girls are here, remember. You know damned well you are here for sex. You are to be used in front of Ellie and Georgina in a variety of interesting carnal ways. I would not have thought that you would want the girls to recognise you. The mask is to hide your identity.'

Of course, she should have realised. Used? She was visited by a shudder of excitement. Her toes curled in her gold evening shoes.

'The garter, however, is quite another thing,' said Brexford. 'You will not discover the reason for it until a little later on.'

211

'I'm wearing it, actually,' Miss Petty told him with a saucy smile. She threw back her head and swallowed a copious draft of wine, trying to calm her nerves.

'Capital. And that garter, my dear Claire, is all you are to wear from this moment on.' Brexford nodded towards a lacquered, Japanese-style cabinet. 'Take off your clothes, if you would. You may stow them in there.'

'What – right now?' This seemed to be altogether too sudden.

'Now,' said Brexford, eyes sliding over her.

'No,' muttered Sophronia. 'I should like to do it.' She stepped up to the headmistress and began to unbutton the front of her light green, fine velvet gown in which she had been feeling so absolutely splendid. As she gulped down more claret, Miss Petty paid close attention to Lady Brexford's busy fingers, fighting to come to terms with what was happening to her, whilst those slim, elegant hands with their diamond and emerald rings and scarlet nails worked their way speedily down the front of her dress to open it up to the floor.

Peeling the gown backwards off the headmistress's shoulders, Lady Brexford draped it over one of her own. She crouched in front of her to remove Claire's evening shoes and to pull down the voluminous, cream cami-knickers as her husband unlaced the whalebone corset. Petters was very quickly clad, apart from the crimson frilled garter, which looked rather fetching a third of the way up her right thigh, in only her chubby birthday suit.

'Put your clothes away where I told you,' said Lord Brexford, nodding across the room.

The cabinet was some thirty feet from her, and the headmistress was imagining the prurient fashion in which the horny lord and his randy lady must have been ogling her plump, juddering buttocks as she padded across the floor in her bare feet to it.

'Now I'd like you to come over here,' said Lord Brexford. He and Sophronia were moving towards the wooden frame. 'Bring the mask.'

With the Brexfords' gazes burning over her wobbling

tits and her dark forest of pubic bush as she approached them, Miss Petty found herself overcome with a most agreeable wave of lust. At last, she thought. At long last it was beginning, and it was not too sudden at all, after all. She eyed the wooden frame with its black leather straps. Its purpose was glaringly obvious. Her stare seemed to challenge it to do its worse.

'Step inside, Claire,' Lord Brexford told her. 'Open your legs and raise your arms. Spread-eagle yourself.'

The two of them strapped her securely in, then Sophronia pulled the hood down over her head. It hung below her chin to drape on her shoulders; she had deliberately arranged her hair in a roll behind her head rather than the bouffant style she preferred so that the yellow hood would fit comfortably. Feeling deliciously, wickedly dirty now that she was trussed with her legs wide apart and her arms in a 'Y' above her head, she looked down at herself. The fancy garter on her thigh seemed to enhance her fleshy nakedness.

Slipping the palm of his hand over both of her tits in turn, twisting and pinching the erect nipples, then crawling his fingers down over Claire Petty's tubby belly to grab a handful of pussy and squeeze, Jeremy told her, 'You will be well advised to utter not a single word when the sport begins. For your voice is most distinctive, and your girls will be sure to realise it is you.'

However, a fact which Lord Brexford was not acquainted with was that Georgina had become Miss Petty's abject sexual slave. There was surely some risk, the headmistress realised, that the girl would recognise her nude body. On the other hand . . . she glanced down at herself as Jeremy's hand left her crotch to grope the insides of her thighs . . . no, it was doubtful she would, with her so stretched; her tits were lifted high, her belly far flatter than usual. She shrugged the minor niggle away. So what if Georgina did happen to twig it was her? The wench was entirely in her power in any case, it hardly seemed it would matter.

The wine punched Miss Petty very squarely in the head,

making her feel happily muzzy. As Sophronia closed in on her to run a tongue over her heavy, dark brown nipples, for an instant her head went out of focus. Lady Brexford made a quick meal of groping all her sexual parts. She licked her lustily once more, from inner thighs to pussy to belly to tits, then the Brexfords abruptly departed, closing the door behind them, leaving their willing victim hanging in more ways than one.

Back in the ballroom, only three couples were dancing, somewhat half-heartedly, to the Blue Danube waltz. The rest of the guests – including Georgina and Ellie who were surrounded by men and being paid sexual attentions of one obvious sort or another – were sprawled in chairs, or loading at the bar, thoroughly primed for sex and impatiently waiting for the orgy to begin.

Their host, as raunchily eager as they, clapped his hands and called an end to the dancing as soon as he set foot in the ballroom. The sextet, blissfully unaware of the shocking, non-musical performance they had been so scurrilously cheated into putting on, began folding away their stands and shutting their instruments into their cases. Even before the musicians were ready to take their leave, Lord Brexford was leading his guests from the ballroom to the drawing-room.

There was a great deal of ribald amusement at the unexpected sight of trussed and naked Miss Petty. When everybody had crowded into the room and the door was locked, Lord Brexford took himself to the side of the wooden stand and, with all eyes upon him, he raised his flattened hand to behind his shoulder and brought it down twice, stingingly hard, across the headmistress's bottom. Her flesh shook, there were two loud grunts from behind the mask as he slapped her, and red smudges appeared on both of her buttocks.

'Before we proceed with what you all know we are to do when I put the lights out,' Lord Brexford then announced, 'I have arranged – as you see – something further to titillate us. This good lady is known as Molly. She is a fallen woman, a lady of the night, a common whore. She is here for us to frolic with as we choose, to do whatever enters our minds, but first she has to be paid, as I have agreed with her. With that transaction in mind ...' He paused, striding to a cabinet from which he produced three long-handled fly swats. 'With that in mind,' he repeated, marching back to Miss Petty and swishing a swat through the air to slap it into her bottom, 'she has on that fat garter. That intriguing little item is tight enough around her thigh to enable it to hold money. You are not obliged to participate, but each one of you who cares to imagine that there is a fly on any part of the tart's person at all, may give it a hearty swat – at the cost of a silver crown in the garter. Now,' – he offered the swatters around, handles first – 'who will be the first?'

There ensued a certain amount of bawdy merriment, accompanying a scramble to have the first swipe. Sophronia meanwhile was easing the garter further up Miss Petty's thigh until it was sunk into the fat just below her pussy – into which she slipped a finger before stepping back.

The headmistress of Chalmers Finishing School for Young Ladies, a pillar of respectability and paragon of virtue – at least as was supposed by the parents of her charges – was relishing her unexpected role as a common prostitute. Behind the silken mask her eyes gleamed as she watched the fly swatters being taken by three, eager, male hands. Three silver-crown pieces were stuffed into her garter, with not one of the men failing to sample her heavy bush with his knuckles as he parted with his money. The swatter heads, Miss Petty noted, were of most fine and floppy red rubber; they were going to sting her very pleasingly, as had Lord Brexford's blow, without bringing more than the minimum of pain.

Gathering all around her, they began with her bottom, lashing away, the swatters going from hand to hand, more and more coins being slipped into the garter. In a very short space of time Petters's trembling buttocks had turned bright pink all over. When it was Lettice's turn, the lewd young lady became more adventurous than the others; she elected to swat an invisible fly on Miss Petty's pubis. That was an encouragement for those who followed to choose areas other than the glowing backside. Blows were thenceforth rained on belly, thighs, tits and pussy, as well as the buttocks. The garter grew fatter and heavier, beginning to bulge all over with money as people had a second turn. Great areas of flesh of the headmistress's body began to turn as pink all over as that of a naked Rubens lady.

Lord Antrim paid for Georgina and Ellie to each have a go. Both of them flinched at the prospect of attacking a tit or the whore's pussy; instead they took a hearty swipe each at the favourite target, the fat bottom, which was glowing a far brighter shade of red than the rest of Miss Petty's abused flesh. Before taking her turn Georgina was visited by the fleeting impression that the trussed woman could be Miss Petty, for the nude body seemed vaguely familiar to her. She dismissed the idea as preposterous – but her swat was as powerful as if the pro had indeed been Petters.

When the overstretched garter began to spill coins on the Chinese rug below the stand, Lord Brexford called a halt. Miss Petty was glad of it. She had had quite enough. Having climaxed several swats earlier she was now, bathed as she was in the languid aftermath of orgasm, feeling the blows too keenly.

'All right. The time we have been most looking forward to all evening is at last upon us, my ruttish friends,' said Brexford, loud enough for all to hear. Walking hurriedly around the drawing-room, he stopped at each of the several gas lamps to put it out. Reaching the final lamp, he stood bathed for moments in its glow, the rest of the room in deep shadow as he announced, 'We are all aware of what we are obliged to do next.'

He switched off the light.

The room went utterly dark. The heavy velvet curtains succeeded in blotting out even the bright flashes from the lightning which was starting to move in from the sea as thunder roared and crashed. The room became alive with rustlings and whisperings and the occasional feminine giggle.

'Is everybody now quite ready?' asked Lord Brexford

after a short while. There was an excited murmur of assent. He relit the lamp beneath which he stood. The light revealed him to be now completely nude from the waist down.

Unhurriedly retracing his steps, cock half erect and proudly swinging, the Lord of Deal rekindled the rest of the drawing-room lamps and a sea of bare, white limbs became more and more scandalously clear to Miss Petty's hooded eyes.

The entire party had taken all their clothing off below the waist. The men, as well as the women, had received their special dress-code instructions from their host well in advance of the ball – the order of the night had been that beneath their tailcoats they were to have on only white dickies – that is to say, false, backless shirt fronts which fastened with buckled cotton, or satin, belts in the small of the back. At the appointed moment, as well as their shoes, socks, trousers and underpants, they were to remove their tailcoats and their false shirt-cuffs.

The reason for the women's two-piece evening wear was now shockingly, arousingly apparent, and the effect in general was, as Brexford had intended and known that it would be, most bawdily erotic with the ladies in black to the waist and nude below it, and the men similarly exposed, but in white, with winged collars and black bow ties, bare-armed and, apart from the dickie belts, barebacked. Male and female genitalia were most erotically on display. Several cocks, including that of the host which had sprung to attention as he lit the final lamp, were already up, some were on the rise, a very few only hung limp.

The scrofulously amused Jeremy Brexford eye surveyed his obscenely apparelled guests. 'Let the climactical action of our little party now commence,' he said. His gaze attached itself thoughtfully to Miss Petty. There was yet another ribald idea running around in his head. He took a firm grip of his hard-on, pointing it at her. 'We who already have a stalk on may fuck whomsoever we please,' he announced, continuing in his role as degenerate master of ceremonies. 'We may do this wherever in the room we desire – on sofas and chairs or on the floor – or up against a wall if we wish. My recommended procedure for those whose cocks need a little help is that they should get them up on our luscious Molly. But once you have a hard-on, do not hog her. You can always screw her later.'

There was very little trouble in the erection department. Many a cock on the rise jumped to attention as its owner watched the orgy getting under way. As the rest took turns to rub their genitals between the ecstatic headmistress's legs, or over and within her buttocks whilst they mauled her tits and leched on the start of the mass copulation around them, they very quickly achieved their hard-ons and left her in search of a pussy, or a mouth, or a bottom hole to stick them in.

Never mind that she had come whilst being whacked with the fly swats. How the once again tremendously aroused and massively frustrated Miss Petty longed to frig herself! Prick after prick was getting solid between her plump thighs against cunt or bottom without actually penetrating her but there was nothing she could personally do to satisfy her mounting lust. The effect upon her of white shirt-fronted men and black-bodiced women without another stitch on between them getting down to heavy sex whilst she was used merely to aid cocks in becoming rock hard before their owners took themselves off to dip them elsewhere was to drive her nearly insane with craving.

But the headmistress was not destined to suffer in that department for long, for the party had been deliberately structured by Brexford so that there were marginally more men than women. Since Sophronia had already cornered Ellie and had her flattened beneath her on a wide sofa close to a huge unlit fireplace, and the pair of them were indulging themselves in a hearty sixty-nine, this temporarily put Ellie out of the running to be penetrated by a man. And Lord Brexford had insisted that, despite his relaxation of the copulation rule concerning his wife for Count Petrovski on the afternoon of the horseback fuck, it was in force again this evening. A tall, youngish earl, new to the house and unaware of that rule, seeking a vacant pussy in which to embed his long cock, had his eye on the succulent target of Sophronia's writhing and bouncing rear end and he was in the act of kneeling behind her on the sofa and positioning his glans for penetration.

Meanwhile, finally deserted – there being no prick left unerect – Miss Petty did not know where to fix her gaze. All the many armchairs and sofas and two of the rugs in the big room were now occupied by rutting, wanking, sucking, groping people. Afraid that she might miss something, her eyes kept darting in every direction in little jerks as her hood rose and fell in the region of her mouth with her shallowly panting breath. They fixed for a moment on the earl as he was trying to introduce his hard-on into Sophronia's pussy above Ellie's probing tongue; Sophronia rudely pushed his loins away. For an instant the young man appeared puzzled and irritated, then he noticed that the trussed whore seemed to be watching him. Holding his slender, but commendably long, erection in his hand, he clambered down from the sofa and approached the headmistress.

'Yours would seem to be the only available minge, Molly,' he muttered, poking two fingers up it. Her legs were spread so wide, and the earl was so tall, that he was obliged to go almost on his knees in order to try and angle his cockhead in her. Giving up that particular attempt, he fetched a pouffe, put it between her legs and knelt on it. The pussy and cock match was now perfect. As his length slid all the way up into the soft wetness Petters groaned in delight.

As the earl began to fuck her, Miss Petty's eyes fell on her sex slave. She could scarcely believe what she was seeing.

In ten short days, Georgina had changed from a fairly innocent virgin whose only experiences of sex had been of the lesbian variety with Ellie Branks and a grope and almost tumble with a stable lad, to a wild and wanton young thing with a rampant craving for anything and everything of a carnal nature. Georgina had become a classic nymphomaniac in the making. Lord Antrim, who had been paying most lascivious attentions to Georgina during the final fifteen minutes in the ballroom, had also been one of the first to sport a cockstand. He had, at the very beginning of the orgiastic proceedings, laid down on his back on a fluffy rug and invited Georgina to straddle him. The girl had done so with great gusto, kneeling astride his hips, handling his hard-on into her pussy and sinking down onto it in a manner which suggested she had been thus fucking for years. As they began to screw, and she sank forward until her tits were jiggling on Lord Antrim's hairy chest, Count Petrovski – another early cock riser – had spotted that her fat, humping bottom presented a delectable target. After greasing his prick and Georgina's ceaselessly rocking bum hole with petroleum jelly from one of the tins Lord Brexford had thoughtfully left scattered around the drawing-room, Petrovski had knelt between Antrim's knees and eased his cock into Georgina's bottom, bringing her initial, tiny stabs of pain and then extraordinarily libidinous pleasure in their wake as the pricks serviced her in two places at once.

So lubricious had Georgina become at this newly discovered, wonderfully kinky diversion, that the idea of filling her third sexual orifice popped into her mind and refused to budge. She had winked lewdly at Jeremy Brexford, who was near by, above her on a chaise longue, beginning to screw a delightful-looking ringlet-haired young lady as the girl gave enthusiastic head to Smythe-Parker. Brexford saw the wink, and then became most intrigued as Georgina poked her tongue at him and licked her full lips suggestively. Grinning hornily, he had uncoupled from the girl. How splendidly he had corrupted the Chalmers wench! Then she should enjoy his cock too, if she so wished.

With Miss Petty observing Georgina's behaviour in lusty amazement while her earl fucked with great vigour, Georgina literally lunged with her parted lips at Brexford's cock, like a dog catching a ball, as he dropped to his knees on the rug on either side of Lord Antrim's head. She sucked the infamous weapon – which was glistening with Ringlet-hair's pussy juice – into her mouth as deeply as she was able. Before her headmistress's randy and astonished eyes, her sex slave became the central feature of the sort of four-way fuck about which many females fantasise but few ever achieve outside their dreams.

Behind Claire Petty, unseen by her, a well-known politician, a short and stocky character, had his greedy eye on her tormented bottom whilst he made use of one of the tins of jelly, smearing it thickly over a rigid cock short and stocky like himself. The first Miss Petty became aware of this man – who had achieved his erection earlier by stroking his cock helmet up and down between her buttocks – was when he shoved the tip of a jelly-coated finger up her backside to the second knuckle and twisted it back and forth in there. Requiring no pouffe to be on a comfortable level with his objective, he positioned his glans between the glowing cheeks and raunchily shoved.

Petters was riding far too great a high to be the least bothered by the flash of pain in her bottom. It in any case passed quickly. Delightfully sandwiched now herself, she leched on what was happening to Georgina as two of the three men servicing the girl's – and their own – needs changed places. Georgina now had Brexford's cock buried in her backside, Petrovski's in her mouth, and that of Lord Antrim pounding her pussy – and she was grunting the first of what were to be a string of little climaxes into the count's immense pole of a prick as her behind rocked and wriggled and her tits were mauled by Lord Brexford's big hands.

The first of the men to come was the politician, who, eyes feasting on Georgina's triple seeing-to, flooded inside her headmistress's bottom hole then sank to his knees behind her, nose buried in the crack of her arse as the vigorously fucking earl's balls bounced between Miss Petty's splayed thighs to knock into his chin each time he rammed his cock home. The next to climax was Count Petrovski – in Georgina's mouth. She swallowed some semen down and the rest dribbled from the corners of her lips as Lord Antrim filled her pussy with his spunk.

All over the drawing-room now, men began to spill their

seed in mouths and bottom holes and in pussies – and over faces, tits, bellies and thighs as the women moaned and shuddered through powerful orgasms of their own. But such an outflow of semen and pussy juice, such an intensity of orgasms, did not signify that the orgy was coming to an end – far from it, for mass carnality tends to feed on itself. This was merely the beginning – and rebuilt erections would last far longer the second time around than the first.

The storm was right overhead now, making an incredible racket. Lightning had hit the conductor on the manor's roof. An old and revered elm tree in the garden had crashed to the ground, its trunk split by a thunderbolt. Several more trees in the forest had been brought down.

Nobody took the slightest notice of the storm, most never even consciously heard it, such was the all-consuming power of their lust. Like the storm, drawing energy from itself, the debauch raged on through the night.

When at last the orgy had worn itself out, Claire Petty – still strapped severely into her frame at four o'clock in the morning – had never been screwed so much, or by so many, in her life. Her sweet charges – for sweet they surely were, sexual behaviour notwithstanding – Ellie Branks and Georgina Tennant, having been sturdily had in every conceivable way by a whole succession of men, were soundly asleep on a blue silk upholstered sofa in one another's arms, innocent smiles on their young but temporarily ravaged-looking faces.

Lord Brexford, despite the fact of being most thoroughly sated, was already planning further lubricious activity at Deal Manor, his jaded eyes wandering contentedly over the shameless scene.

NEW BOOKS

Coming up from Nexus and Black Lace

One Week in the Private House by Esme Ombreux
June 1995   Price: £4.99   ISBN: 0 352 32788 X
Jem, Lucy and Julia are new recruits to the Private House – a
dark, secluded place gripped by an atmosphere of decadence
and stringent discipline. Highly sexual but very different
people, the three women enjoy welcomes that are varied but
equally erotic.

Return to the Manor by Barbra Baron
June 1995   Price: £4.99   ISBN: 0 352 32989 0
At Chalmers Finishing School for Young Ladies, the tyrannical
headmistress still has her beady eye on her pretty charges; the
girls still enjoy receiving their punishment just as much as
Miss Petty enjoys dispensing it; and Lord Brexford still
watches breathless from the manor across the moor. But now
there's a whole new intake for Miss Petty to break in.

The Image & other classic stories of submission by Jean de
Berg and Juan Muntaner
July 1995   Price: £4.99   ISBN: 0 352 33006 6
Anne is an apparent novice in the ways of sex, and Jean finds
himself irresistibly attracted to her. On closer examination,
though, she is revealed to be the devoted slave of the inscru-
table Claire. The new edition of this classic tale of domination
also features two erotically charged stories by Jean Muntaner
and a preface by the author of *The Story of O*.

Conduct Unbecoming by Arabella Knight
July 1995   Price: £4.99   ISBN: 0 352 33007 4
Unbeknown to the brave lads at the front, some of the women
at home played an invaluable role in Britain's war effort. The
all-female unit at Walnut Tree Farm, for example, interrogated
women suspected of sleeping with enemy officials. Their
methods of persuasion – usually involving leather and naked
flesh – were as successful as they were unusual.

The Seductress by Vivienne LaFay
June 1995   Price: £4.99   ISBN: 0 352 32997 1
Rejected by her husband, Lady Emma is free to practise her prurient skills on the rest of 1890s society. Starting with her cousin's innocent fiancé and moving on to Paris, she embarks on a campaign of seduction that sets hearts racing all across Europe.

Healing Passion by Sylvie Ouellette
June 1995   Price: £4.99   ISBN: 0 352 32998 X
The staff of the exclusive Dorchester clinic have some rather strange ideas about therapy. When they're not pandering to the sexual demands of their patients, they're satisfying each other's healthy libidos. Which all comes as rather a shock to fresh-faced nurse Judith on her first day.

The Stallion by Georgina Brown
July 1995   Price: £4.99   ISBN: 0 352 33005 8
Penny Bennett has an overriding passion for showjumping, but she needs a top-class horse before she can perform well. She'd do anything for a fine thoroughbred stallion. Taking her at her word, Alistair Beaumont and his sister put the dark-haired Penny through a series of bizarre and kinky trials.

Crash Course by Juliet Hastings
July 1995   Price: £4.99   ISBN: 0 352 33018 X
Kate nearly resigns when she's asked to run yet another assertiveness training course by her demanding boss. But on discovering that three of the four trainees are well-proportioned young men, she rapidly changes her mind. This is an ideal opportunity to try out her rigorous training techniques on willing new subjects.

NEXUS BACKLIST

All books are priced £4.99 unless another price is given. If a date is supplied, the book in question will not be available until that month in 1995.

CONTEMPORARY EROTICA

THE ACADEMY	Arabella Knight	
CONDUCT UNBECOMING	Arabella Knight	Jul
CONTOURS OF DARKNESS	Marco Vassi	
THE DEVIL'S ADVOCATE	Anonymous	
DIFFERENT STROKES	Sarah Veitch	Aug
THE DOMINO TATTOO	Cyrian Amberlake	
THE DOMINO ENIGMA	Cyrian Amberlake	
THE DOMINO QUEEN	Cyrian Amberlake	
ELAINE	Stephen Ferris	
EMMA'S SECRET WORLD	Hilary James	
EMMA ENSLAVED	Hilary James	
EMMA'S SECRET DIARIES	Hilary James	
FALLEN ANGELS	Kendal Grahame	
THE FANTASIES OF JOSEPHINE SCOTT	Josephine Scott	
THE GENTLE DEGENERATES	Marco Vassi	
HEART OF DESIRE	Maria del Rey	
HELEN – A MODERN ODALISQUE	Larry Stern	
HIS MISTRESS'S VOICE	G. C. Scott	
HOUSE OF ANGELS	Yvonne Strickland	May
THE HOUSE OF MALDONA	Yolanda Celbridge	
THE IMAGE	Jean de Berg	Jul
THE INSTITUTE	Maria del Rey	
SISTERHOOD OF THE INSTITUTE	Maria del Rey	

EROTIC SCIENCE FICTION

FANTASYWORLD	Larry Stern	
WANTON	Andrea Arven	

ANCIENT & FANTASY SETTINGS

CHAMPIONS OF LOVE	Anonymous	
CHAMPIONS OF PLEASURE	Anonymous	
CHAMPIONS OF DESIRE	Anonymous	
THE CLOAK OF APHRODITE	Kendal Grahame	
THE HANDMAIDENS	Aran Ashe	
THE SLAVE OF LIDIR	Aran Ashe	
THE DUNGEONS OF LIDIR	Aran Ashe	
THE FOREST OF BONDAGE	Aran Ashe	
PLEASURE ISLAND	Aran Ashe	
WITCH QUEEN OF VIXANIA	Morgana Baron	

EDWARDIAN, VICTORIAN & OLDER EROTICA

ANNIE	Evelyn Culber	
ANNIE AND THE SOCIETY	Evelyn Culber	
THE AWAKENING OF LYDIA	Philippa Masters	Apr
BEATRICE	Anonymous	
CHOOSING LOVERS FOR JUSTINE	Aran Ashe	
GARDENS OF DESIRE	Roger Rougiere	
THE LASCIVIOUS MONK	Anonymous	
LURE OF THE MANOR	Barbra Baron	
RETURN TO THE MANOR	Barbra Baron	Jun
MAN WITH A MAID 1	Anonymous	
MAN WITH A MAID 2	Anonymous	
MAN WITH A MAID 3	Anonymous	
MEMOIRS OF A CORNISH GOVERNESS	Yolanda Celbridge	
THE GOVERNESS AT ST AGATHA'S	Yolanda Celbridge	
TIME OF HER LIFE	Josephine Scott	
VIOLETTE	Anonymous	

THE JAZZ AGE

BLUE ANGEL NIGHTS	Margarete von Falkensee	
BLUE ANGEL DAYS	Margarete von Falkensee	

Please send me the books I have ticked above.

Name . . . .

Address . . . .

. . . .

. . . .

. . . . Post code . . . .

Send to: **Cash Sales, Nexus Books, 332 Ladbroke Grove, London W10 5AH.**

Please enclose a cheque or postal order, made payable to **Nexus Books**, to the value of the books you have ordered plus postage and packing costs as follows:

UK and BFPO – £1.00 for the first book, 50p for each subsequent book.

Overseas (including Republic of Ireland) – £2.00 for the first book, £1.00 for the second book, and 50p for each subsequent book.

If you would prefer to pay by VISA or ACCESS/MASTER-CARD, please write your card number and expiry date here:

. . . .

Please allow up to 28 days for delivery.

Signature . . . .